# THE
# FAMILY
# MAN

# THE FAMILY MAN

*A Rosedale Investigation*

## LYN FARRELL

CAVEL
**PRESS**

Kenmore, WA

## A Camel Press book published by Epicenter Press

Epicenter Press
6524 NE 181st St.
Suite 2
Kenmore, WA 98028

For more information go to:
www.Camelpress.com
www.Coffeetownpress.com
www.Epicenterpress.com
www.LynFarrell.com

Cover design by Scott Book
Interior design by Melissa Vail Coffman

*The Family Man*
Copyright © 2024 by Lyn Farrell

Library of Congress Control Number: 2023945710

ISBN: 978-1-68492-137-9 (Trade Paper)
ISBN: 978-1-68492-138-6 (eBook)

"The Family Man," is dedicated to all the family and friends who have helped with, read and vastly improved my writing: my family and especially my daughter and co-author Lisa, daughters Shauna, Linda, Jacquie, son Mark, my grandchildren and especially Melody, the MSU Creative Writers, and so many more who have taken the time to read the books. You are what makes my writing happen.

# ACKNOWLEDGMENTS

I'D LIKE TO ACKNOWLEDGE AND THANK Jennifer McCord, Executive Editor and Phil Garrett, Publisher, Epicenter Press for their guidance, support and for making my stories into beautiful books. Jennifer focuses her keen eye on what makes a perfect mystery and with her impressive skills has honed and sharpened my prose. She has been my mentor and colleague through this journey and it is her cutting-edge suggestions that make my books successful. I'm grateful to my friend Nicky D, who suggested using 23 & Me. Micah Walker, a family friend, and excellent copy editor, read and made necessary changes to the whole book. It was his idea that my missing person, James Browning, needed to make a cameo appearance. He was right and Chapter 19 was added because of his insight. Linda Nuttal did the final content edit and invariably asks the right questions. Dr. Robert Stuart was, as always, helpful in making the medical details correct. If there are errors in medical matters, they are mine, and not his.

# ONE

Spring had been dramatic in its onset that year. Daffodils, the bright harbingers of the season, had arrived in wild profusion by the end of February. A huge golden yolk of sun rose each morning and spilled its warm light down on the little town of Rosedale, Tennessee.

Miss Billy Jo Bradley, the youngest employee of Rosedale Investigations, was in an excellent mood. Under the tutelage of her work-mom and fashionista, Investigator Dory Clarkson, she had acquired a small professional wardrobe, styled her luxurious dark hair in a shoulder-skimming cut and learned how to apply make-up to her curly eyelashes and heart-shaped face. Taking the outfit she'd selected for the day from her closet, she laid it out on the bed. She'd decided on black slacks, low-heeled black shoes and a shell pink twin-set with black hematite jewelry.

Once dressed, she gave herself a quick check in the full-length mirror before walking out on the landing and closing her door. Walking down the stairs from her apartment on the second floor of the business, she felt quite pleased with herself. Although she had experienced moments of ambivalence about her job in the past, that morning she felt she was on the right path.

When CEO Detective PD Pascoe gave her the responsibility of choosing which cases the agency should investigate last fall, she'd been thrilled. Since then, she had learned a set of probing questions to ask would-be clients. As a private detective agency, they couldn't take on criminal cases. Those belonged to the sheriff's office, although once it was determined no crime was involved, they were often referred to Rosedale Investigations. It was a logical decision, since two of the principals in the agency had worked for the sheriff's office prior to their retirements.

Over the years since its establishment, the agency had built a fine reputation for finding missing persons and property, as well as providing something other agencies never gave its clients. Rosedale Investigations stayed with its investigations until the cases were fully resolved and their clients completely satisfied. It had paid off in client loyalty and repeat business. Four staff members were employed by the agency—two detectives, one investigator, and Billy Jo, who did the office computer work. Detectives PD Pascoe, Wayne Nichols and Investigator Dory Clarkson were partners in the firm. Despite broad hints, pleading glances and the three years she'd been with the agency, Billy Jo had never been considered for partnership. It was a sore point.

THE FIRST POTENTIAL CLIENT THAT MORNING, Mrs. Jessica Browning, was due to arrive at 8:30 a.m. She'd called the agency the previous day to request the appointment. Her husband was missing, she said, and the Rosedale Sheriff's office had decided there hadn't been a crime. Other than keeping an eye out for his car, the sheriff wasn't going to pursue the case. They had referred Mrs. Browning to Rosedale Investigations.

Billy Jo had completed her background checks on both the husband and wife, covering the period of the previous decade. Neither James nor Jessica had police records. James was a salesman who sold space for hauling items across the state for a company called Fast Freight Deliveries. Jessica was a stay-at-home mom. They had one child, a little boy. Wanting as much information as possible before their newest client arrived, she placed a call to the sheriff's office.

"Morning, Billy Jo," Detective Rob Fuller said when he picked up the call. "In answer to your question about James Browning, I did a fair bit of checking on the guy when his wife came in to report him missing. At that time, he hadn't been home in a week, which she said wasn't unusual. He hadn't been taking her calls, though, and that was *not* his normal pattern. She had already called his boss who said James might be out of town on a buying trip. However, since he didn't seem sure and her husband hadn't mentioned the trip, she was understandably concerned."

"I presume you triangulated cell towers in the area for his phone calls."

"Naturally. He'd been moving around a bit but mostly between Rosedale and our sister city of Mount Blanc. I'm well aware that someone else could be using his phone, but I checked his credit card purchases and they were all from places he'd previously shopped—grocery stores, movie theaters, restaurants, hardware stores, drug stores and the like. Seemed to me like he was avoiding going home. Unfortunately, he has now either turned his phone off or it's out of power."

"Was there anything about the case that particularly piqued your interest?" asked Billy Jo. If something struck Detective Rob as off-kilter, she wanted to hear about it.

"Just one thing. Whenever a husband is turned in as missing, I always ask if there could be a possibility the person is seeing someone else. It's a difficult question to put to the spouse, but often yields good information."

"What did Jessica say?"

"It was what she didn't say that pinged my antennae. She told me she didn't believe so, but there was a significant pause before she answered."

"I'll follow up on that. Thanks, Rob."

SINCE NONE OF THE SENIOR PARTNERS had arrived by the time she finished the call, Billy Jo checked the office voicemail and heard the gravelly voice of Detective PD Pascoe, her boss and CEO of Rosedale Investigations.

"I won't be in until around noon today. Hope all the members of the team will be in-house then as I have something important to tell y'all."

*Interesting*, Billy Jo thought and smiled to herself. She and PD were close (other than his stubborn reluctance to make her a partner) and some time ago she had adopted him as her grandfather. She had checked the legality carefully before preparing the documents, which PD happily signed.

The next message was from Dory saying, "I'll be in around ten o'clock. Checking on the whereabouts of a possibly unfaithful wife."

The last voicemail was from Detective Wayne Nichols who left a message saying, "I have a confidential informant to see this morning. Will be in around eleven."

Billy Jo checked the time and walked into the kitchen. Starting a pot of coffee and plugging in the electric teapot for tea, she glanced out the window into the back yard. Sunshine lit the row of golden daffodils she and Dory had planted the previous autumn at the base of the Rose of Sharon shrubs that encircled the lawn. The daffodils were fully open and the bright blue hyacinths were budded. It was going to be a beautiful day.

A few minutes later, the doorbell rang and Billy Jo opened the door to see an attractive woman standing on the front porch.

"Good morning, Mrs. Browning. Please come in. You can hang your coat up on that hook just inside the door. Lovely day with all this sunshine, isn't it?"

Jessica Browning nodded, but she looked weary and had failed to respond to Billy Jo's comment about the weather. She was about five feet five inches tall and elegantly slim, with blonde hair in a pageboy style and large gray-green eyes. Attractively dressed in a lilac blouse and black skirt, she was striking.

*Most men who ditched their marriages did so for younger, prettier partners. A woman as stunning as Jessica shouldn't have any trouble hanging on to a husband,* Billy Jo thought.

"What can I get you to drink this morning?" she asked.

"Do you have tea?" Jessica's voice was low and husky. It sounded like she had been crying.

"Sure do. Follow me into the kitchen. We have a selection."

Having prepared Earl Grey tea with sugar and lemon, the two women walked down the hallway to the conference room. Once they were both seated, Billy Jo asked Jessica to tell her about the situation. She reiterated what she had told the sheriff's office, saying her husband had been gone over a week at that point and she was terribly worried. Their six year-old son, Trevor, had been asking for his dad.

"I understand your concerns, Mrs. Browning, and we're going to do all we can to help you. Do you have the make and model of his car? We'll need that, plus his license plate number, cell phone number, credit card numbers and a good photo," Billy Jo said.

"I can give you the photo and cell phone number now and I'll stop by later today with the rest."

"Thanks. Now, can I ask you to think back to the last day your husband was at home? Did anything unusual happen that day? Did he have any appointments he mentioned? Get any phone calls that seemed to trouble him?"

Jessica Browning frowned, looking thoughtful. "There was one call. We were having breakfast when it came in. I remember him saying, 'I've been expecting this for a long time.' I asked him who it was and he said it was work, but his tone of voice was odd and something about his face didn't look right."

"You thought he was lying," Billy Jo said, looking intently at the woman.

"Yes, that's what I thought," she said and took a deep breath. "Detective Rob Fuller from the sheriff's office asked me if he could be seeing someone else. I told him I doubted it, but I've been thinking about his question since and there's some history about us as a couple you should know."

She paused and time seemed suspended in the silence. Golden sunlight slanted through the clerestory windows, making long rectangles of light on the conference room table. They could hear birds chirping outside and smell the blossoming lilacs through the open windows.

"Go on," Billy Jo said gently.

Jessica inhaled and said, "James is my second husband. I married my first husband, Chris, in 2016. He was killed by a drunk driver only a year after our wedding. We hadn't even had our first fight," she hesitated and rubbed her hands across her eyes that glistened.

"That's just awful. I'm so sorry," Billy Jo said, and her eyes were filled with compassion.

Jessica took a shaky breath before saying, "Chris and James are first cousins. I met James at Chris's funeral. James told me later that he'd promised Chris he would be a father to his children, if anything were to happen to him. My husband must have had some premonition that he would pass away early because I was already pregnant. Anyway, one thing led to another and James asked me to marry him before Trevor was born."

"I understand. Your first husband died; you were alone and pregnant. James was there and proposed. But, I can feel your love for your first husband when you speak of him. It makes me wonder if you had any hesitancy in accepting James's proposal."

"No, not for a moment. I was deeply in love with him by then and James is a wonderful father to Trevor, very dedicated."

"Tell me a bit more about your husband, will you? It could help us find him."

"He looks quite a bit like Chris and is similar to him in many ways, but James is more romantic. He asks me on dates and buys me flowers for no reason when he goes to the grocery store. He's very handy and fixes items around the house. I have a bulletin board where I post a list of things for him to do. He never seems to notice things that need repair, but is Johnny-on-the-spot, once he is told what needs doing," she said with a pensive smile.

Billy Jo nodded for her to continue.

"My husband has a characteristic that has all but disappeared in men today—to him all women deserve to be adored. He told me he struggled to get past his mother's death and felt as hollow as an empty shell for years afterwards. He has a deep-seated need for a woman to love him and provide him direction. I think he would be lost without me," Jessica said.

"I can see why you love him. Doesn't he have a downside?"

"There is only one thing about James that troubles me sometimes. In the years we've been married, I have grown to love him deeply, but sometimes, when he looks at me, he seems . . . very far away," Jessica blinked back her tears.

Billy Jo handed her a tissue, patted her on the shoulder and said, "You can leave it to us now. Don't worry. We'll find him. Rosedale Investigations has a great track record in locating missing persons."

# TWO

BY NOON THE ENTIRE FOUR-PERSON ROSEDALE TEAM had assembled in the kitchen. Detective PD Pascoe arrived looking windblown and cheerful. Although he was usually dressed in a suit and tie, that morning he was wearing jeans, a plaid shirt and a blue windbreaker. Tall and thin, he had wrinkles around his dark boot-button eyes and thin white hair that touched his shoulders.

Dory Clarkson, an older African American woman, looked disgruntled. Her search for evidence on the unfaithful wife hadn't panned out, she told them.

Detective Wayne Nichols came in with sandwiches for the team. He had broad shoulders, a stocky physique and hazel eyes that seemed to probe the conscience of everyone he questioned.

"I'm going to dispense with the case updates today because I have an important announcement to make. I'm turning seventy-five in a month, and I've decided to retire," PD said. "I've beaten prostate cancer and have been lucky enough to make it through two decades as a cop in a big city and ten years as a PI without dying a violent death. Lately, I have the sense that my luck is running out. I want to spend whatever time I have left in peace, walking in the fields around my cabin and sharing time with my grandchildren."

A brief silence greeted his words. Wayne and Dory glanced quickly at each other. Billy Jo could hardly catch her breath.

"Does this mean you're closing the agency?" Dory asked with a worried note in her voice.

"No, I'm handing the business to you and Wayne to run. My grandson, Liam, has been accepted to the University of Tennessee at

Knoxville. He had a year of college previously and now wants to finish his degree. I'd like to purchase a two-bedroom condo there—where he can live while he's in school and I can stay when I visit. I'm keeping my cabin here as well, so I will be able to spend time with all of you but especially you, Billy Jo," PD smiled at her.

She found herself unable to respond.

"Do you want us to buy you out of the business?" Dory asked. As CFO of Rosedale Investigations, she was responsible for the finances.

"I'm leaving that up to you, but I need enough cash for the down payment on the condo and monthly disbursements from our retirement account. Hope you can figure out how to manage that," he said.

"Well, it's a tall order. I'll have to see what we can do."

"You know, PD, I had a feeling this was coming," Wayne said with a rueful look. "I guess congratulations are in order, but I'm sure going to miss you, Buddy. You've been a good friend and partner." He clapped him on the back.

"The feeling is mutual. I'm planning on living at my cabin during semester breaks, over the Christmas holidays, and all summer. Hope you will all come out to for visits and pizza on the deck. How about it, Billy Jo?" PD asked, looking directly at her.

She swallowed, struggling to know what to say. The words seemed trapped in her throat. PD reached out to hug her and after a moment's hesitation, she hugged him back.

"One piece of business before I take off. I know you met with a new client this morning. Do you recommend taking on the case?"

She cleared her throat before saying, "Yes, sir. The sheriff's office decided James Browning was alive and well. They thought it likely he had taken up with another woman. His wife Jessica is dropping off his license plate number, credit card numbers, etc. later today." Her comment was as level as she could manage, but it took a distinct effort to control the quaver in her voice.

"Good work. I'll stop back in the next couple of days to discuss the money details. Okay, Dory?"

"I'm sure going to miss us working together," she said in a husky voice. PD reached out and hugged her. He turned to Wayne, who gave him a manly shoulder hug, and with a brief backward glance at the business he had developed from scratch after he retired as a detective from the Nashville police post, PD departed.

Watching the door swing shut behind him, Billy Jo felt a sharp stab of loss. *Would their relationship be the same once they weren't working together? Would PD's decision make Wayne and Dory think about their own retirements? Would she still be his granddaughter?* She suddenly felt terribly alone.

An old reminiscence hit her with a punch. It was one of the few recollections she had of the man she believed was her father. She was four when he stopped coming around. One of her last memories was of him wearing a blue cardigan and smelling sweetly of pipe tobacco. When he leaned down and kissed her on the head, he said he was leaving but would be back . . . someday. She'd raised her chubby dimpled hand to touch his face, feeling the stubble on his chin.

RAIN STARTED AROUND TEN O'CLOCK THAT NIGHT and continued until dawn. Gray clouds scuttled across the sky the next morning and raindrops were spattered on windows and car windshields. The daffodils stood in mud halfway up their bright green legs. Looking out the kitchen window, Billy Jo felt distinctly morose. Sunny days lifted her spirits, but the downpour made her depressed and PD's news had only intensified her sorrowful mood. The office just didn't seem the same without him telling her to put on her *dang* shoes, help him find things on the computer, asking for updates and being part and parcel of her everyday life.

Dory was in her office working on PD's buy-out plan, muttering and cussing from time to time. Wayne stopped in and took the photo of James Browning. He said he planned to go by Fast Freight Deliveries where the man worked and speak with his boss.

Billy Jo tried to focus on her computer, but found her mind wandering. She texted Mark Schneider, her boyfriend who did IT work for the Nashville PD, asking if he would meet her for dinner. He texted back *yes* and suggested their local tavern. She experienced a brief rise in spirits. Mark always helped her remember that her glass was half-full.

Wayne called in later saying he'd visited the warehouse where Browning was employed. They hadn't seen him or heard from him in over a week. It seemed a sad, but all too-usual situation. James Browning had seemingly left his wife, and apparently his job, for some unknown reason, possibly another woman.

"You're going to have a tough conversation with Jessica Browning—if our suspicions prove to be true," Wayne said.

Being unwilling to speak to Jessica until they knew more, Billy Jo called the couple's cell phone provider and requested a list of James Browning's calls for the last two weeks. When the fax arrived, there was just one number that raised her eyebrows. His last call was to a number she recognized. It was to the main phone number of the Nashville police post. Maybe Mark could find out who Mr. Browning spoke to on the day before his phone went dead.

By late afternoon, Billy Jo decided to call it a day. She walked upstairs to her apartment, deciding to change into jeans and a comfy blue sweater before joining her boyfriend for dinner. She smiled thinking of his nickname, Dragon Boy. It was what the partners at Rosedale Investigations called him, due to a large fire-breathing dragon he had tattooed on his back. Mark had blunt features, a good build and dark eyes that went soft when he looked at her. She adored him. And to her delight, it was mutual.

THE YOUNG COUPLE DISCUSSED PD'S RETIREMENT over a meal at their local restaurant called the Bucket. It was an ancient building that fronted the main street in the little southern town of Rosedale. Over the years it had been home to many businesses, but its current incarnation had lasted for a decade. Despite the dated décor (brown wooden booths with hard leather seats, red asphalt-tile floors and license plates nailed to the walls) it was filled with noisy, jovial customers. Mark and Billy Jo both ordered the burger and beverage special.

"I get that you're worried about what's going to happen with PD retiring," Mark said. "And I understand your fears about the other partners possibly leaving, but I can't see Dory ever quitting work. She would lose her mind."

"You're probably right, but I wonder about Wayne. When PD said he felt like his luck was about to run out, I saw him resonate to that," Billy Jo said.

"I've heard lots of older cops, hanging on until they got their twenty years in, say the same thing. They feel like they have escaped death by the skin of their teeth so many times they need to get out. They all believe in the old saying, *when your number's up, your number is up.*"

"Speaking of numbers, our missing client James Browning called the Nashville post the day he disappeared. It was at nine o'clock in the morning a week ago. Could you try to find out who he talked to?"

"Sure thing."

"Do you ever have that same feeling, Mark, like you will know when your life is coming to an end?" she asked.

"Heck no. I'm just a gear head. The only time I was ever in danger was when we were trying to stop the Brookovers from burning the cursed painting. What did you call that case?"

"In the Frame."

"That's right. I felt like I was going to pass out when you confronted Mr. Brookover. I started running toward you as fast as I could, before he gave it up. Don't you ever do that to me again," he said looking at her intently.

"I won't," she said. "Can't believe I stood up to him like that, when I knew he still had bullets in his gun. Once it was all over, I couldn't stop shaking."

"Thank God that's in the past. Anyway, try to look on the bright side of PD's decision. I think it could improve your relationship."

"Really? Why would you say that?" Billy Jo asked with a confused frown.

"Well, as your boss, the two of you had quite a few conflicts. You always wanted to become a partner in the business, and he never agreed. Plus, PD is a *nose to the grindstone* type of guy and you pushed his buttons from time to time by leaving early, coming to staff meetings barefoot and dressed in your pj's, etcetera."

"I know, but for some reason I feel . . . like the lights have gone out in my life," Billy Jo said wistfully, and Mark reached for her hand.

In her mind, she stood alone on a precipice, fearful if PD's retirement caused the other partners to close the business, she would tumble down into the life she lived before they met. As a result of her mother and grandfather dying within days of each other the summer she turned seventeen, she'd been homeless for two years before that magical day when PD walked into the little pizzeria where she waitressed asking if anyone knew a girl named Billy Jo Bradley.

Mark's voice broke her train of thought saying, "I think you're borrowing trouble, as my mother would say. You two are going to be just fine." He smiled at her as the waitress walked up with their orders.

They were seated at a booth by the window. Turning away from the table to look outside, Billy Jo saw her face reflected in the glass. The raindrops on the window looked like tears running down her face. There was something about this big change in her life that made her remember things she'd walled off for years and dreaded resurrecting. Taking a deep breath, she forced her mind back to what Mark was saying.

"What did you say?"

"I said, I bet this summer we will all be out at PD's—grilling chicken and toasting his retirement."

"I guess," she said softly, but remembering the tiny wisps of white fog rising from the ravine below the deck in the evenings and how the inky darkness blew them away like smoke in the wind, she grimaced.

# THREE

DETECTIVE WAYNE NICHOLS RETURNED TO THE OFFICE of Fast Freight Deliveries for a second visit the following day. He felt he hadn't gotten as much information as he could have on his initial conversation with the boss and planned to speak with an employee. The sliding metal door to the large warehouse was open and he walked inside. A young guy who was sitting at a desk in front of floor-to-ceiling metal racks filled with boxes asked, "Can I help you, sir?"

The kid looked to be about nineteen years old, had slicked back short hair and was wearing an orange baseball cap with the logo for the Nashville Predators. His name tag read Richard.

"Good morning, Richard. I'm Detective Nichols," he said, pulling out his PI identification card. "We're trying to locate a man named James Browning. I understand he works here. Has he come into the warehouse recently?"

"The salesmen don't often come into the warehouse. They work from home on their computers, but he's been online. I'm responsible for scheduling the truckers' merchandise pick-ups, once I get the orders. Browning has been placing orders to ship food to a chain of grocery stores throughout the state."

"Has he called?"

"Yup. He called this morning to check whether a shipment was going to Oleffson's Groceries in Mount Blanc. They had complained because they didn't receive their fresh vegetables on time last week."

"Do you mind giving me his phone number?" Wayne said. Although Jessica Browning had given them her husband's cell number, it was dead when he tried it. He was pretty sure any calls the business received since would be from a new phone or a burner. Those damn things were impossible to trace.

"Sorry, Sir. Can't give out phone numbers," Richard said, looking very determined. His jaw was set and Wayne decided to ease back.

"I understand. No problem. Is Browning's car still here? Mrs. Browning asked us to keep an eye out for it," Wayne said.

"Nope. Young blonde picked it up yesterday," Richard said with a slightly sheepish smile.

"A looker, was she?" Wayne asked, recognizing the face of a young man appreciative of female beauty.

"Sure was. I wasn't certain she was old enough to drive and asked her to show me her license."

"Good thinking. Do you remember her name by chance?" Wayne asked.

"It was Samantha Leigh. I assumed she was a relative of Browning's, maybe even his daughter, although her last name wasn't the same. Almost asked for her phone number before I realized she'd just turned sixteen. I don't date underage girls," Richard said, shaking his head.

"Good decision. Do you remember her address by chance?" he asked.

"Sorry, I don't."

"No problem. Appreciate the help."

Wayne walked out through the open door of the warehouse into cool sunlight. The rain had moved off leaving the air sweetly moist. The faces of the blue pansies planted in wooden tubs near the warehouse door looked freshly washed. Climbing into his truck, he dialed the office.

"Morning, Billy Jo. I got something you might be able to use on the Browning case. I went back to the place James Browning works this morning and learned that a girl named Samantha Leigh picked up his car yesterday. She's a blonde sixteen-year-old who just got her license."

"Then the Department of Motor Vehicles should have an address for her. I'll try to pry it out of them. Might be best to go over there in person," she said.

"If you get an address, I'll go talk to her," Wayne said. "What's Dory up to?"

"Still trying to figure out how to get PD enough money to buy the condo in Knoxville. She had me call the Rosedale Citizen's Bank this morning."

"What department?" Wayne asked.

"Mortgages," Billy Jo said. "Sorry, have to go." He clicked off the call.

DESPITE TALKING TO EVERY EMPLOYEE WHO WORKED for the Department of Motor Vehicles saying she was searching for a *missing person*, Billy Jo got absolutely nowhere. Nobody would give her Samantha Leigh's driver's license number or address. She gave up in exasperation and headed over to the sheriff's office. On her way there, she stopped at the Rosedale Nursery. She hoped to raise her spirits by enjoying all the flowering plants they stocked in spring. An amethyst heliotrope caught her eye. She purchased the plant and carried it with her into the sheriff's office.

Mrs. Coffin, the oddly-named dispatcher for the office greeted her saying, "Hello, Billy Jo."

"Good Morning, Mrs. Coffin."

"That's such a pretty little plant."

"It's a heliotrope. I thought it might brighten up my desk at work. Hope you can help me with something. I'm looking for an address for a newly-licensed driver. She's local and her name is Samantha Leigh."

"Why do you want to find her?" Mrs. Coffin asked. "Does that flower have any scent? So many don't these days."

"It does. Here, take a whiff," she said handing the plant to the woman. "I think it smells like cherry pie."

Mrs. Coffin took a long, luxurious sniff. "To me it smells like a grape popsicle. Just delicious," she said, reluctantly handing the flower with its arching purple racemes back to Billy Jo.

"I'm not sure if you were in the loop when Jessica Browning came in to report her husband missing. Detective Rob didn't find any evidence of a crime and referred the case to us. Mr. Browning's car was left at the warehouse where he works, but a young girl named Samantha Leigh picked it up yesterday. We'd like to talk to her in case she knows where he is."

"I remember Jessica. Poor woman. Sorry, but I'm pretty busy today, Billy Jo. Might be a couple of days before I can get to your request," Mrs. Coffin said, casting an oblique look at the plant.

Billy Jo, who recognized a request for a bribe when she heard one, held the heliotrope out to her. "Here, it's yours. Let me know if you can come up with an address, will you?"

"Oh, thank you. I surely will. Might even get to it later today," she said, giving Billy Jo a cheeky grin.

"I just thought you might," Billy Jo said with a matching grin of her own.

ONCE BACK AT HER DESK IN THE OFFICES of Rosedale Investigations, Billy Jo found Dory gathering up her purse and keys.

"Glad you're back," she said. "There's a new client coming in right after lunch. Her name is Annabelle Browning. She's also got a missing husband."

"Hmmm. That's odd. Same last name as Jessica. It's going to be hard keeping the cases separate," Billy Jo said.

"I left you a note with her husband's social security number, their address and a copy of her driver's license. Can you do her background check? I've got an appointment at the bank."

Dory was dressed in a state-of-the-art sharkskin sheath and silver-gray heels. Her shiny earrings were so long they brushed her shoulders. Although she was easily forty pounds over her optimal weight, she'd always refused to reveal how much she weighed—or her age. She had a gift for amusing comebacks and caustic one-liners that kept everyone in the office in line.

"Getting a mortgage?" Billy Jo asked.

"Hope so. This building is paid for, so if the bank approves a new mortgage on the property, we could give PD a large chunk of cash for his condo purchase in Knoxville."

"Bummer, I had hoped you wouldn't be able to figure it out and he'd have to stay," Billy Jo said with a sigh.

"I noticed yesterday that PD's retiring was hitting you particularly hard," Dory said. "Tell you what, after my meeting at the bank, we can talk over lunch. I'll meet you at that new little sidewalk café outside the Rosedale Florist at noon."

"Okay," Billy Jo said, but Dory heard the plaintive note in her voice.

"You look like you need a hug." She reached for the girl whose tears suddenly overflowed.

AFTER DORY LEFT, BILLY JO SAT down at her work station, grabbed a tissue and wiped her eyes. The hug had helped her feel a bit better. Putting her fingers to her keyboard, she dug in. Three hours later she had the new client's background done. Annabelle Browning was forty years old and married to James Browning, age forty-three. Her driver's license number showed she had blue eyes, blonde hair, was five foot four inches tall and weighed 160 pounds. She was employed at the Rosedale County Administration Building where she handled voter registration and recruited election volunteers. The woman had one child, Samantha Leigh.

She then called the County Administration Center and bare-face lied to Friendly Voice who, when she requested Annabelle's address for a fictional flower delivery, said Annabelle lived at 6700 Park Lane, townhouse number 16, in the city of Mount Blanc.

"Did Samantha pass her driver's test? The flowers are for congratulations," she said.

"Yes, Samantha just passed her test just fine," Friendly Voice said.

Billy Jo thanked her and clicked off the call, deep in thought. Odd that the names were the same. Both women married to a Jim or James Browning, both men missing and both apparently working at the same place. *The Browning name wasn't that unusual*, she thought, *but Samantha Leigh's name was less common*. And Samantha was the girl who had picked up James Browning's car from work. It was baffling. Thinking Dory might be able to shed some light on the conundrum, Billy Jo put the office phone on voicemail and headed to the Rosedale Florist's café.

# FOUR

Billy Jo arrived at the Café before Dory appeared. The rain from the previous evening had dwindled away and the sun was emerging, a good thing as the restaurant was a mere strip of tables in front of the florist shop that had a glass facade like a garage door that rolled up into the ceiling. The door was fully raised at the moment and the glorious scent of ivory trumpet lilies drenched the air.

Each table and set of chairs for the restaurant were placed under a brightly flowered pink umbrella. Unsurprisingly, given that the grill was located outside the florist's shop, all of the tables were decorated with potted plants, mostly pink Peruvian lilies and paper-white narcissus. Piped music floated outside. It was Caribbean Calypso and reggae which Billy Jo enjoyed, not as much as opera of course. She adored opera.

The outdoor kitchen stood at the end of the line of tables and the lovely aroma of coffee brewing was luring in the customers. An aproned waitress approached and, when learning there would be a second diner, placed two menus on the table.

"What do you want to drink?" she asked.

"Iced tea, minimal sugar and lemon," she replied. "And my friend will have a flat white coffee."

"Got it," she said and disappeared. As she walked away, Billy Jo noticed that she wore her tied-back hair in a high bun. Some strands of her hair stuck up in a perky rooster tail.

Despite the sunshine and pleasant eatery, Billy Jo continued to struggle to control her painful reaction to PD's decision to retire. She knew it was irrational. Obviously, the man would have had to retire at some point. Mark tried to cheer her, insisting that her relationship with PD would improve, once he wasn't her boss. Dory had noticed her gloomy demeanor and gave her a hug, but Billy Jo remained down in the dumps. Like she told Mark, she felt as if someone had switched off the lights in her life.

The memories of her homeless years kept intruding. When PD appeared at the counter on that momentous day (a skinny old white guy who asked if a girl named Billy Jo Bradley worked there) her first reaction was to feel apprehensive.

"What do you want with her?" she'd asked him in a hostile tone. When he said he'd been a friend of her grandfather's and had been looking for her for a long time, she admitted she was Billy Jo. Although PD had zero resemblance to the handsome knight from fairy tales, he had rescued her from a truly dreadful situation. For that act alone, he would always be a prince to her.

For so long she'd pushed the recollection of those homeless days to the far reaches of her consciousness, while relishing her new life as the cherished youngest among the partners at Rosedale Investigations. Hers had been a rags-to-riches Cinderella story and the time she mentally called her *orphan years* had faded away. She'd never wanted to resurrect the sad urchin she was then, but with PD's announcement, her ragamuffin self had reappeared, lurking in the darkened stairwells of her mind.

Dory appeared and plumped down opposite Billy Jo. Noticing her arrival, the waitress walked over and set down her flat white coffee.

"Thanks," she said. Then turning to her lunch partner, she added, "The bank's going to give us a mortgage on the building. We will be able to give PD what he wants. Now, what seems to be the problem with you? Did you think PD was going to work himself into the grave just to make you happy?"

"Dory, don't be mad at me, please," Billy Jo wailed. "I can't help how I feel."

"Clearly you need to get some things off your chest. Let's decide what we want to eat and then you can tell me what going on in that pretty head of yours."

Dory turned her attention to the menu and shortly thereafter signaled the rooster-tailed waitress, who reappeared, order pad in hand. She ordered a BLT sandwich with fries. Billy Jo ordered a gyro and a Greek salad. Then the perfectly-groomed Miss Dory turned her full-bore attention on Billy Jo and said, "What's really going on? Talk to me, girl."

Billy Jo took a sip of her tea and said, "What have I told you about my life before PD found me?"

"Not a lot. I know it was pretty tough. Your mother died of ovarian cancer when you were a teenager. Your Grampa Aaron had been living with you, but he died around the same time. You never told me what that was like, losing both of them, and it must have been just awful. And I don't think we've ever talked about how you managed to keep a roof over your head until PD tracked you down," Dory said, narrowing her eyes and looking keenly at the girl.

Billy Jo swallowed. Dory's instincts as an Investigator had honed in on the very time she wanted desperately to forget. It was as if she'd pressed on a painful bruise.

The waitress came up with their sandwiches and served them. Both women began to eat and nothing was said for a bit, except for "pass the salt," and "how's your sandwich?"

HAVING FINISHED HER LUNCH, Billy Jo took a deep breath and said, "My mom and I were always close. My father appeared from time to time, but never came back after I turned four. I didn't really miss him because I was so young and Mom was such an upbeat person. She always made life fun, although we didn't have much money and the doctor's practice where she worked provided little in the way of benefits. Looking back, I think her sunny disposition was probably put on for my benefit," she said, looking forlornly at Dory.

"Even without a father, or much in the way of money, it sounds like you had a pretty happy childhood," Dory said. "There are lots of single moms in the black community. They do a great job."

"The best times for me were when we went to visit my mom's parents. They lived out in the country beyond Rosedale and had a little farm. I remember seeing the fluffy baby chicks in the spring and holding them in my hands. They had a barn and a white cat who had kittens in the haymow every year. Grandma was a good cook and taught me how to make a few simple meals, like spaghetti and mac 'n cheese. Once school let out for the year, I spent summers with them. It was something I looked forward to all year. Sadly, my grandmother died of some type of cancer when I was eleven. Grampa Aaron sold the farm and moved in with us after she passed."

Dory nodded, signaling for the waitress who brought her another coffee and topped up Billy Jo's iced tea. "Go on," she said.

"It all changed one day at the end of 11<sup>th</sup> grade. I remember coming home from school and finding the apartment dark. I called for my mother. There was no answer and instinctively I felt something was wrong. I tiptoed down the hall to her room and opened the door. The curtains were shut and she was asleep. I don't think I'd ever seen her take a nap during the day before. She was always busy, cooking, cleaning and singing. I couldn't figure out why she wasn't at work." She cleared her throat, trying to dampen her sorrow.

Dory nodded and Billy Jo's husky voice continued, "She stopped going to work that day and I never heard her sing again." She swallowed. "I'm sorry, Dory, but I can't talk about this any longer. I've made those years disappear with everything I had in me, and it hurts to dredge it all up again."

Dory looked at her for a long moment before saying. "I get it now. Losing your grandmother, your grandpa and then your mom made you grow up way too fast. That's why you reverted to being such a ditzy kid after PD found you. Having him retire rocks you and makes you feel that your life will return to that time. But it won't because I'm not ever leaving you. You're stuck with me," Dory said and her nut-brown face was so loving that Billy Jo's tears spilled over. She reached for a napkin and dabbed her face.

Just then her phone rang and she pulled it from her pocket. "Hello," she said and then added, "Thank you. I appreciate your help."

"Who was that?" Dory asked, signaling for the waitress and signing the check.

"Mrs. Coffin from the sheriff's office. Wayne discovered that a sixteen-year-old girl named Samantha Leigh picked up Mr. Browning's car yesterday from the shipping company where he works. I asked her to find Samantha's address so we could check it out. She lives in a condo in Mount Blanc. The address is 6700 Park Lane," Billy Jo said, looked intently at Dory.

Dory frowned. "Hold on a minute. Isn't that the same address I got for our newest client, Mrs. Annabelle Browning, the woman who is coming in later today?"

"It is," Billy Jo said. "When I did her background, I found out that Annabelle Browning has a daughter named Samantha Leigh."

"Wait, I'm confused. Our new client, Annabelle, is the mother of Samantha Leigh who picked up James Browning's car yesterday from where he works? But, isn't James Browning married to Jessica?"

"So she said. The Browning name isn't that uncommon, and James is an ordinary name, but I'm struggling to understand what is going on here."

Dory's mouth twisted. "It's perfectly clear to me. It seems that our cheating rascal Mr. Browning has found himself a new girlfriend. He's ditched Jessica and moved in with Annabelle." She hesitated and frowned, "But, no. That can't be right, because Annabelle also says he's missing."

Driving back to Rosedale Investigations, Billy Jo kept thinking about the situation. Could it be that the men were twins? No, twins wouldn't have had the same first name. Despite the identical names, Dory was probably right. The simplest explanation had to be that James had left Jessica for Annabelle. Since she'd been working at Rosedale Investigations, Billy Jo learned that while women left their husbands for a variety of reasons, the usual reason for a man to leave his marriage was another woman.

*If you hear hoof-beats it's always better to think horse than zebra,* PD often told her.

# FIVE

BILLY JO, DORY AND WAYNE WERE WAITING in the kitchen of Rosedale Investigations when Annabelle Browning arrived that afternoon. She wore a shapeless faded lavender lounge suit and sneakers. Her dishwater blonde hair was stringy and her whole slump-shouldered demeanor projected an image of smoldering resentment.

Following her down the hall to the conference room, Billy Jo's confusion deepened. Annabelle was both older than and not nearly as good-looking as Jessica. If Dory was right and Browning had left Jessica for Annabelle, it didn't add up.

The team got seated with their beverages and Wayne nodded to Dory to begin.

"It's nice to meet you, Mrs. Browning. Please tell us what we can do for you today?"

"My husband, Jim, is missing," she said.

Billy Jo and Dory made brief eye contact.

"How long has he been gone?" Wayne asked.

"A little more than a week," Annabelle said. "I know it's not very long, but he said he would be home by the weekend. We had a family celebration planned for my daughter, Samantha, because she got her driver's license. The party took place without him ever showing up. It's worrying because he's a very devoted father."

"When did you see him last?" Dory asked.

"The last day we spoke was the morning I got a phone call from the bank. They said we were late with our mortgage payment, but Jim handles the money and I didn't know about the issue. I called him and he said he'd take care of it."

"And you haven't heard from him or seen him since?" Wayne asked.

"Not a word. Late that same evening he texted Samantha, asking her to pick up his car from the office and bring it home. It seemed odd. She just got her license and is pretty inexperienced as a driver. I was surprised he'd ask her to drive at night."

"Would you say you have a good marriage?" Wayne asked in a gentle tone of voice. His hazel eyes held hers.

Annabelle sighed and said, "I don't think marriage is a walk in the park for anyone. We've certainly had our ups and downs. James and I split up for a while and we only got back together after he came here to Mount Blanc. I think, more than anything else, James needs direction. There's a hunger in him for a woman to give him purpose. Without me telling him what to do, he goes . . . off track." She shook her head, sounding exasperated.

"Does Jim work at Fast Freight Deliveries by chance?" Billy Jo asked, with a quick sidelong glance at Wayne.

"Yes, he sells space on semi-trucks that deliver goods to stores, especially perishable goods like fresh fruit and vegetables."

Billy Jo frowned. It couldn't be a coincidence that two men named Browning worked at the same place doing the same job. And none of them believed in coincidences in investigations.

"Unfortunately, we can't help you yet, Mrs. Browning," Wayne said. "Missing persons have to be reported to the law and they have to decide there hasn't been a crime and refer the case to us before we can look into the matter. In your case, that would be city police in Mount Blanc. Did you already report your husband missing to them?"

"I did, but the detective I spoke with told me adults could live anywhere they wanted to. He also mentioned that Jim hadn't been missing very long. They'd keep an eye out for his car, but it wouldn't be high priority."

"I thought he had Samantha bring his car home," Dory said, narrow-eyed.

"She did, and said she put it in our carport, but it's not there now," Annabelle said in a tight voice.

"I'll call John Granger for you. He's the police chief in Mount Blanc. Maybe, I can light a fire under things over there. Once Captain Granger's officers have looked into it more thoroughly, and if your husband hasn't turned up by then, we'll be happy to take your case," Wayne said.

"Do you have a picture of him for us?" Billy Jo said.

The woman rummaged around in her purse and came up with a family photo.

"Thanks. We also need the license number of his car, credit card numbers and his cell phone number. We can't formally investigate until Mount Blanc determines that no crime has been committed, but if we spot the car, we have your contact information and we'll let you know."

"You might also talk with Samantha again. If she and her dad are close, she might recall something significant he said. Be sure to check your home voicemail and your cell phone texts and email messages too," Dory said.

Annabelle thanked them and picked up her purse. "I'm sorry to have bothered you this morning. It's probably nothing."

"Don't be silly. We will be glad to help once a crime has been ruled out."

"God only knows what the jerk has gotten up to this time," Annabelle said, shaking her head. Her body language loudly telegraphed her disgust.

"I'll show you out," Dory said and the two women left the room. Annabelle said good-bye as she walked out the front door. Heading back to the conference room, Dory was astonished to hear delighted peals of hilarity coming from the conference room. Billy Jo and Wayne were both laughing wildly and she was pleased to think the girl's gloom had lifted. Opening the conference room door, she said, "What's so darn funny?"

"Take a look at these two photos, Dory. See what you think," Billy Jo said, stifling a grin, as she passed the pictures Jessica and Annabelle had provided of their missing husbands across the table.

Dory looked at both carefully before raising her face and shaking her head. "Oh, my God. It's the same guy."

"We think so too," Wayne said grinning.

"Well, well, well. It appears we have our first case of bigamy," Dory said and chuckled.

"I agree, but I still have a question," Billy Jo said after managing to control her laughter. "Where is Mr. James Browning now? Clearly, he's not with Annabelle or with Jessica."

"And he's not at work either," Wayne said. "When I stopped by the warehouse, the young man I spoke with said that the salesmen usually worked from home. He said Browning has been online and sending in orders. So, he must be working from some third location because neither Annabelle nor Jessica have seen him."

"The man might just have had it up to here trying to please two wives," Dory said, rolling her eyes. "I understand from my male friends that a lot of women are pretty demanding. Not me, of course," she said grinning. "Men just worship me."

"I don't get what this guy has going for him to get two women to marry him," Wayne said with a confused frown. "He looks pretty ordinary to me."

They all looked at the photos again, seeing a rugged-looking man with close-cut hair and a trim mustache. In the photo Annabelle gave them, she was standing behind Browning with her hand on his shoulder. Jennifer's photo showed all three of them in a seated position. In that picture, James had little Trevor in his lap.

"Well, he does have a kind of cute smile," Billy Jo said.

"But a weak chin," Dory said. "Does nothing for me."

"There's something more than bigamy going on here, because I got the distinct impression Annabelle Browning wasn't telling us everything," Wayne said.

"When both women find out they're married to the same guy, there's going to be one hell of a catfight," Dory said with a lifted eyebrow.

"Maybe the guy just absconded. Remember, he is behind on his mortgage," Wayne said.

"Would he have run though? He doesn't sound like the type. Both these wives made a point of saying how loving a father he is. Maybe he's been assaulted or even . . ."

"Murdered," Wayne's mouth flattened into a line. "I'll call Captain Granger."

"This man of two families is going to take some finding," Dory said.

Billy Jo snapped her fingers. "It's the *Case of the Family Man*," she said with an amused grin.

BILLY JO WAS HARD AT WORK ON HER COMPUTER that afternoon when Wayne reappeared.

"I'm back," he called as he hung his leather jacket up on the hooks just inside the hall.

"Could you make me some coffee?" she asked without looking up.

"Sure can. What are you working on so diligently this afternoon?"

"I've encountered a serious stumbling block."

Wayne walked into the kitchen and made a pot of coffee. Taking a cup to Billy Jo, he set it on her desk. "It must be a pretty big problem to slow you down. You have rock-star computer skills."

"Not today, it seems," she said and scowled at her monitor. "Do you remember when we were working on the Blind Switch case and I couldn't find that horse trainer James Walters?"

"You transposed his name to Walter James and found him as I recall."

"That's right, but James or Jim Browning is proving to be much more of a challenge."

"How so?"

"I decided to look into Browning with both first names, Jim and James as a combined search, not separately. It's definitely the same person, with the same social security and driver's license number. But, I can only go back ten years. Before that all I found was an infant named James Browning who died fifty years ago."

"This tells me that Browning must have assumed the identity of a dead child for some unknown reason, and I'm betting it's connected to his disappearance." Wayne frowned as he added, "It's no wonder you can't find him. You're chasing a ghost."

"A ghost who just shows up ten years ago out of nowhere," she said and sighed.

"Because he was behind on his mortgage payments, see if you can find where James banks."

"Now that I can do," Billy Jo said with a determined expression and got back to it.

# SIX

DORY AND BILLY JO LEFT THE OFFICE TOGETHER the following morning travelling in Dory's car. They were on their way to the town of Mount Blanc. It was the sister city to Rosedale and the place where Annabelle and her daughter Samantha lived. It was a lovely spring day and Billy Jo made a valiant effort to cheer herself up by looking at the flowering trees ablaze in nearly every lawn. The dogwoods were in full bloom and many were surrounded by colorful skirts of pink azaleas. The magnolia tree blooms looked like brandy goblets—chalices created from ivory, pink and cream petals. She rolled down the car window and caught their citrusy scent. Some of the rhododendrons planted around the historic estates were enormous, probably a half-century old. Taking a deep breath, she told herself to *lighten up*. PD was only retiring after all. He wasn't dying, moving away or selling his cabin. *Thank God.*

They found the townhouse complex fairly easily, but almost immediately Dory was driving in circles. The names of the roads were all the same, except for the last word. There was Park Lane, Park Street, Park Avenue and Park Drive. Each road in the complex had at least three iterations.

"Certainly no imagination applied to street names here," she groused.

"Streets are supposed to connect buildings and run east to west. Avenues run north and south. A drive is a winding road and a lane is a narrow trail that lacks a median," Billy Jo said.

"How the heck do you know that?" Dory asked, casting her a quick look as they continued to prowl around the complex.

"A good education," Billy Jo said.

They happened upon Park Avenue almost by accident but once found, it was relatively straightforward to find number 6700 and unit 16. They checked the carpark across from the townhouses, but didn't see James' car—a blue 2017 Oldsmobile Cutlass.

"Tell me again why we came here at this time? It's after ten. With Annabelle at work and Samantha at school, we won't be able to talk to either of them," Billy Jo said.

"Because most complexes have at least one nosy neighbor, and they are normally at home during the day," Dory said. "We need a lot more information about this situation before talking with Browning's two wives again."

"How do you know this stuff?" Billy Jo asked.

"A good street education," Dory said, grinning. They parked the car, walked to unit number 16 and knocked. No answer. They proceeded to knock on each door until the door at number 21 opened.

"How can I help?" the woman asked cheerfully. She looked to be early retirement age, with hair expertly styled. She was slim and wore black slacks, a crisp turquoise blouse and Zuni animal fetish earrings. Smile lines curved around her lips with their shiny peach lipstick. A young cat with a tortoiseshell coat twined himself sinuously around her feet.

"I'm Investigator Dory Clarkson and this is my colleague, Billy Jo Bradley," Dory said, holding out her Private Investigator card. "We are looking for Mr. Browning of Number 16. We're hoping you might be able to help us. May I ask your name?"

"Lorelei Vail," the woman said. "I know the Browning family. Come in and I'll pour us some sun-tea. I just made it." She smiled, turned around and both women followed her into her townhouse, giving each other amazed raised-eyebrow looks. Most people weren't so hospitable to private detectives. As a general rule, folks were downright wary.

Lorelei's townhouse was narrow with an open concept kitchen/dining/living room and a powder room on the main floor. A spiral staircase with black metal steps rose to the right of the entryway leading to the bedrooms on the second level. The complex was new; the kitchen had pale gray cabinets, quartz countertops and stainless steel appliances. The walls had been painted a grayish beige. The whole place had been done in monochromatic tones and the effect was calm and restful. A clear glass vase on the island held a dozen yellow jonquils.

"Take a seat at the island," Lorelei said with a smile.

Dory and Billy Jo took their seats at wrought-iron barstools with wooden seats. The top of the island was cut at an angle on each end like a picture frame, and descended all the way to the floor. The white and gray streaks on the highly polished surface gave it a waterfall effect. After serving them fragrant English breakfast tea with lemon in near-translucent cups, Lorelei joined them.

"How can I help you?" she asked.

"We work for Rosedale Investigations and Annabelle Browning reported her husband Jim missing yesterday. She said he'd been gone over a week at that time," Dory said.

"So, eight or nine days now," Lorelei said thoughtfully. "As you probably noticed, my unit is across from the carports. I can see Mr. Browning's blue Olds easily from my kitchen window. It wasn't there for several days, but then I saw Annabelle's daughter, Samantha, drive the car in the other evening. She parked in their regular spot."

"Go on. This is very helpful, Ms. Vail."

"Call me Lorelei. I'm retired now, but was a buyer for an upscale women's clothing store in Nashville for years. Helping customers find clothes that fit well and enhance their appearance, I learned to focus on details. I pride myself on my observation skills," she said with a satisfied smile.

"Browning's car isn't there now, we noticed," Billy Jo said.

"Yes, and watching it leave was interesting. I always get up bright and early. Buttons here expects his breakfast early," she said, gesturing to the cat who stalked from the room with his tail held high. "Mr. Browning had a suitcase with him, so I assumed he was leaving town. And he was wearing a suit and tie which he rarely wore."

Walking out to their car a bit later, the two women looked at each other in astonishment.

"I will never doubt your instincts again, Dory. I didn't think we'd learn anything and we struck gold," Billy Jo said.

THE TWO WOMEN WERE SIPPING LEMONADE and having sandwiches at the picnic table behind Rosedale Investigations around noon when Dory's phone rang. She put the call on speaker so Billy Jo could listen in.

"Hi, Wayne. Yes, in fact we got quite a bit of information from a curtain-twitcher who observed Browning leaving his Mount Blanc condo early in the morning one day last week. He was wearing a suit and tie and had a suitcase with him."

"Interesting. I wanted to let you know I won't be in tomorrow morning. Lucy has started a Street Medicine program for her medical students and residents."

"What the heck is street medicine?" Billy Jo asked.

"It's a program to provide care for the homeless. Lucy wants her residents, who usually come from well-to-do families, to see the conditions under which these people live. Most of those folks don't come into the ER unless they're accident victims. They know they will be turned away if they are only looking for a place to sleep. I don't like the idea of my wife and a couple of trainees going to the places where the homeless tend to congregate, so I'm going along. Lucy had backpacks made for the students with the words Street Medicine printed on them. She says she has one for me with the word Detective on it," he chuckled. "I'll be back in the office in the afternoon."

"See you then, partner," Dory said and hung up the call.

# SEVEN

THE EVENING BEFORE THE STREET MEDICINE PROJECT was due to start, Wayne and his wife, Lucy, were studying an unfolded map of Rose County on their kitchen island.

"I managed to get both medical school and hospital approval for taking my students out on the street. If it goes well, I hope to make this experience a standard component of the Emergency Medicine clerkship," she said. "Can you point out the spots on this map where we could see the most homeless people?"

"See this place where the overpass crosses the river on the way to Nashville?" Wayne asked, pointing to the map. "I've seen tents set up there, and with the availability of fresh water, it's a magnet for the indigent. The Nashville cops call it Homeless City."

"Are there women and children living there?" Lucy asked. Her eyes reflected the concern in her voice. She was dressed in Wayne's favorite robe, silky white with red roses trailing down the sleeves. Her dark brown hair was long and wavy. Wayne was proud of Lucy's passion for the poorest in society and invariably moved by her beauty. They had been married for less than a year.

"There is zero political tolerance for leaving women and kids on the streets, especially in the winter. But, I have seen young teen-agers in the area and some of them are being used as drug runners by gangs that are unfortunately spreading to Rosedale from Nashville."

Lucy shook her head in dismay. "If we encounter any kids under eighteen, I'll get Child Protective Services to step in. I have permission to bring anyone needing emergency care we can't deliver on-the-street to the ER," she said. "It was a bit of a hard sell, as the hospital usually doesn't get reimbursed for those patients."

"What kinds of problems would require hospital treatment?" Wayne asked.

"Broken bones, pregnant women on the verge of delivery and festering wounds that require i.v. antibiotics. I've loaded all the backpacks with Covid and pregnancy testing kits. If asked, I can give vaccinations and write prescriptions for birth control."

"What about gunshot wounds?" Wayne asked.

"Ever the detective," she smiled. "Well, if it's what you call a *thru-and-thru* with no bullet imbedded, I can treat those on the street. If the bullet is still in the body, they need to come to the hospital. Sounds like we should start at Homeless City. Thanks, Honey."

LUCY'S CONCEPT FOR A STREET MEDICINE CLINIC had spread like wildfire through the hospital and six medical students, two residents and two nurses had signed up to join the group. Three cars set off in a convoy and after a short drive parked near the bridge where a crumbly cement pad, dotted with burn barrels and trash cans, was the site of a makeshift town. Wayne trailed his physician wife as she led her small band, all wearing lime green backpacks, to the place where the homeless congregated. Someone had rigged a broom handle across two metal barrels and hung a blue plastic tarp over it. Rocks held the tarp down at the corners, creating a wholly inadequate shelter. Wayne shuddered to think of anyone sleeping there in the winter.

A big man with a buzz cut who had been sitting on a straw bale smoking a cigarette stood up and walked purposefully toward Lucy. He was dressed in dirty Army fatigues and high boots. Wayne stiffened.

"Good morning, sir," Lucy said cheerily. She was dressed in green scrubs with her stethoscope draped around her neck. The wind blew her shiny brown hair back from her face. "I'm Dr. Lucy Nichols and my students, residents and nurses are here to help with any medical problems your people have. What's your name, sir?"

He didn't answer right away and Wayne walked closer—prepared to intervene if necessary.

"Roscoe," the man finally said, but he looked at her suspiciously. Wayne watched his hands. If the man reached for a gun, he was braced to throw him to the ground. He felt like an idiot for leaving his own gun at home. Having it on his person, even unloaded, which it usually was, helped control such situations.

"What's your rank, Soldier?" Lucy asked.

"It's Sergeant," he said.

"Sergeant Roscoe, could you ask any of the folks here who have injuries or infections to form a line? We are going to set up our clinic here," she said, indicating an area mostly free of pieces of dirty paper and old food wrappers that swirled around in the brisk wind. Cars rumbled past on the overpass overhead. The sky was dark with rain clouds that lay like heavy bands of gauze across the sky.

One of the residents set up a small folding table. A nursing student moved forward to unfold a couple of chairs. The two of them sat down at the table, removing bandages and syringes from their backpacks. Sergeant Roscoe hadn't asked the group to come forward and they sat together or loitered in small groups. One of them lit the trash in a burn barrel. It smoldered, sending a plume of bitter blue smoke into the clouded air.

"Could you please tell them we aren't interested in drug use or illegal aliens? We just want to patch everyone up," Lucy said in a bright voice.

"Do as the doctor says right now, Soldier," Wayne ordered in a low commanding voice.

Roscoe glanced briefly at him, no doubt registering him as a cop, before calling out to the group. "It's okay. You can come over. Just a bunch of medics."

People stood up and shambled slowly toward the table. They were dressed in layers of dirty clothes and stank of cigarettes and alcohol. Poverty dominated the group, encasing them in a near-visible cloak of hunger, hopelessness and despair.

An hour later, all of them had been treated. Some were non-English speakers and Wayne was interested to see how much could be communicated about a medical problem with gestures. The group started packing up. They were about to leave for the second site on their route, when he spotted a teen-aged boy who'd ducked under the overpass. He touched Lucy's shoulder and pointed. She glanced at the youngster who was holding his left arm at a funny angle.

"You there, come over and let me take a look at that," she called out clearly. When he didn't move, she looked at Sergeant Roscoe.

"Move it, kid," Sgt. Roscoe said.

The boy looked uneasy, but walked closer. When Lucy told him to take off his sweatshirt Wayne grimaced. His right arm was swollen and he saw a bit of jagged bone poking out of the skin near his wrist. One of the medical students swallowed and turned away when he saw the broken shaft of bone.

Lucy felt the boy's arm carefully and asked one of the residents to get an arm sling for the boy. "What's your name?" she asked.

"He don't talk much, Miss," an old woman said in a high cracked voice. "Goes by the nickname of Nightshade."

Wayne wondered if the boy might be part Native American. His skin was reddish in tone and his shiny black hair was gathered in a ponytail. He felt a twinge of recognition. The kid looked a lot like he had at that age, pointed on the cusp of manhood, alone and already damaged.

"How long since he broke the arm," Lucy asked the woman who had spoken for the boy.

"We had a late cold snap about a month ago. He slipped in a puddle and put out his arm to break his fall. I told him he needed a doctor."

"You have to come with me now," Lucy said firmly. "I can't treat this here." She turned to her residents and said, "This young man has what we call a FOOSH injury. Do any of you know what that acronym stands for?"

One resident spoke up saying, "It means a *fall onto an outstretched hand.*"

"That's correct. Well done, Kristyn. We're going to take him with us to the hospital. For those of you who aren't close enough to see, Nightshade has an untreated compound fracture of the left radius and the ulna. Without an X-ray, I can't be certain, but I'm pretty sure both bones are broken."

Wayne took the boy's good arm and helped him into the back seat of Lucy's car, laying a hand on his head to be sure he didn't bump it. It was a common cop gesture and the boy's eyes widened.

"It's okay. I was a police officer a long time ago, but I don't do that work anymore. The doctor's just going to fix your arm."

Nightshade nodded but his shiny narrowed eyes never left Wayne's.

# EIGHT

BILLY JO WAS RETURNING FROM LUNCH when she saw a pretty, teen-aged girl standing on their narrow porch. She was wearing a halter sundress printed with lemons, had a pair of sunglasses perched on her blonde head and sandals on her feet.

"Is there something I can do for you?" Billy Jo asked, walking up the sidewalk.

"I hope so," the girl said softly.

"Come on in. It's getting hot out here. We have some iced tea in the fridge." Billy Jo preceded the girl into the entry, walked past her workstation and entered the kitchen. "How do you like your tea? Sweet? Lemon?"

"Iced tea with both, please," the teenager said, adding in a quiet voice, "I've come to talk to you about my father, Jim Browning because . . ." She swallowed and stopped speaking for a moment. "My mother didn't tell you the whole story. I'm Samantha Leigh by the way." She took the cold glass of tea in her hands.

"You better have a seat," Billy Jo said. There was a small round table in the kitchen, just big enough for two chairs. The window was open and a light breeze lifted the white organza curtains. The lovely scent of hyacinths waved into the room. The girl took a seat, but was perched on the edge of the chair, looking as if she might leave at any moment.

Billy Jo reached across the table and briefly touched the girl's hand. "I promise, whatever you say will be kept completely confidential," she said, meeting the girl's cornflower blue eyes with her own.

Samantha inhaled shakily and said, "Mom and I originally lived in Bellevue, Washington. Dad was with us then, but he left when I was six. We moved here four years ago."

"What can you tell me about your father's situation?" Billy Jo asked.

"I probably shouldn't have come," Samantha said, looking around nervously.

"You can trust me," Billy Jo said. "All we are trying to do is find him."

"Me too," she said softly. "The truth is that my mother knows why he left and probably where he is now. All of this—him going missing and our moving here, relates to a crime that took place ten years ago. We were parked in back of the grocery store when I heard the shots. A man collapsed on the pavement and I saw the blood," she grimaced. "Mom told me later that the murdered man was a police officer."

"You witnessed a murder as a child," Billy Jo whispered quietly, thinking it would have been a terrible thing for a six-year-old to see. She sat very still, fearing any movement on her part would send Samantha flying.

"I have to go," the girl said, standing up and dashing out of the kitchen. She left the door to Rosedale Investigations open as she darted from the building. Billy Jo reached the front door just as the girl jumped into her car, backed out of the driveway, turned and sped down the street.

Standing on the porch, Billy Jo pulled her cell phone from her pocket and dialed Dory's number. When she answered Billy Jo said, "I need you to come to the office. Samantha Leigh was here. She says her mother knows where her husband is and why he left. It all relates to the murder of a police officer that occurred ten years ago."

"I'll call Wayne," Dory said.

"PD, too?" Billy Jo asked hopefully.

"Yes, given this involves a cop killing, he'll probably come in."

THE ENTIRE FOUR-PERSON ROSEDALE INVESTIGATIONS TEAM arrived within the hour. Billy Jo had made a pot of coffee, knowing it would be an intense session. She was cheered to see PD and he mentioned he wanted her to come out to the cabin soon. She had begun to think that Mark was right, his retirement might just improve their relationship, until she remembered the big question that loomed in the back of her mind. *Why had it taken PD so long to find her after her grandfather and mother died?*

"You said you had some information for us," Wayne said, looking at Billy Jo.

"I certainly hope *you* got something useful. I struck out," Dory said. She was beautifully dressed as usual. Today's outfit was in shades of purple and blue. Her heels were indigo and her earrings were sapphire and amethyst. She patted her complex braided hair-do.

"I had a visit from Miss Samantha Leigh about an hour ago. Her mother, Annabelle, didn't tell us the whole story. Apparently, all of this is related to a police officer who was murdered ten years ago. Samantha witnessed the killing from the back seat of Browning's car. He disappeared from their lives a few days afterwards."

"Poor kid," Dory said sympathetically.

"After my sojourn with Lucy and her students this morning for the Street Medicine clinic, I had a thought about Browning's car," Wayne said. "I called one of my old Confidential Informants. He's an ace at spotting missing vehicles, ran a car theft ring until I caught up with him. I'd asked him to keep an eye out for Browning's Olds and he got lucky. The vehicle was left in long-term parking at the private airport in Mount Blanc."

"Since the man was a witness to murder, I'll ask the sheriff if he can get a warrant to get into the car. He'll probably agree to have his forensic techs go over it with a fine-tooth comb," Dory said.

"Should I ask Annabelle Browning to come in again?" Billy Jo asked.

"Yes. Let's have her come back in ASAP so we can have a crack at her," PD said, rubbing his hands together.

"I thought you were retiring," Dory said, frowning.

"I am, but this is beginning to sound like a pretty unusual case—what with a man who has two wives, witnessed a cop's murder and has now disappeared," he said.

"What if Mrs. Browning won't talk to us?" Billy Jo asked.

"I'll make her come in," Wayne said, and his mouth tightened.

"Hold on a moment, you two. We were engaged to find the man. We now know he's left the area alive and well. The sheriff is likely to say our job is done," Dory said.

"As you know perfectly well, Dory, there is no statute of limitations on murder. Because Browning saw the murder of a police officer, the sheriff will want to talk to Annabelle. I'll ask if one of his deputies will come with me to collect the woman," Wayne said. His jaw was clenched.

Needing an officer of the law to lend him authority when all he wanted was to bring a person in for an interview was galling. For so many years he had *been* the law. Being a PI lacked many of the privileges he'd taken for granted as a detective. PD, who knew exactly how he felt, gave him a commiserating glance.

# NINE

Sheriff Bradley's Aunt Cornelia was a Judge for Rose County, but she hesitated when the sheriff requested a warrant to search James Browning's car. It was first necessary, she told him, to determine whether the Mount Blanc Police had jurisdiction over the airport. As it turned out, the airport was just outside the city limits and therefore fell under the purview of the sheriff whose writ ran to all of Rose County. Once the jurisdiction issue was settled, and the Judge learned the missing man had been a witness to a murder of a police officer, she was persuaded. The sheriff called Wayne the following day to say his warrant was ready.

After thanking the sheriff for his help, Wayne and George, the Sheriff's Deputy, drove to the Mount Blanc airport. They quickly spotted Browning's car parked in the long-term lot. George popped the car door open with a slim piece of metal that fit between the door and the window. Luckily, a key to the ignition had been left under the driver's seat. George offered to drive the car to the forensics bay at the sheriff's office where the lab techs would go over it thoroughly.

After the Deputy left, Wayne walked into the airport office. "Good morning," he greeted the pretty girl at the counter.

"Are you here to rent a plane?" she asked him. "Beautiful day for flying."

"No, just for information. I'm Detective Wayne Nichols and I'm a private investigator." He pulled his PI identification from his wallet and showed it to her. "I'm working a missing person's case. A middle-aged man either flew a plane from this airport himself, or was flown from here by a private pilot about a week ago. I'm hoping we can figure out when the plane left the airport. I've got approximate dates."

"Sure thing," she said with a wide-eyed expression.

After carefully eliminating the people who rented space to keep their planes in the hangars, and pilots who weren't licensed to fly passengers, they found him. A Mr. John Brown (an obvious alias) had been flown out of Mount Blanc airport at ten o'clock p.m. a week ago by a private pilot. The flight plan showed his final destination was Bellevue, Washington.

"You have been very helpful and I want to thank you. Did you get a chance to speak with Mr. Brown before he left? Or overhear anything he said to the pilot? He could be in danger and we're trying to save his life," Wayne said.

"Oh, wow! Poor guy." She sounded shocked and then added, "I didn't hear much except that he was in a hurry to get to a meeting with a Prosecuting Attorney. They needed his testimony for a trial. Does that help?"

"It sure does. Thank you again," he said and departed.

DRIVING BACK TO THE OFFICE, Wayne reviewed the case in his mind. Each bit of evidence swirled like a shard of brightly colored glass in a kaleidoscope that tumbled and rolled. Mentally turning the wheel on the device, he brought what he knew into focus.

Ten years ago, Browning had witnessed the murder of a police officer in the parking lot behind a grocery store. James was probably getting out of the car, intending to lift Samantha from her car seat, when he heard the gunshots. He would have seen the police officer fall to the pavement, blood spreading from his wound. At that point, the killer probably glanced around to see if anyone had witnessed the shooting. He and Browning would have made eye contact. Perhaps the killer even took a shot or two at James before fleeing the scene. Immediately thereafter, Browning left the state, no doubt afraid the killer would track him down. Four years later, Annabelle Browning and her daughter relocated from their home in Bellevue, Washington to join him in Mount Blanc, Tennessee.

There was a definite hiccup though, because as far as Wayne could tell, before Annabelle and Samantha arrived, Browning had married Jessica and become a father, wildly deviating from what seemed to be a deliberate "under the radar" existence. Presuming Browning was hiding from a killer who wanted him silenced, he shouldn't have done anything that brought him unwanted attention. *A bonehead move.*

Then just over a week ago, Browning drove to the private airport near Mount Blanc and was flown from there to the state of Washington. They perpetrator of the murder he'd witnessed must have come up for trial. The Prosecuting Attorney needed Browning's testimony. Wayne felt a rise of satisfaction as the pieces in the kaleidoscope stopped spinning and clicked into place. He knew where Browning had gone and why he left. He called the office.

"What's up, big guy?" Dory asked.

He relayed the sequence of events to her and asked, "What do you think is going on?"

"I'd say the Prosecuting Attorney is concerned about whether Browning can reliably identify the shooter after all this time. If your timeline is correct, it was shortly after Browning witnessed the shooting that he skedaddled all the way here," she said.

"It crossed my mind that the murdered officer might have been undercover. Unless it was an undercover operation, it shouldn't have taken ten years to get to trial."

"My God, could this case get any more complicated?" Dory said in an exasperated voice.

WAYNE WAS COOKING DINNER THAT EVENING. He'd recently learned how to stir-fry veggies and was giving it a shot. He poured a small puddle of cooking oil into the round-bottomed wok heating on the stove and added garlic and salt. Just before the garlic turned brown, he tossed strips of sweet red pepper, round slices of zucchini, diced Bok choy and some long green onions into the pan. He'd cooked the chicken earlier and set it aside. The rice was bubbling in the cooker when he heard the garage door open. He set two wine glasses on the polished granite surface of the island and poured Chardonnay into their glasses.

"Smells delicious, thanks for cooking," Lucy said. She took off her raincoat and hung it up, pulling off her boots and stashing them under the bench in the back entryway.

Wayne looked up, intending to kiss her hello, before noticing a young man standing in shadow behind her. It was the boy from the Street Medicine clinic. He was wearing green scrubs and carried his old clothes in a bundle under his left arm. His right arm was in a cast.

"Hello," he said in a level tone, wondering what the heck the kid was doing in their kitchen. Then, glancing at Lucy who gave him a *don't ask* look, he added, "Glad you could join us for dinner. I was thinking we'd eat out in the sunroom."

"Nice idea. I'll get the plates and glasses," Lucy said. Telling the boy to put down his clothes and bring the silverware and napkins, she led the way to the glass-walled sunroom that overlooked their backyard. Wayne could hear them talking before she returned to the kitchen.

He raised an eloquent eyebrow and Lucy whispered, "I got orthopedics to set the arm. It was a very difficult surgery as it had been untreated for so long."

"Why is the kid here?" he asked in a low tone.

"Long story. Let's eat and then we can take a walk and I'll tell you all about it."

Wayne carried the veggies, meat and rice out to the sunroom table and they tucked in. The boy looked suspiciously at the meal at first, but after one bite, a huge smile lit his face. He positively shoveled it down. When asked if he liked the food, he nodded but so far he hadn't said a word. Dinner finished, they cleared the table and added the dishes to the dishwasher. Lucy told the boy they were going for a walk and said he could make himself at home.

"You're going to be sleeping in the second bedroom down the hall. If you're still hungry, there's ice cream in the freezer. I'm throwing your grungy old clothes in the wash."

A SAFFRON-COLORED LIGHT FROM THE SETTING SUN spread across their back yard and a breeze ruffled the grass as the couple stepped out their back door. A split-rail fence, turned silver-gray with age, marked the boundary between their property and a cornfield. They walked toward the fence hand-in-hand. From decades in law enforcement, Wayne knew how to wait. However, hearing nothing from his beautiful wife for nearly five minutes, he finally broke the stalemate.

"Honey, is this kind of like bringing a lost puppy home?"

"Kind of," she smiled sweetly, reaching up and giving him a kiss. Wayne felt a rise of frustration. His wife was using her womanly wiles on him. And, it was working.

"Here's what happened. Before his surgery, the O.R. nurse bundled Nightshade into the shower with a bar of soap and some shampoo, telling him to take his time and not to come out until he was totally clean. When he was done, she gave him a towel and some green scrubs," She looked up at him with a complex glance, part pleading, part proud.

"Go on."

"They had to give him a long-acting general anesthetic to keep him under for the length of the procedure which took four hours. Once the orthopedist was finished, Nightshade was taken to recovery. Knowing he'd be unconscious for some time, Channing, my ER nurse, and I headed to Homeless City. When we got there, I didn't see Sergeant Roscoe, but the little white-haired woman named Rosie was there. Do you remember her?"

"I do," he said with a slight edge to his voice.

"Anyway, she said Nightshade has been with the group for three years. When he first arrived, his mother was with him, but she overdosed on heroin and died. Since then, the group has watched out for him. But from that day to this, the boy hasn't spoken to anyone other than the residents of Homeless City."

Wayne frowned at his wife and said, "Am I to understand, in complete defiance of the law, you have brought the boy here to our home? What happened to Child Protective Services? Isn't he underage?"

"Well, yes. He's fifteen, according to Rosie, but I just couldn't take him back to that awful place." She flushed, raised her eyes and said, "He really should still be in the hospital, but they discharged him." She straightened her shoulders and her eyes flashed. "I'm simply not sending him back on the streets with an unhealed compound fracture, Wayne."

She crossed her arms across her chest and he knew he was beaten. Once Lucy played the doctor card, he had few options. Only one occurred to him. "Okay, but just for the night, and then you need to start the process of getting him into foster care. You could get into big trouble otherwise. In fact, your license to practice medicine could be in jeopardy."

Lucy nodded, but Wayne wondered if her nod meant she agreed with him, or only that they had reached a temporary cease-fire in what could be a long, drawn-out war.

As it turned out, a follow-up skirmish was unnecessary. The next morning when Lucy opened the door to the guest bedroom, it was empty. The bed hadn't been slept in. She had washed the boy's clothes the night before and set them, clean and folded, on a chair outside his door. The green scrubs he had been wearing were left on the bed and his own clothes were gone.

"He'll need cash. I'll check the drawer," Wayne said and walked to the little chest in the front entryway. The money they kept there was for fundraisers for schools, local sports teams or the paperboy. A student had stopped by after dinner the previous evening asking for support for the high school football team. Lucy told Nightshade to give the student a $20 bill from the chest. There should have been $50 left in the drawer, but it was empty.

They looked at each other and she said, "Well, that seems to be that. I'm going to the hospital."

"And I have a client to visit," Wayne said, looking at his watch.

# TEN

WAYNE AND DORY ARRIVED AT THE HOME of Annabelle Browning before eight o'clock that morning. Knowing she was employed at the township office, they wanted to catch her before she left for work. When they rang the doorbell, nobody answered. Wayne was about to start pounding on the door when they heard a voice from behind them.

"Investigator Clarkson, are you trying to reach Annabelle?"

It was Lorelei Vail, the observant (some might even say meddlesome) neighbor. She was out for a walk dressed in a perfectly tailored purple jogging suit with white sneakers.

"Good morning, Lorelei. This is my partner, Detective Nichols. We have some information about Mrs. Browning's husband and want to speak to her," Dory said, just as the front door to the condo cracked open.

"I don't have time to talk this morning," Annabelle said and started to close the door.

Wayne put his big size eleven foot in the opening. "This isn't going to take long."

With gritted teeth, Annabelle opened the door, and they walked inside. Without being invited to sit down, Wayne and Dory took their seats on the couch. Annabelle was still standing with a hairbrush in her hand until Wayne told her to sit down. It was his cop voice that did it. She sat.

"We have some important information about your husband. His car was left at the private airport here in Mount Blanc a week ago," Wayne said.

"You could have left me a message about that," Annabelle said, looking irritated and put-upon. She brushed her hair angrily.

"Your husband was flown out of town by a private pilot," Dory said.

"That's all I needed to know. I don't need any more help from you now," Annabelle said. "I have to get to work."

Wayne's eyes bored hers as he said, "He was flown from here to Bellevue, Washington. Would you know anything about why that was his destination?"

Annabelle flushed.

"I asked you a question," Wayne said in a dark voice. "We have information that your husband left here to speak with the Prosecuting Attorney in the city about a murder he witnessed a decade ago."

Annabelle seemed to crumple like a beaten dog. She put her hairbrush down on the coffee table and started to cry.

LUCY ARRIVED TO FIND THE ER SURPRISINGLY EMPTY. She checked with the attending physician, saying she had an errand to run, and asking if it would be okay if she left for an hour. He told her to go ahead. After telling her chief resident he could page her if necessary, she walked out to her car. She would be within fifteen minutes of the hospital if she got a call. There was time for what she planned to do.

A quarter of an hour later, she was parked at the side of the highway above Homeless City. From her position on the lay-by, she could see people moving about, talking and smoking. She looked for Nightshade but didn't see him. Then a big mangy mutt walked into the area and to her surprise was called over and petted by several people. Food was always scarce for the homeless, and they wouldn't tolerate most animals, especially those who would have to be fed daily. The dog sat down outside the little shelter she had seen before, the one created by hanging a faded blue tarp over a broom-handle resting across two burn barrels.

A hand reached out and pulled the dog into the shelter. Lucy's mouth tightened. There was no doubt now in her mind who owned the dog. She'd seen a white cast. Sergeant Roscoe walked over, stooped down and spoke to the occupant. He was handed a wad of bills. She had no doubt it was the money from their house.

Lucy got out of the car and walked down the hill directly toward the blue tarp shelter. Rosie noticed and moved quickly to intercept. She was a small bent-over old woman who had what used to be called a dowager's hump. The proper medical term for it was hypokyphosis, meaning an excessive curvature of the spine. It was caused in older people by fractures in the vertebrae and was exceptionally hard to treat. Despite her disability, Lucy had noticed the previous day that Rosie was one smart cookie. Her black-currant eyes reflected a shrewd intelligence.

"I'm here for Nightshade," Lucy said firmly, continuing to walk toward the blue tarp, despite a tugging on her sleeve.

"He's not here," Rosie said.

"Somehow, I doubt that, Rosie. What's the dog's name?"

"Huck," she said.

"Come here, Huck," Lucy called, and the dog peeked out of the shelter. "I have a treat for you."

The huge dog emerged. He was part German shepherd and part Australian Cattle dog, scrawny and filthy. He was so thin, you could see his ribs. He'd been in a fight and one ear was damaged. Lucy scrounged through her jacket pockets and came up with a package of oyster crackers. She removed the wrapping and gave a cracker to the dog. "I'm giving Huck a treat," she said loudly, and the flap on the blanket shelter opened.

Nightshade, his cast grimy with dirt, crawled out. When she pointed to his cast and frowned, he hung his head.

"You are coming with me," she said in a blunt tone.

"Have to bring my dog." He'd spoken so softly she hardly registered his words. Rosie's eyes widened, hearing the boy speak.

"Now that I see it up close, I can tell that your cast is cracked. The orthopedist is going to have to remove it, check the wound for infection and make you a new one. This is serious, Nightshade, unless it's treated immediately you could lose the use of that arm."

The boy turned and gave a low musical whistle in Huck's direction. When the dog came over, he grabbed hold of the remnants of a mangy collar and looked at her.

Lucy took a deep breath, suppressed her irritation with difficulty and said, "Fine. Huck can come."

They stopped at a dog-grooming place on the way to the hospital and took the dog inside.

Luckily, a groomer was available who agreed to give the dog a bath, cut his nails and comb him out.

"We have a vet practice next door. I'll have him take a look at his ear," the young man said.

"Good idea. Ask them to give him a rabies shot and please feed him, too. We'll be back to pay for the vet services, the grooming and the food," Lucy said and taking Nightshade firmly by his unbroken arm, led him to the car.

DRIVING TOWARD THE HOSPITAL WITH THE BOY in the passenger seat, Lucy recalled hearing the orthopedic surgeon, who had spent hours cleaning the wound and setting the arm say, "It's vital he keeps the cast clean."

*How on earth was she was going to ensure that Nightshade followed his instructions? Especially living in Homeless City?*

That had been the moment, the exact instant in the moving stream of time, when she knew she had to take the boy home with her. Now they were going back to the hospital for a second surgical procedure. She could just imagine the look on the orthopedist's face when he saw the filthy cracked cast.

"Your surgery cost a bundle, which luckily the hospital absorbed, but I'm on the hook for the grooming and vet care for Huck, plus the $50 you *stole*. If I take you home, and I'm stressing the word *if*, are you going to stick around long enough to pay us back?"

"Can Huck come?" he asked.

Feeling frustrated, Lucy strove for calm. "Well, I guess the dog can stay with us for a while. He's used to living outdoors, so we can make him a bed in the garage. We have some yard work that needs doing and that's how you are going to pay back our money and for Huck's care. Are we agreed?"

Nightshade nodded.

"A nod isn't quite good enough, young man. You need to say you agree."

"I agree," the boy said, but his voice broke.

"What else do you say when someone does you a huge favor?" she asked, taking her eyes briefly from the road and giving him a penetrating look.

"Thank you," Nightshade said and held his slender brown hand out to shake hers.

JESSICA BROWNING HAD BOOKED A FOLLOW-UP APPOINTMENT with Rosedale Investigations. Her husband was still missing and she wanted to know what they had found out so far. Billy Jo felt a bit anxious about the encounter. Afraid she might say something the partners would rather be kept confidential, she called PD.

"I'm sorry to bother you when you aren't *working* here anymore," she told him with a touch of resentment in her voice. "Jessica Browning is coming in this morning, and I don't know what I am allowed to tell her."

"Call Dory and Wayne," PD said.

"Already did. They are talking with the *other* Mrs. Browning and then are headed to the sheriff's office."

"Hmm. In that case, I'll drive over," PD said and hung up.

He arrived half an hour later, grabbed a cup of coffee, and pulled a chair up to Billy Jo's desk. "What are you working on?"

"I'm struggling to fill in Browning's background. There's nothing in the system about him prior to ten years ago."

"Let it go. It's almost time for Jessica's appointment. I'll take the lead on the interview. You can be present, but only as an observer," PD said firmly.

JESSICA ARRIVED RIGHT ON TIME. The woman was sharply dressed as usual, but her face looked pale and she was thinner.

"Come on back to the conference room," Billy Jo said, after offering her tea or coffee, which she declined. Once there, PD introduced himself as CEO of Rosedale Investigations.

"I've been called in due to the seriousness of your situation," he said.

"Thank you," Jessica said softly. "I'm terribly worried about my husband and appreciate you taking the time to meet with me."

"Happy to do it," PD said, sounding mollified. "Here's what we have learned. We believe your husband to be alive and well. He was flown out of the Mount Blanc airport in a private plane a week ago, headed to Bellevue, Washington. We are of the opinion that he was taken there to assist the Prosecuting Attorney in preparation for a trial."

"What?" Jessica looked stunned. "James couldn't possibly know anything helpful. He works here and takes orders for grocery delivery. Are you sure you have the right person?"

"We are, because it seems your husband witnessed the murder of a police officer before he moved here," PD said.

"My God," Jessica said. She looked like she'd been struck.

"What can you tell me about your husband's life before you two married?"

Jessica took a deep breath before saying, "Not very much really. James is my first husband Chris's cousin. We met at his funeral. I was desperately sad at that time and worried about money. James offered to move in and help me financially. He'd always wanted a family, he told me. I got the feeling he'd had a family once, but that they were estranged. I said he could move in with me, but told him I wasn't ready for another intimate relationship. He honored my wishes. When I discovered I was pregnant with my first husband's child, although it was his cousin's baby and not his own, James proposed and I accepted."

"Did he ever tell you what he had been doing for work before you met?"

"No, but he said Chris asked him to serve as our child's father if anything should happen to him. When I agreed to marry James, I felt I was honoring my deceased husband's wishes."

"Everything I've told you so far, Jessica, is speculative, except for the fact that your husband is alive and well. Whatever he's doing in the state of Washington, I'm quite sure he will be back home when his participation is no longer needed," PD said and patted Jessica's shoulder.

"Thank you. I'll tell my son this. Hopefully it will help him, too. Please let me know anything else you find out," she said.

AFTER JESSICA LEFT, BILLY JO TURNED to PD with a wounded look and asked why he hadn't let her participate in the interview.

"Use your head, Billy Jo. This guy Browning is involved in some very heavy stuff. And let us not forget that he's married to two women, both of whom could be involved in whatever he's up to. You need to keep quiet unless one of the partners tells you it's okay to bring something up."

Billy Jo gritted her teeth as she fought back tears. Resentment burned in her throat at the putdown. She'd be damned if she'd keep quiet when she'd worked for Rosedale Investigations for three years and was majoring in criminal justice at the University. She stomped into the kitchen for coffee. PD followed her.

"I know you're mad," he said. "But having your feelings hurt is a lot better than exposing you to danger and this whole case reeks of major crime."

Billy Jo looked at his face and felt his love wash over her like sunshine, warm and palpable as the coffee cup in her hand. Despite the put-down, she knew he was only being protective. It was annoying, but apparently part-and-parcel of any cop's duty toward their family.

"How about a hug?" he asked and when she nodded, he gathered her into his arms.

WATCHING THE SKINNY OLD MAN WALK OUT to his truck later, Billy Jo felt a stab of loss.

A sudden memory of the day the landlord told her she had to move out of their apartment rose in her mind. It was shortly after the deaths of both her mother and grandfather. The landlord said she hadn't paid her rent and he'd a found a new renter. "You, young lady, are a squatter," he said.

"But where am I supposed to live?" she'd asked pitifully.

"Not my problem, girl. Get your stuff and be out of here by five o'clock."

Looking around the apartment, with all its memories of her dear mother and grandfather, she struggled to decide what to take. Tears falling, she grabbed a plastic trash bag and stuffed it with her clothes. She added her winter jacket, a pillow, a puffy quilt and her mother's pink flannel nightgown. It was the last thing she wore before her final surgery. Raising the nightgown to her face, Billy Jo inhaled a trace of her mother's lily of the valley perfume. Sobbing, she added the nightgown to the plastic bag and went into the kitchen. There wasn't much in the cupboard, but she found a loaf of bread, a jar of jam and some peanut butter. It was all she could carry.

Walking out to the parking area in a softly falling rain, Billy Jo put the trash bag, pillow and blanket, as well as the food in the back seat. Then, taking a final look at what had been her home for as long as she could remember, she started the car, turned on her windshield wipers and drove off. That night was the longest of her life. She woke up shivering in the gray early morning light and for a moment didn't know where she was. Then she remembered.

She was homeless . . . and an orphan.

# ELEVEN

BILLY JO WAS MAKING HERSELF A CAPPUCCINO in the kitchen the next morning when she heard the doorbell tinkle. "I'll get it," she called. Opening the door, she saw Lorelei Vail standing on the front porch and invited her to come inside.

"Good morning, Lorelei," Dory said, as she came out of her office and spotted their visitor. "I wondered, after you just *happened* to show up outside the Browning's residence yesterday, if you had more to tell us. Let's get some coffee and go to the conference room."

After they all took their seats, Lorelei said, "I managed to waylay Samantha after school yesterday. Nice girl, Samantha. Anyway, I learned that Annabelle never changed her last name when she married Browning. Her first marriage was to Darrell Leigh. James Browning and Annabelle Leigh got together when Samantha was just a baby."

"Good information, Lorelei. Did the marriage to Mr. Leigh end in divorce?"

"Yes, it did. However, I'm not sure she is legally married to Browning, and neither was Samantha."

"In my search of his background, I discovered that they were married," Billy Jo said, defensively. It was irritating that this woman had found information contradicting her work. She was the credentialed IT person for the business after all, not this nosy clothes buyer.

"Are you familiar with the state of common law marriage?" Lorelei asked.

"I am, although I'd need to review its current legality," Dory said. "As I recall, if a couple presents themselves to friends and family as married, live together and have shared bank accounts, they are considered married under the law after co-habiting for a certain period of time."

"That's correct and I believe that James and Annabelle are a common law couple. That made me wonder if Annabelle used his last name when she got the job at the township office, so I checked. Her employment file lists her as Annabelle Leigh," Lorelei said. She tilted her bird-like head to the side and pursed her lips, looking smug.

"How the heck did you get ahold of her employment file?" Dory asked. *The woman was a wonder.*

"Samantha checked it for me. She works part-time as a student helper for the office. And there's more."

"Somehow, I knew there would be," Dory said. Rosedale Investigations seriously needed to hire this woman. She was a born Confidential Informant.

"Apparently, when Browning relocated here, Annabelle didn't come with him. It was several years before she joined him."

"Did Samantha tell you this? She was only ten when they came here, so she might not be considered the most reliable source," Billy Jo said, realizing how cross she sounded.

"I find her totally believable," Lorelei said firmly. "She told me she'd overheard a phone conversation between her parents. Annabelle told James she'd gotten a visit from the cops. They thought the shooter was back in the area. James said they should come to Mount Blanc and join him."-

"Are you looking for a job?" Dory asked with a chuckle. "I'm an Investigator with a private detective agency, and I've got to admit feeling pretty inadequate right now."

"Actually, I've been thinking about going back to work. I have some extra time on my hands and I'm bored. Let's talk," she said. Dory agreed and shooed Billy Jo out of the room, despite her protests.

LUCY'S CAR WAS IN THE DRIVEWAY when Wayne pulled in that evening. Getting out of his truck, he was startled to see a large dog asleep in a dog bed placed in the far corner of the garage. There was a white bandage on the animal's left ear. The dog raised his head and growled in a low rumble. He was leashed to the tool cabinet. Given his size, it was a relief.

"Lucy, I'm home," he called as he walked into their kitchen. He could hear voices coming from the sunroom. With curiosity growing about the voices (and the dog) he walked through the casement arch at the back of their house and stepped down onto the polished stone floor of their recently-added sunroom. Skylights had been built into the roof of the extension and beautiful rectangles of light fell upon the bottle green sofa, his wife and the boy who was seated with her. Lucy got up to kiss him hello.

Wayne had been relieved to find Nightshade gone that morning, assuming the young intruder had returned to Homeless City. When he found the money missing from the hall table, he thought it was a small price to pay to detach Lucy from the kid. Now the boy was back.

Obviously, it wasn't going to be that easy to dislodge him.

"Let me get you a glass of wine," Lucy said and left the room.

"I assume that's your dog in our garage," Wayne said gruffly, looking at Nightshade.

The boy nodded and said, "Huck."

"Is that the dog's name, Huck?"

Nightshade nodded.

"Looked like he'd been in a fight. Is he aggressive?" he asked, a note of worry in his voice. As a cop, he'd been accosted many times by large dangerous dogs.

Before he got an answer, Lucy returned with two wine glasses and a can of soda.

"Let's take our wine outside," she said, and Wayne nodded. They left Nightshade sipping his soda on the couch and walked through their back yard to the edge of their property. Bright green shoots of young corn were coming up in the field. Beyond the field was a pine forest illuminated by the setting sun. The view was Wayne's favorite. No houses, no streets, no stores, no crime. Looking across the cornfield normally gave him a feeling of serenity, but not today.

"I thought we agreed you would contact Child Protective Services," he said in a gravelly voice.

"I decided it was best to have Nightshade stay with us for a bit. Since he made off with our cash from the table in the front hall, he needs to work off that debt."

"And the dog?" Wayne asked pointedly.

"Well . . . he wouldn't leave Homeless City without him. He's had the dog since he was a puppy, Honey. It's his only family."

Wayne took a deep breath. "How on earth did you get Child Protective Services to agree to this? You did call them, right?"

The color rose in Lucy's cheeks and she gave him a brief guilty smile before saying, "I did. But you know that adolescents, especially minority teens, are very hard to place. Protective Services is underfunded and understaffed. They were relieved by my offer, especially after I told them he was a relative."

"A relative of yours?" Wayne asked, frowning.

"No. Yours, of course. I didn't think they would buy a genetic connection with me. I'm Swedish, which is about as white as it's possible to be. I think Nightshade's part Native American, and I told them about your ancestry."

"What the hell, Lucy? Couldn't you have called me about this life-altering decision of yours? We're supposed to be a team and I don't for a second buy that he's only going to be with us a few days."

"Do you remember the conversation we had before you proposed? The one when I said I'd like to be a mother someday?" she asked with a sweet smile.

"I do, of course, but does it have to be this boy? He's a street kid and probably has a record. He could be violent for all we know. He comes with lots of baggage we know nothing about. I know you want to be a mother, but I thought we would adopt, maybe a younger child. I'm sorry, Lucy, but I never agreed to this." He shook his head.

Then with no warning at all, she started to cry. Not with red cheeks and loud sobs, but silently. With tears that never seemed to stop running from uplifted brimming eyes, she said, "Are you really going to say 'No' to the son God has sent us?"

Wayne put his arms around her, suppressing his frustration. He just knew he was going to end up being a father to a troubled teenage boy who had careened into their lives with an unknown past and damn dog the size of a mountain lion.

# TWELVE

PD PASCOE WAS DRIVING TO HIS CABIN OUTSIDE ROSEDALE. It was spring break from the University and Liam, his grandson, had a week off from classes. They had recently closed on the purchase of a condo in Knoxville. With the help of Liam and several of his buddies, they'd orchestrated the simple move. The unit was now minimally furnished, had beds in the bedrooms, a folding table and chairs in the kitchen, and a TV and a couch in the living room. They had purchased the furniture from second-hand stores along with a set of dishes, glassware, silverware, pots and pans.

As he drove, PD smiled to himself. His retirement dreams of having time to spend observing the abundant nature around his cabin and enjoying his two grandchildren were actually coming true. Having Billy Jo and Liam come into his life in his old age was a totally unexpected blessing. He'd been asked to take care of Billy Jo when her grandfather, Aaron, was dying. It took him two years to locate her, a fact that still caused him to feel a pang of guilt, but things had worked out well since.

In a sad turn of events, some time ago PD got a call from the Rosedale Funeral parlor, and learned he had a son who'd passed away. They wanted him to claim the man's ashes. Once he contacted the man's widow and found he had a grandson, he couldn't wait to meet him. The corners of his mouth rose in pure delight.

He could still have a decade or more to live—days and nights filled with tranquility, seeing the sun rise, watching the stars come out at night and seeing the deer and wild turkeys on warm summer evenings. When autumn came, the three of them could sit out on his deck as colored leaves tumbled from the trees. He looked over at Liam, who had fallen asleep. The young man was tall and thin. He had an uncanny resemblance to PD's older brother, who had died in a car accident at sixteen. He felt the past slide seamlessly into the present and rode a cresting wave of fulfillment.

BEFORE LEAVING KNOXVILLE, PD LEFT A MESSAGE on the Rosedale Investigations voicemail saying he was headed home to the cabin. Hearing the message, Billy Jo decided to drive out there after work. She was looking forward to having some time alone with him. Lately, memories of the time she'd been homeless kept pushing to the surface of her mind, raising questions she'd never had the courage to ask before.

Had her biological grandfather, Aaron, been eligible for any military benefits from his Army service? Did he have a life insurance policy? If so, who was the beneficiary? Would it be her late mother? Having worked for Rosedale Investigations for several years, she'd learned that there were primary beneficiaries and subsidiary beneficiaries who inherited in the case where a primary beneficiary had passed away.

There were also some harder questions that troubled Billy Jo, some that would put PD in an awkward position. Why had it taken him two years after her grandfather died to find her? Those were desperate times when she was homeless and living in her car. The man was a detective, for heaven's sake. Couldn't he have tracked her down sooner?

She'd been so elated to be rescued, given a beautiful free apartment and a job, it hadn't occurred to her to question him before, but PD's decision to retire had brought it to a head. She knew she should be grateful for her recent life with all its benefits, but felt a sword-thrust of resentment in her heart. Because their deaths virtually coincided, neither her mother, nor her grandfather, had made any provisions for her, other than her mom saying there was an old Army buddy of her grandfather's who had promised to help. It was two years before she learned the Army buddy was PD. Why had it taken him so long to honor his promise to help her? Didn't he care? The questions burned like a maddened swarm of wasps in her mind.

IT WAS SUNDOWN WHEN BILLY JO REACHED THE TURN-OFF to the gravel lane that wound through a poplar and beech forest to PD's place. She'd brought pizza, beer and wine, planning to reheat the pizza in the oven. Pulling into the circle drive in front of the cabin, she saw PD's car. She didn't see Liam's red motorcycle and heaved a sigh of relief. Her adopted grandfather was out walking. And he was alone.

She'd tried hard to be a good sport about sharing PD with Liam, but it had taken an effort. Not that Liam was a bad guy. He was all right, but he had a blood tie to PD and she didn't. Liam had appeared on the scene when the Rosedale Funeral Home called asking PD to pick up the ashes of a son he'd never known existed. When he contacted his son's ex-wife, he learned about Liam and now they were close. She worried about that.

*Would PD feel something for Liam that he could never feel for her? She was only the granddaughter of an old Army pal after all. Liam was his biological grandson. Would PD slowly slip away from her—like a child's sandcastle washed away by a wave? Was she on the verge of losing a second family?*

Taking a deep breath, Billy Jo walked inside, set the food on the counter and started the oven to pre-heat. She put the beer in the fridge. Sliding the pizza into the oven, she set the timer. Pouring herself a glass of wine, she grabbed a fuzzy cuddle blanket from the couch and walked out onto the deck that floated above a deep ravine. Four Adirondack chairs, red, green, blue and purple, were placed in a half circle. She took the blue one. Sipping her wine and feeling the warmth of the evening sun as she snuggled under the blanket, she recalled the last thing her mother said to her before going into the OR for what she had told her was a minor procedure.

"In case I don't make it," she said, "Grampa has made arrangements with a friend of his to take care of you. You're going to be all right. Remember to count your blessings." Her voice had been all but inaudible, blunted by the anesthetic administered prior to her surgery.

It was only when the surgeon came out to speak with her after the procedure that she learned her mother had been battling ovarian cancer for over a year.

"I'm very sorry, young lady. There was a sudden cardiac event that happened when your mother was on the table. She didn't survive," the surgeon said.

"What? No, that can't be. It just was a cosmetic procedure," her voice cracked.

The surgeon's eyes softened as he said, "Perhaps that's what she told you, dear, but the surgery today was her last hope. Your mother had metastatic ovarian cancer. Her life expectancy was only about six months. It would have been a hard death; perhaps in some ways this was a blessing for her, although not for you, of course. I'm very sorry for your loss."

It had been the worst day of her life.

Now she wondered if she should even raise the questions that tormented her about why PD had failed to come for her. The past was gone and her present existence brimmed with love, but it was as if she heard a door squeak as it swung open in the back of her mind—a door that led to an anguished past which caught her in its grip. She was no longer the happy-go-lucky kid who had everything she needed. Now her heart was filled with both the bitter and the sweet.

Billy Jo heard two male voices as they approached the cabin. Hoping to find that Wayne was with PD, she got up from her chair on the deck and walked into the kitchen. The timer rang, and she opened the oven door. The pizza was bubbling. Then her face fell as PD and Liam walked into the cabin.

"Hi, Billy Jo," Liam said, pleasantly. "I didn't know you were coming out."

"I didn't either, but you're always welcome," PD said smiling. "We were just wondering what to have for dinner. I'll get the plates and glasses."

They sat down to eat at the table in front of the glass sliding door that led out to the deck. As they downed the pizza, the two men talked happily about the trails they were cutting through the fields, a herd of deer they had chased up and some wild turkeys they'd seen.

"This property is an oasis for wildlife," Liam said. He looked relaxed and happy, dressed in jeans and a t-shirt that read, *Photographers never lose Focus*. He was taking classes to become a professional photographer, a passion he'd shared with PD.

*Something else I don't have in common with him*, she thought grimly.

"It's because the property has been left to Mother Nature for decades. It was a farm once in the distant past, but it's too hilly for modern agriculture. White-tailed deer, wild turkeys, songbirds, raptors and even foxes live here now. I'm thinking this summer we might put up a couple of blinds to observe the hawks and eagles. You could get some really good shots. What do you think, Liam?"

Billy Jo picked at her food. It wasn't fair that the two of them were engaged in projects that didn't involve her. PD was supposed to be *her* grandfather. She excused herself from the table, put her dishes into the sink and walked out to the deck. The sun lit the little lake at the bottom of the ravine staining the surface of the water pink. The last lip of sun had fallen below the horizon and only rose-colored clouds floated in the sky.

"*I may as well leave as I'm clearly not wanted here.*" Just as she reached the back door, PD got up from the table.

"Please don't go yet, Billy Jo," he said. "I'm sorry if we left you out of the conversation. I tell you what, let's walk down the lane. There's a pileated woodpecker on the cottonwood tree I want to show you."

"Okay," she said, thinking she'd be given a perfect opportunity. They strolled down the gravel two-track, up a rise and then down a small hill before she said, "I have something to ask you."

"Look, there he is," PD said. The large black and white woodpecker was hanging on the side of a half-dead cottonwood, boring holes into its deep interior for worms and bugs. The bird must have heard their voices because he stopped working, flew straight toward them and rose into the air over their heads. They could hear its wings beating and see his vivid red, white and black coloring.

"How about that, Billy Jo. Isn't he spectacular?"

"I said, I have a question." At the serious note in her voice, PD turned toward her, his deeply lined face troubled. "I want to know if my biological grandfather, Aaron, had life insurance. Or received any benefits from his Army service?"

PD took a deep breath. "Is there anything else bothering you, Billy Jo? I could tell you felt left out at dinner."

"Does the fact that I'm not related to you by blood, and that Liam is, does it matter?" Her face crumpled and her voice broke.

"Of course not. You are . . . essential to me," PD said and held out his hand for hers.

So it began, but at the end of their conversation, as they walked back to the cabin with the moon rising, the mourning doves cooing and the croaking of bull frogs, Billy Jo learned PD had been the beneficiary of her grandfather's life insurance policy. Grandpa Aaron had left PD the money for him to use to cover the costs of her support and education. The decision was infuriating and painful, as if neither one of them trusted her to use the money sensibly.

Noticing the look on her face, PD said, "I think it's time for me to give you control of the money Aaron left. I'll do that soon."

Driving away from the cabin as the full moon floated in the sky, she asked the universe the seminal question, the one she still hadn't dared to ask PD.

"How could you take the money, even using it as you did, and not find me?"

# THIRTEEN

Knowing it would be several weeks before any more progress could be made on the Browning matter, the team decided to take on a second case. A woman named Hilary Broadchurch-Miller had been requesting their services. She wanted to discuss a troubling situation with her brother.

Dory was standing on the front porch, sipping her coffee and enjoying the beautiful sunny morning before it got too hot to be outdoors. Passing Billy Jo's workstation earlier, she'd noticed the girl was professionally dressed which hopefully meant she was getting used to PD's decision to retire. Although when asked about her visit to his place the previous evening, the girl just shrugged and said, "It went okay."

At that moment, their newest client drove into the driveway and Dory walked down the porch steps to meet her.

"You must be Hilary. I'm Investigator Clarkson and I'll be getting your details this morning." They walked inside. She took Hilary's jacket, hung it up and escorted her into the kitchen. While getting her some coffee, she introduced her to Billy Jo.

Once the three of them took their seats at the conference table, Dory said, "When you called, you said you were concerned about your brother, Grant. Is that the reason for your visit?"

"Yes, it certainly is," Hilary said, in a tone ringing with barely suppressed resentment. She was slim, with a pleasant face, curly brown hair and an upturned nose awash with freckles.

*It would have been a lovely face,* Billy Jo thought, *if only her teeth weren't clenched.*

"Tell me a bit more about the issue," Dory said.

"My brother is engaged in an inappropriate relationship," Hilary said. "It's with his yoga instructor."

"Is the woman of age?" Dory asked in a suspicious tone.

"Yes, she's twenty-one."

"Then I'm sorry, Hilary, but we can't help you. You may not approve of your brother's choice, but Rosedale Investigations is not the *Love Police*. We don't look into relationships between unmarried adults. I'll show you out." She stood.

"Please, wait just a moment," Hilary said.

Dory sat back down and said, "We can assure you whatever you tell us is in complete confidence."

"It's just that Grant promised to cover the cost of sending my two sons to college," Hilary said in a piqued voice.

"I see. And you're concerned if he marries or has a child with this young woman that your brother will renege on his promise to cover the cost of college for your boys. Is that right?"

"I know it seems selfish, but my husband and I have been counting on his support."

"Rosedale Investigations works with a family attorney in Rosedale named Evangeline Bon Temps," Billy Jo said. "She could draw up a contract about the college support. If your brother is willing to sign it, you could stop worrying about his relationship with this girl."

"Thank you, I'll do that, but I'd still like you to look into the situation. The woman's name is Aimee Anderson."

"Toward what end?" Dory asked. "Is there something going on here that you haven't told us?"

"I think she might be blackmailing him," Hilary said in a barely audible tone.

The nasty word hung in the air and Billy Jo inhaled sharply.

"Do you have any evidence of that, Hilary? Blackmail is against the law."

"I know, and if I had any hard evidence, you would tell me I should pay a visit to the sheriff."

"Not you, Hilary. If this girl is blackmailing your brother, he's the one who needs to report it," Dory said.

"How long has this relationship been going on?" Billy Jo asked.

"It started two months ago, right after Aimee got back from Mexico. Grant told me she went there to complete her yoga training and get certified as an instructor. As far as evidence is concerned, all I have is my intuition which tells me something is going on between my brother and this girl and that it's going to be a problem for me. Could you please see what you can find?"

"What could she have on your brother? Does he have a record? Is he involved in anything illegal? Drugs? Theft?" Dory asked.

"Nothing like that, I assure you," Hilary said.

"Well, it's likely to be a dead end, but we will see what we can find. What studio employs her?"

"It's called Power Zone and it's in the new strip mall in Rosedale."

"We'll get started today, but if we dig up evidence that Aimee is actually blackmailing your brother, he will have to report it. That's not the job of private investigators. Blackmail falls under the bailiwick of the law."

"Thank you. Please let me know what you find. I'll stop back in a few days," Hilary said.

As the door closed behind their newest client, Billy Jo said, "I presume this means I'm going to Power Zone."

"Yup, and signing up for a yoga class with Aimee Anderson."

"Would you be okay with me taking the lead on this one? Since this case involves a young woman my age, she might feel more comfortable talking to me. I will keep you and Wayne in the loop."

"Actually, yes. Please do. I have a lot to do to get PD's retirement payout finalized. And I'm still trying to get some evidence on Molly, my presumably unfaithful wife," Dory said.

ANNABELLE BROWNING STOPPED BY THE OFFICE late that afternoon, paid her bill and officially informed the office she wanted no further investigation done into the case of her missing husband. Dory tried vigorously to dissuade her, to no avail.

"Will you inform us when he reappears?" she asked, and Annabelle nodded. After the woman left, Dory walked into the kitchen. Billy Jo was standing there, gazing out the open window. She turned around when Dory came in, but she couldn't quite disguise the shine of unshed tears in her eyes.

Grabbing a tissue, Billy Jo blew her nose. "Did you know that PD thinks both Annabelle and Jessica could be involved with James Browning in the criminal case under investigation?"

"Having met both women, I doubt Jessica is involved. For one thing, she keeps dropping by here nearly every day to ask whether we have made any progress toward finding her husband. I think it's sweet. She's like those little old ladies who go to the doctor every week, whether they need to or not," Dory grinned. "On another note, have you heard from Wayne?"

"He just called. Lucy's been helping a homeless boy they met the day of the Street Medicine event. The kid is staying with them and I got the sense that our Detective was not exactly thrilled about it. But, he's had some luck on the Browning case. He contacted the local newspaper in Bellevue. It's a medium-sized city outside Seattle where Annabelle and James originally lived. The paper is called the Endeavor and Wayne's been talking to a reporter whose been giving him information."

"What has he learned?" Dory asked.

"Browning is staying in a hotel in Bellevue. Drew, that's the name of the reporter, told Wayne that he is going to be a key witness in the trial of the man accused of shooting the police officer."

AFTER CHANGING INTO EXERCISE CLOTHES, Billy Jo was about to leave for Power Zone that evening, when she heard wild pounding on the front door. Running down the stairs, she opened the door to a flushed and frantic-looking Jessica Browning.

"I have to talk to you right now," she said, pushing her way into the entryway.

"What's going on?" Billy Jo asked.

"I got a letter from my husband."

"That's good news, isn't it?" She felt confused about why Jessica would be so perturbed. Getting a letter should reassure her that her husband was alive and well.

"Just look at this," Jessica said holding the letter out to Billy Jo who took the sheet of paper and read the letter.

"*Dear Jessica, I'm so sorry I left without telling you where I was going. I've been asked to meet with the Prosecuting Attorney here about a case of murder. I miss you and Trevor. Give the little guy a hug for me. When I get back, I have something important to tell you. It's very difficult for me to talk about and I'm sorry I never told you before. When we got married, I was separated from my first wife. I have another family. Please forgive me. Love, James.*"

"What the hell does he mean *another family*?" Jessica asked in an anguished voice. Her pretty face was mottled with tears.

"I'm sorry, Jessica. I don't know," Billy Jo said.

"You do know something. I can see it in your face." Jessica's eyes flashed.

Billy Jo took a deep breath and said, "I think it's best that your husband tells you himself when he gets back."

"Tells me what? What the hell is going on here? I'm a paying client. You have a duty to tell me what you have found." She pointed her finger at Billy Jo, her voice hard and accusing.

Thinking desperately, Billy Jo said, "I'm just the IT person for the agency, Jessica. You will have to speak with Investigator Clarkson or Detective Nichols if you want more information."

"To hell with this. I'm going to call your CEO, PD Pascoe. He is going to tell me what my husband meant by his *other family*." With that she flounced out the door.

Billy Jo reached for her cell phone and dialed PD. When he didn't answer, she left a message telling him about the letter from Browning and Jessica's insistence on speaking with him. Having done what she could to mitigate the oncoming storm, she walked outside to her car and headed for Power Zone. Parking her car in the lot for the gym, Billy Jo left a text message for both Wayne and Dory about the seriously agitated Jessica Browning. Dory immediately sent back a return text saying, *Wonder if Annabelle got a letter too?*

POWER ZONE WAS LOCATED AT THE END of a recently built line of shops on the outskirts of Rosedale. The entrance doors to the studio were bracketed by black wrought-iron urns planted with dark red calla lilies. Sycamore trees had been installed in open squares cut into the concrete sidewalk outside the building. The wind rose and the tree's stiff leaves clattered in the breeze, clicking against each other as if they had been made of metal.

Observing the activity in the two-story building through its expansive glass front, Billy Jo saw people riding on exercise bikes and using other equipment. On the mezzanine, an exercise class was in session. She opened the door and walked up to the front desk.

"Can I help you?" the receptionist asked.

"Yes. I'd like to sign up for a yoga class. I've heard good things about Miss Anderson and would like to take a class from her."

"Perfect timing. She has a new class starting this evening at 7:00 p.m.

You're lucky to get in. This is her last slot. Here's the brochure about it."

Looking at the multi-colored brochure with photos of healthy-looking men and women, Billy Jo reached for her wallet and handed the receptionist the office credit card.

"The first class is free; after that it's $70 per class, but if you pay for the whole six-week course it's only $325. Shall I charge the whole amount to this card?"

"I'll decide after tonight's class," Billy Jo said, taking back the credit card. She completed the paperwork the receptionist handed her and asked, "Mind if I look around?"

"Not at all. The yoga classroom is upstairs. The earlier class is just ending. You can take an elevator or the stairs over there." The woman gestured to the right side of the building.

As BILLY JO WALKED UP THE TWO-STORY STAIRCASE, the yoga students streamed past her. They were talking happily to each other, discussing a current movie and a recent concert. Thinking of their client's brother, Billy Jo wondered why he would pursue a relationship with a woman half his age. *Grant should appreciate his blessings,* she thought.

*But aren't you doing the same dumb thing?* She took a shaky breath. *If she confronted PD about why it took so long to find her, would she be going against her mother's last words? Failing to appreciate her own blessings?*

Reaching the top of the stairs, Billy Jo walked down the hall to the yoga studio. She opened the door to an empty room with a shining corkwood floor. A pretty blonde woman in yoga pants and a halter top walked over with her hand outstretched.

"Hi, I'm Aimee. You're early for the class, but very welcome," she said.

# FOURTEEN

THE NEXT MORNING BILLY JO AND DORY were making coffee and discussing the previous evening's yoga class, when the phone rang. Dory grabbed it and even though it wasn't on speaker, they could both hear the outraged screeching of the person on the other line. "It's Annabelle," she whispered, switching the phone to speaker.

"So, you got a letter from your husband? What's got you so upset?"

"The bastard has another family! That's what the letter said, that he had *another family*. After everything I have done for that man. I am so mad I could spit!"

"Can you read me the whole letter, Annabelle?"

"Yes, hang on. I left it on the kitchen counter. On top of everything else, Samantha found the letter this morning. She's upset, but more understanding than I am. She's been learning about the justice system in school and wants the perpetrator who killed the narcotics cop tried for his crime."

Dory frowned. "You didn't tell us before that the guy who was killed was a narc."

"He was undercover apparently. This is what it says." Annabelle began to read.

Her letter was pretty much a duplicate of Jessica's. Dory stalled on telling her what they knew, but the angry woman was not to be put off. She virtually demanded a meeting with the whole Rosedale staff later that day.

"Whew," she said, hanging up the phone. "That is one seriously pissed woman. I'll have to talk to Wayne and agree on our strategy before she comes in. What did you tell Jessica about her letter?"

"I stalled as well, but Jessica said she was going to track PD down and insist that he tell her what's going on about her husband's *other family*."

"We better get the entire staff together this afternoon then," Dory said. "Now, what did you learn at yoga last night?"

"It was a good class. Aimee Anderson knows her stuff. Hilary's brother, Grant, was there. He's not very good at yoga but was manfully trying to keep up. When the class was over and the rest of the students left, he stayed behind. I hovered outside the door and overheard a bit of their conversation. She said finding out about his blood type had been terribly upsetting and she was struggling to decide the right thing to do."

"Finding out about his *blood type*? That's what she said?"

"Yes, and peeking in through the crack in the door, I saw that he'd placed his hand on her shoulder. It wasn't a sexual gesture, though, more like comforting."

"Good work. Have you done a background on Aimee yet?"

"No, that's my task for this morning. Luckily, her phone number was on the brochure I got from the receptionist. I'll request a report on her most recent phone calls from her cell phone carrier."

"Don't forget to do the financial checks too. I'd be very interested to know if there have been any large deposits made to her checking account recently. Can you do that?"

"Dory, you know I can't do that," Billy Jo said, rolling her eyes. "It's unethical and I wouldn't do it even if I could. But I'll check her credit cards to see if she's made any large purchases."

"While you are doing that, I'll round up our male partners for this afternoon's meeting. We have some serious cogitating to do about what to tell the two wives of the bigamous James Browning."

ACROSS TOWN AT THE NICHOLS' RESIDENCE, Lucy roused the sleeping Nightshade from bed, saying, "Wake up. You need to take a shower. I'm cooking breakfast." She placed a stack of newly purchased clothes (underwear, socks, a shirt, pants and a light windbreaker jacket) on the bed. "Bacon and eggs are on the menu this morning."

"You don't usually cook this much for me," Wayne said in a mildly irritated tone when Lucy returned. He was sitting at the table sipping his coffee. The Rosedale paper was unfolded in front of him. It was open to the weekly crime summary.

"I'm going to let your complaint go, as it is unworthy of you," she said, frowning. "I found out some more information about Nightshade yesterday. The boy's proper name is Henry Knight, it's the word knight spelled with a K. I got his birthday too, it's September tenth, 2009. He'll be turning sixteen in the fall. Can you stick around this morning? I want to get him started on the landscaping jobs and he'll need supervision. We're crediting him $10 per hour toward what he owes us."

"Ten dollars an hour! That's way too steep for grunt labor," Wayne groused.

"You, my friend, are totally out of step with modern times. We should really be paying him $15, but since he's reimbursing us for the money he *stole*, I didn't want to be that generous. Do you know what he needs to do?"

"Not a clue."

The next few minutes were spent with Lucy explaining that mulch was being delivered, what flower beds needed weeding prior to mulching, where the garden gloves were that would fit the boy, the careful handling of weed killer and the like.

"Make sure he's wearing his windbreaker. If he gets his cast dirty again, the orthopedist will literally put me against the wall and call in a *firing squad!*"

When Nightshade appeared with wet hair and dressed in his new clothes, he said he was hungry. Lucy smiled and the three of them sat down to breakfast.

AFTER HIS WIFE DEPARTED, WAYNE TOLD NIGHTSHADE to clear the table and load the dishwasher. Then he listed the jobs that needed doing. Just as he was finishing explaining the assignment, they heard the beeping of a large dump truck from Pure Nature Lawn Company backing up their driveway. "Go outside and have them deposit the mulch on the concrete, not the lawn," Wayne said. Watching Nightshade through the window as he gestured to the truck driver backing up the driveway, he dialed Detective Rob at the sheriff's office.

"Morning, Wayne. What can I do for Rosedale Investigations this morning?"

"Lucy has hired a young man to do some gardening jobs for us and I'd appreciate you checking on whether he has a record. His name is Henry Knight, birthday 9/10/09. No permanent address."

"No problem. I'll text you what I find this afternoon. By the way, the cop gossip mill has gone wild," the Detective chuckled. "The rumor is that your wife has acquired a kid from Homeless City and wants to keep him. Is that right? We're all finding this most diverting."

"You people don't have nearly enough to do if you're spending time gossiping about me. Appreciate you checking his record, Rob." Wayne hung up.

He poured himself another cup of coffee and walked outside to a lovely morning filled with birdsong. The Pure Nature company truck was pulling away, having deposited the mulch on the cement driveway. Nightshade was filling the wheelbarrow with mulch but he hadn't done a lick of weeding. Lucy had been clear that the beds were to be weeded prior to adding mulch.

At that moment, Wayne's phone made the incoming text beep and he saw a message from Dory. All four members of the staff needed to be in the office that afternoon. Both of Browning's wives were coming in for an appointment. Annabelle and Jessica had received identical letters revealing the existence of a second family.

WAYNE, DORY, BILLY JO, AND PD WERE STANDING in the kitchen tossing several ideas around about what they could ethically share with Annabelle Browning. She was scheduled for 4:00 o'clock. Jessica was coming in an hour later.

"What do you think our approach should be, PD?" Wayne asked.

"I think we have to stick to our guns and say that Browning will be back soon. He has to be the one to tell them."

"*Au contraire*," Dory said, grinning. "I'm tempted to get the two women together, just to see the fur fly. Those letters really set the cat among the pigeons."

"I'm not getting into that catfight," Wayne said, raising his arms in the air. "I'm having enough problems with the opposite sex as it is."

"We heard you have a young man who's moved in with you," Dory said, squashing her amusement with difficulty.

"I'd appreciate you wiping that smile off your face, Investigator Clarkson. It's not funny."

"Well, it's just a bit funny," Dory said. Her eyes were twinkling.

"Drop it, you two," PD said. "I think we need to plead ignorance. James has to be the one to give them both the information. Billy Jo, do you agree?"

"I certainly do. Jessica put me on the spot earlier. I stalled, but she could tell I was keeping something back. She thinks you will tell her what's going on, PD, because you met with her earlier."

"I can think of only one circumstance under which we could ethically share the information about the two families with the women," Wayne said with a dark look.

"What circumstance? I can't think of a single one," Dory said.

"Me neither," Billy Jo said.

"If Browning were dead, we would be obligated to tell them," PD said meeting Wayne's eyes.

The four of them looked at each other for a long moment, just as the front doorbell rang.

# FIFTEEN

ALL FOUR MEMBERS OF THE ROSEDALE INVESTIGATIONS TEAM felt wrung-out after the tense meetings with Annabelle and Jessica. The discussions had been further complicated by Jessica arriving early and Annabelle walking past her as she was leaving. Billy Jo had barely managed to keep the two women apart. Exhausted from the tight-lipped effort of keeping what they knew about Browning's "other family" confidential, they headed for the kitchen and pulled four bottles of hard lemonade from the fridge.

"So, you managed to keep them from speaking to each other?" PD asked.

"Just barely," Billy Jo answered. "Annabelle was shooting daggers at Jessica, and I walked her all the way to the car for fear she would come back inside. She'd immediately assumed that Jessica was the other wife and was fuming as she screeched out of the driveway."

"Jessica, on the other hand, couldn't stop crying," Wayne said. "I felt sorry for her."

"If Dory's unofficial informant, Lorelei Vail, is right, the marriage to Annabelle is a common law marriage. Browning married Jessica in a legal ceremony at City Hall here in Rosedale. He may believe he hasn't committed a crime, but he has," PD said.

"Either Annabelle or Jessica could sue him, but it would only be a civil matter."

"On another subject, PD, I wanted you to know we have taken on a second major case," Dory said. "Our newest client, Hilary Broadchurch-Miller, suspects Miss Aimee Anderson, a local yoga instructor, of blackmailing her brother. Billy Jo attended her class last night. She'd like to take the lead on this one."

"Okay by me. What did you learn, Billy Jo?" Wayne asked.

"Aimee is an excellent instructor and Grant Broadchurch is in the class. He stayed after the other students left and I listened in on their conversation. Hilary is correct that there's something going on between the two of them, but I don't think it's a love affair. As Dory mentioned, Hilary suspects blackmail. It's possible, since Aimee's been charging higher value items to her credit cards recently. Plus, she's been going out to dinner at expensive restaurants. That's a departure from her earlier pattern."

"If you give me the names of the restaurants and the dates, I'll go to the eateries and see if any of the wait staff remembers Aimee. Does she have a boyfriend?" Wayne asked.

"She does," Billy Jo answered. "His name is Phillip Easton. He's twenty-five and just graduated with a master's degree in business. My source told me they have been dating for almost a year and it's a serious relationship. My bet is those fancy dinners are with the boyfriend but paid for on Grant's dollar."

"Have you checked Venmo yet?" Dory asked.

"Planning to do so."

"What the heck is Venmo?" PD asked.

"It's an app that connects bank accounts. It's a way of sending money. Every time you send money on that site, you have to provide a reason, even if it's made-up. I'm going to check whether Grant is sending Aimee money and the reasons he lists."

"Well done," Wayne said. "That sounds like partner level work to me." He shot a look at PD.

"I agree," Dory said.

Billy Jo looked pleadingly at PD, who took a deep breath and said, "Now that I am retired, and only here as a consultant on the Browning case, I think decisions about partnership are no longer mine to make. It's up to you two." He looked at Wayne and Dory.

"In that case, Billy Jo, I'd like you to prepare an application for partnership in which you list the cases you've worked on and your contributions to each. Can you get that to us by early next week?" Wayne asked.

"Oh, I sure can." Billy Jo's her heart-shaped face turned pink.

"On a separate personnel matter, I'd like to discuss putting Lorelei Vail on the payroll as a Confidential Informant," Dory said.

"I always trust your instincts, but I need to meet her first," Wayne said.

"Of course."

"If we're done with business for the day, it's Friday afternoon and I'm inviting all of you, plus significant others, to come out to my cabin for pizza. How's eight o'clock sound?" PD said.

"Sounds good to me," Dory said and turning to Wayne with an innocent look, she added, "I assume you will be bringing the newest member of your family."

Wayne scowled.

AFTER THE PARTNERS LEFT THE OFFICE, Billy Jo took a moment to look at the Venmo app. She added the app to her phone, put in her checking account information and entered her name. Once her account was open, she was amazed to see that she could simply type in the name of the person she wanted to send money to. No password was required. She entered Aimee Anderson's name and her Venmo account came up. There was no mistake because her picture was visible in the little circle beside her name. A recent transaction had been posted with the reason listed as, "Birthday Money from Mom." All the rest of the money she'd received was from Grant Broadchurch. He had been sending her money every week for the last two months. In the little box for the reason it said, "For our future."

Billy Jo frowned, wondering what he meant. Glancing at the clock on her computer, she saw it was 6:30. Picking up the brochure she'd gotten at Power Zone, she saw that Aimee was teaching a yoga class starting that evening at 7:00. She ran upstairs to change into exercise apparel. Given the need to buttress her application for partnership, it couldn't hurt to put the woman on the spot about why she was receiving money every week from wealthy Grant Broadchurch.

BILLY JO PULLED INTO THE PARKING LOT in front of Power Zone fifteen minutes later. She was reaching into the back seat for her gym bag when Aimee drove in. Getting out of her car, she walked over to the instructor.

"Are you here for the 7:00 class?" Aimee asked. She was wearing what looked like a designer yoga suit. It fit her like a glove.

"I am. You are a really good instructor. I've learned a lot already. That outfit fits you perfectly, by the way. Where did you get it?"

"This one was custom-tailored to my body," Aimee said, pulling her jade-green yoga matt from the back seat of her car.

"I haven't had a chance to introduce myself to you yet. My name is Billy Jo Bradley and I work for Rosedale Investigations. I'm the IT person for the business, but I also interview initial clients in order to decide if we should take their cases."

"Sorry, Billy Jo. I'm late so don't have time to chat. I need to get the room set up for the class tonight."

"I'll help if you like."

They entered the mostly empty facility and walked upstairs to the yoga room. It was beautifully designed for the purpose with one floor-to-ceiling mirrored wall, bamboo paneling on the other walls, a large ceiling fan, and cork floors.

"You can get out the rest of the yoga mats and set up the chairs, if you don't mind. This is a chair yoga class," Aimee said.

Billy Jo helped set up chairs and put down mats for those clients who preferred floor work. No one else had appeared so far. It was the perfect opportunity to speak with Aimee alone. "Do you mind answering a question for me?" she asked.

"No, go ahead," Aimee said. She had pulled some wide, brightly colored wide elastic bands from her gym bag before starting the music using her cell phone and a portable Bluetooth speaker.

"What is your relationship with Grant Broadchurch? Are the two of you having an affair?" Billy Jo asked quietly.

Aimee swung around with a stunned expression on her face. "My personal relationships are *none* of your business and I don't appreciate being asked about something private at work. I have a boyfriend who would be incensed if you made that accusation."

"Would you rather I spoke to Phillip Easton about this?"

"What the hell is this? How do you know his name?"

"I'm just doing my job, Aimee. Rosedale Investigations has been asked to investigate you. I have been looking at your Venmo account and Grant Broadchurch has been sending you money every week for the last two months. If you aren't sleeping with him, why is he giving you money?"

"I refuse to discuss this. We have security in this building and unless you are out of here in the next two minutes, I'm calling them." Aimee's olive green eyes blazed. Sweat broke out on her forehead. Some tendrils from her blonde bangs had partially escaped her hairband and a few wet strands lay on her forehead.

"Okay, okay. I'm leaving, but if there is an innocent explanation for the money, I won't need to inform the police."

"The police? What the hell do the police have to do with this?" Aimee yelped. Noticing that a few students had entered the room, she instantly stopped talking.

"Blackmail is against the law," Billy Jo said. She'd spoken in a nearly inaudible voice, but the offensive word carried. The incoming yoga students who had been chatting broke off their conversations to stare at the two of them. The room was suddenly silent.

"I'm calling security," Aimee said and entered a code into her phone. She touched her speaker, and the music came to an abrupt stop. Her voice was loud enough that everyone heard her say, "I need assistance in the yoga room ASAP. You need to remove a client who's here under false pretenses."

"I'll go, but this isn't over," Billy Jo said and fled from the room.

Walking to the front desk, she mentally scolded herself for being so confrontational. She had obviously botched the job and felt frustrated about mishandling things. No doubt Dory or Wayne would have been able to get information without getting the woman's back up. She stopped at the front desk and left her card. Then she pulled a small yellow sticky note from a pack on the counter and wrote the yoga instructor's name and the words, "Call me if you don't want the police involved." Given the content of the message, she was pretty sure someone would make sure she got the note.

Driving out of the parking lot, she called her boyfriend, Mark. When he answered she said, "Are you coming out to PD's house for pizza tonight?"

"Yes, just about to leave. I can pick you up if you like."

"Please. I'm on my way back to the office. I'll meet you there."

"You sound upset. What's going on?" he asked.

"I'll tell you about it on the way. I just screwed up an interview and it's probably doomed my hopes for partnership," she said gloomily.

# SIXTEEN

THE PARTY AT PD'S HOUSE WAS IN FULL SWING when Mark and Billy Jo drove up to the cabin that evening. With the car windows down, they could hear music floating out to meet them on the cool night air. It was the famous Beatles song called "All My Loving." Mark angled the front end of his car into the brush and turned off the key.

"You've been quiet all the way out here, Billy Jo. Want to tell me what's going on?"

"It's the whole situation. After PD got this new grandson, he decided to *live* with him for nine months of the year! It's because Liam showed up that he decided to retire. He chose him over me and it hurts."

"You said there was one good thing that came out of that situation though," Mark said calmly.

"There was. I have a real chance at becoming a partner now that PD decided it's up to Wayne and Dory. At least that's what I thought, before I totally annihilated my interview with Aimee Anderson."

"That's the yoga instructor, right? Could you go at it from another angle?"

"What are you thinking?"

"Maybe you should talk to Grant Broadchurch directly. If you can get him to come into the office, you could challenge him about the blackmail. He might crack."

"Cracking suspects is more Wayne's job," she said, sounding defeated.

"You've watched him plenty of times. I'm sure you could imitate the technique. Or you could call Broadchurch's sister and have her stop by again. People often remember things in a second interview they forgot to say initially. That's what Nashville's Finest tell me anyway."

"True, good ideas. Did I tell you I need to make a list of times where my ideas helped solve the agency's cases? It's part of my application for partnership."

"You were the one who actually identified the killer in the case you called the Blind Switch. That was an excellent catch."

"That was pretty good, wasn't it," Billy Jo said, and the corners of her mouth rose a bit.

NIGHTSHADE WAS RIDING IN THE BACK SEAT of Wayne's pick-up. Lucy had said they were going to a party. He asked if his dog could come, but they both said "no." He didn't want to go if Huck couldn't come, he said, but Wayne said he didn't have a choice. They weren't leaving him alone in the house.

He knew it was because he had bailed on the first night and returned to Homeless City. That, and taking their $50, meant they weren't about to trust him on his own. He sulked about being made to go, but the big detective took him by the arm and walked him out to his truck. It wouldn't pay to get into a tussle with that guy. He outweighed by a hundred pounds and none of it looked like flab.

After a half hour in riding silence while listening to Wayne and Lucy talk quietly in the front seat, Nightshade asked, "Where's this place we're going?"

"It's Wayne's partner's cabin. He lives on forty acres in the woods. It's a get-together for all the people who work at Rosedale Investigations," Lucy said.

"We didn't have dinner," he said, sounding hard-done-by. He'd watched Dr. Lucy filling a big pin-wheeled tray with olives, cheeses, crackers, deviled eggs, black cherries and strawberries. It made his mouth water. Once all the crescent shapes in the tray were filled, she'd covered the circular dish with silver foil. When she turned away, he peeled up the edge slightly and reached in for a deviled egg. She'd caught him.

"This is for the party," she said firmly. "Hands off."

He assumed he would be fed eventually, but his stomach ached so badly he felt like he was going to pass out. He'd been hungrier in Homeless City, but having three square meals a day seemed to make the wait between meals last forever. "How long before you take me back to Homeless City?" he asked in a grumpy tone.

Lucy glanced at Wayne, who didn't answer. Nightshade picked up on the tension between them. The woman had done a lot for him, fixed his arm and let him keep Huck. She'd been kind, but the man didn't seem to like him.

"We haven't decided," she said.

"If I'm staying for a while, what am I supposed to call you?" he asked.

"You can call me Dr. Lucy. What should he call you, Wayne?" she asked. Turning toward her husband with a grin, she said, "Don't say, Detective."

"How about, Wayne?" Nightshade asked.

"It's not really polite to call an adult by their first name, so it's Mr. Nichols for the time being," Lucy said.

He wondered what she meant. *Would he be required to call him something else in the future? The man had been a cop. When Lucy called him Detective it meant he wasn't just an ordinary cop. Detectives were higher in rank, Sgt. Roscoe had told him that. Would Wayne have checked his police record? He'd have to be careful not to steal . . . for a while at least. He'd turn sixteen in the fall and if he got nailed again, it wouldn't be Juvie. It would be the adult prison. But it didn't really matter what he called them. He wasn't going to be with them that long.*

He'd been in two foster care homes in the years since his mother died and nobody came after him when he returned to Homeless City. This couple wouldn't either. He'd be free again, but knew what that meant. He'd be hungry, always hungry. Sometimes when he crawled into his cruddy old sleeping bag under the tented tarp in Homeless City, when he pressed down on his stomach, he thought he could feel his backbone.

A HALF HOUR LATER, WAYNE TURNED INTO A NARROW TRAIL with fields on one side and a forest on the other. A cornfield rolled away in the distance and Nightshade remembered a day when his mother was still alive. They had stolen sweet corn from a field like this. He remembered the milky juice from the kernels as it ran down his chin and how the little rows of kernels had looked like baby teeth. They'd laughed at each other as the delicious corn filled their empty stomachs.

The truck bumped down the track and as they approached a little wooden cabin, he could hear music coming from inside. It was a song his mother used to sing called "Fire and Rain." His mood improved as he climbed out of the pick-up truck and caught the scent of hot bubbling pizza. As long as he got fed, it wouldn't be so bad putting up with these people. Maybe he could filch a beer or two.

There would be time enough to return to Homeless City when his arm was healed. That would be in about six weeks, Dr. Lucy said. It seemed like a long time, but at least with these people he got fed. And Huck seemed to like it there. Dr. Lucy said the dog could come into the house at night to sleep by his bed after he'd finished the obedience training she'd signed him up for. When it came time to leave, Huck might not want to go, Nightshade realized. He'd already started putting on weight.

"Howdy folks," a man's voice rang out as he held the door open for them. "Glad you could come. I'm PD. You must be Nightshade," he said, shaking hands with the young man.

"Pizza's ready," a girl's voice called from inside. "Come in and help yourself to a slice or two. Plates are on the counter, salad is in the bowl, silverware and napkins too."

Walking into the kitchen, he saw a young, pretty girl with dark curly hair. He wondered what she was doing with all these old people. Then he noticed a tall guy standing behind her. He had a dragon head tattooed on his neck and looked protective. Probably her boyfriend.

"After you get pizza and salad, come over here and help yourself to beverages," a heavy-set African American woman announced.

After grabbing a plate, four pizza slices, and nodding to the girl who said her name was Billy Jo, he walked into the dining area. A big aluminum washtub filled with ice was on the table. It contained soda cans, wine bottles and beer. He reached his hand in and scooped out a can of beer.

"You, son, are a minor," the black woman said firmly, grabbing hold of his wrist. "I know one when I see one. Help yourself to anything non-alcoholic. You're Nightshade, right? I'm Dory."

Putting the beer back in the washtub and taking a soda, he slunk out to the big deck that floated above a heavily forested valley. Looking toward the bottom of the hill, he noticed someone had hauled wooden pallets down there and made a kind of walkway. He traced it through the woods with his eyes, seeing it lead to a small reed-fringed pond. The sun was going down and a golden bar of light lay across the water. He looked for Dr. Lucy and saw her chatting with the girl who said her name was Billy Jo. They glanced in his direction, and he thought they were talking about him. Standing beside the beverage table, Wayne and the guy called PD were talking to the black woman named Dory.

Nobody was looking at him and he circled around the end of the deck and stood with his back to the exterior wall under an open window.

"How's it going with Nightshade?" Dory asked.

"Just as I suspected, he has a record." It was Wayne's voice. He sounded unsurprised.

"For what?" That was PD's voice.

"Just minor theft. He was put in Juvenile Detention for three months. He only stole food and a set of walkie-talkies. Nobody felt very good about the sentence."

"I'm sure they didn't. I'm surprised they put him in Juvie. First offense stuff is usually handled with a warning."

"It was probably because he was homeless," Dory said. "How does Lucy feel about him having a record?"

"I haven't told her yet," Wayne said.

"Better tell her soon," she said.

"Any recent news on the Browning case from your reporter at the Bellevue newspaper?"

"The trial is coming up shortly. Once Browning testifies, he'll be free to come home."

"His freedom could just be the death of him, literally," Dory said. After her comment, she laughed.

"If he manages to escape the people he's testifying against and comes back here, both his wives will definitely murder him," PD said and chuckled.

"It's no laughing matter. I know how the man feels," Wayne said gloomily.

"At least you've only got one woman who will kill you if you don't support her about the boy," Dory said.

"Browning was a nutcase to marry two women," Wayne said. "I've got enough trouble with one."

"Do you think Lucy wants to be a foster mom to the kid?" Dory asked.

"I'm afraid she wants to make it permanent," Wayne said.

Nightshade walked off the deck into the nearby forest and stood looking down at the small lake, now ablaze with sunset colors. If Dr. Lucy wanted to keep him permanently, he needed to know what that meant. He'd already been a foster kid and it hadn't worked. Did Wayne mean she wanted to adopt him? If so, he would need to leave sooner than he had planned. Their house was comfortable, the food was good, and he had Huck, but it was a prison all the same. All that pampering would make him soft and you couldn't be soft if you lived in Homeless City. Sergeant Roscoe told him he wouldn't always be around to protect him. He said he had to be tough . . . if he was going to survive.

# SEVENTEEN

WAYNE WAS SOUND ASLEEP WHEN THE phone rang the next morning. He grabbed it on the first try. Decades of being a cop meant always being available. "Hello?" he said, trying to erase the sleepiness in his voice.

"Is this Detective Nichols?"

"Yes."

"This is Drew. I'm the reporter for the Endeavor in Bellevue."

"Of course. I recognize your voice, Drew. What's happening?"

"The trial ended in a hung jury. Browning's identification of the defendant was demolished by the defense attorney. He kept hammering away on how long it had been, that the shooting happened at night, how the lighting was poor, etc."

"Browning's on his way back here now, I assume," Wayne said.

"He is. I followed him into the airport and he was waiting in the gate for a plane to Tennessee."

"You've given me some great information. Once Browning gets back here, I'll give you everything we find out from him. Could be a major scoop for you."

"I can just see my byline now," Drew said happily and thanked him.

Clicking off the call, Wayne looked at the clock. It was almost eight in the morning. He glanced at the other side of the bed. The pillow next to his showed the indentation of Lucy's head. She'd left early for her shift.

Getting out of bed, he thought through the information he'd gotten from Drew. Ten years previously, Browning was the sole witness to the murder of a narcotics cop. Since then, he'd relocated to Tennessee, probably afraid the killer would come after him. Having seen him at the trial, the killer now knew James Browning's identity and whereabouts. He could track him down. Browning would be poised to run again. *Poor guy*, Wayne thought. *All he did was witness a murder, and now he's on his way home to Rosedale to face the second battle, the one he has coming to him from his women.*

He showered, dressed and walked out to the kitchen. Pouring himself a cup of black coffee, he was about to leave the house when he saw Lucy's note.

"Please take Nightshade with you to the office today. I don't want him alone in the house. He needs a haircut. That's the usual province of the male head of the family." He looked around but didn't see or hear the boy. In fact, he'd nearly gone to work without remembering they had a third person in the house. Walking down the hall to the guest bedroom, he opened the door. Nightshade was sleeping deeply, his long dark hair spread out on the pillow. Wayne shook him by the shoulder. "I need you to get up. You're going with me to the office today."

The kid made a series of inarticulate irritable noises before pushing the blanket off his body, sitting up and setting his bare feet on the floor.

"On your feet, Soldier. After you shower, pick up the room and make your bed," Wayne said. He saw the boy's eyes widen when he called him soldier and recalled it was what Sergeant Roscoe of Homeless City called him. Perhaps the use of the word meant he had found an opening into the boy's so-far closed mind. He needed to get to know this young man who, it seemed, was now part and parcel of his life. *The things I do for love*, he thought.

BILLY JO AND DORY WERE HAVING DONUTS. They were fresh and still slightly warm from the donut store. Dory was having her favorite, blueberry. Billy Jo was indulging in cherry with chocolate frosting. When they checked the answering machine, they heard Wayne's message saying Browning had finished testifying and was heading back to Tennessee. He wanted them to check Lyft and Uber and find out where the driver dropped him off.

"Our big guy sure doesn't want much, does he," Dory drawled. "You're looking good this morning, Kiddo. Love those dark blue skinny jeans and white blouse. Nice addition of the navy jacket. Cute little bluebird earrings."

"Thanks. You too. Looking hot in that red sarong dress. Very flattering to the *voluptuous older female*." She grinned and Dory frowned. Dory resented any reference to her age or weight which had been so carefully redacted they might have been state secrets. "Wayne's crazy. There's no way to find out which home James chose to go to. On another matter, I didn't get the chance to tell you very much last night, but I totally botched my interview with Aimee Anderson. She got so furious, she called security to escort me out of Power Zone," Billy Jo said, her face flushed with embarrassment.

"Unfortunate, but you're not down and out yet. I gathered it hadn't gone well, so I called Hilary. I asked her to come in and she'll be here shortly. Do you want me to talk to her? Or do you want to?"

"I'll do it. Might be able to redeem myself," Billy Jo said as the bell on the front door tinkled and Wayne and Nightshade came into the building.

"Good morning, you two," Dory said and offered Nightshade one of the donuts from a box originally containing a dozen. He crammed it into his mouth and reached for a second.

"Hilary Broadchurch-Miller is on her way in," Billy Jo said.

"Do you have your approach thought out?" Wayne asked.

"Yes, I'm going to ask about Grant's prior romantic relationships. With what I overheard Aimee say about his blood type, I'm thinking she's a relative, possibly his daughter."

"Okay. Meanwhile, we'll get out of here before all those donuts are inhaled. I'm taking Nightshade to the barber shop."

"What? No, I don't want my hair cut," Nightshade said. His expression was shocked and dismayed.

"Not your choice. Dr. Lucy left marching orders this morning," he said, propelling the surly teenager out the front door. They passed Hilary Broadchurch Miller on the sidewalk.

"Good Morning, Hilary," Billy Jo greeted the woman when she opened the door to the building. "Thanks for coming in this morning. We have some fresh donuts if you would like one. Coffee's hot as well."

"Thank you, they do look delicious," she said and helped herself to the last blueberry donut (Dory frowned, they were her favorites) and a cup of coffee with cream.

"I wanted to give you an update on our investigation so far, and ask a couple more questions, if that's okay," Billy Jo said.

"Certainly," Hilary said.

"I joined Aimee Anderson's yoga class. She's an excellent instructor, but unfortunately, I got nowhere with my questioning. She absolutely denied sleeping with your brother, and I thought she was telling the truth. She was equally outraged when I asked her about blackmail. I even threatened to report the situation to the police. Didn't seem to faze her."

"Hmmm. Anything else?"

"She almost had security toss me out of Power Zone," Billy Jo said with a grimace.

"Did you check to see if she's receiving any money from Grant?"

"I did and you're right. You brother's been giving her money every week for the last two months."

"That's exactly what I thought. He's sending her money and I want it stopped! When Grant dies my sons will inherit a sizeable estate. He developed some software around the time they were born. It's still very profitable and he's made them his beneficiaries. I'm not letting my brother change his will for this money-hungry upstart." Hilary's face was flushed.

"You'll have to talk to him about that. Changing the subject, I wonder if Grant ever had a serious girlfriend when he was in his twenties."

"When he was in college he had a girlfriend named Cindy. She was a cute blonde and a communications major, I believe. He's probably dated other women since, but none that he introduced to me."

"Do you remember the college girlfriend's surname?"

"Her maiden name was Taylor, but she's probably married now. It's likely she has a different last name. Why do you want to know about old girlfriends?"

"I'm thinking his college girlfriend might have gotten pregnant and that Aimee might be his daughter," Billy Jo said.

"That couldn't have happened."

"Why not?" Billy Jo asked.

"Because I asked Grant once if he wanted a family. I said he'd better get busy if he did. He wasn't getting any younger. He told me he'd never be able to have a family because he was sterile from a case of mumps when he was a boy."

*So much for that direction*, Billy Jo thought and felt the sting of frustration. "Would you mind asking your brother if he knows Cindy's whereabouts and her last name?"

"No problem, but I'm telling you it's a dead end."

"You said earlier that Aimee could be blackmailing your brother. What do you think she could blackmail him about?"

"Money. It's the only thing I can think of. Possibly there's been some mishandling of the income from his software," she said.

"Okay, I'll see what I can find," Billy Jo said, but inside she felt even more discouraged. She had no idea how to find out about income from computer software. It was way outside her wheelhouse.

# EIGHTEEN

IT WAS A WARM SUMMER NIGHT AND FIREFLIES WERE BLINKING like little green lanterns above the blossoming roses in the upscale neighborhood of South Rosedale Estates where Dory and Billy Jo were surveilling the home of Molly Powell. Molly's husband, George, a good-looking black attorney, had contacted the agency some time ago requesting their services. He suspected his wife was having an affair with Dr. Jack Manning, the doctor who was head of the clinic where Molly worked.

Rosedale Investigations preferred the more engrossing cases involving missing persons or property, and helping the sheriff's office with major crime. However, the documenting of unfaithful spouses was the bedrock of their business. They hadn't done much work recently on George Powell's suspicions, due to the time spent on other cases, but he'd called that morning, saying he was going to be out of town for several days.

"Molly might take my out-of-town trip as a chance to be with her lover," he said bitterly.

Dory agreed and she and Billy Jo had been parked at the edge of the Powell property for three hours.

"I have to pee," Billy Jo said.

"Lordy Pete, didn't you go before we left?" Dory said, exasperated.

"I did, but I really have to go again."

"Nothing seems to be happening anyway and it's past ten. It's unlikely Lover Boy will arrive this late, so you can go behind that shrub on the edge of their yard."

Billy Jo nodded and got out of the car. She had pulled down her very tight jeans and was squatting behind a shrub when the front porch light came on and Molly Powell came out on her porch. To her horror, Billy Jo could see she was carrying a flashlight.

"Who's out there? What are you doing in my front yard?" She waved her flashlight in Billy Jo's direction.

"Get back in the car right now!" Dory hissed from the open window.

Molly started walking directly toward the bush where Billy Jo was frantically trying to pull up her pants. Mosquitoes were whining around her. She jumped when one stung her on her bare bum. *Could this get any more embarrassing*, she thought. She felt frantic to get back in the car, but when she tugged up her jeans, her undies remained tightly wrapped around her thighs and she was forced to do a rapid waddle.

Dory opened her car window and trying to distract the woman called, "We are having car trouble. Could you help us?"

Molly Powell stopped in her tracks and turned her flashlight in the direction of Dory's voice.

At that moment, Billy Jo managed to crawl into the back seat of the car, still struggling with her stupid underpants. "Drive!" she whispered fiercely.

Dory started the car and pealed out of the subdivision. Billy Jo was hunched over in the back seat, holding onto the handle of the car door that hadn't fully closed. After a few minutes, they came to a stop and parked in a nearby retail lot.

"Next time wear a skirt and skip the undies. Tight jeans are a rookie move on a stake-out. You should know better by now, *Birdbrain*."

"God, what a mess. So humiliating. When she shone the flashlight on me, I thought I'd die," Billy Jo said. "Can you take me home? I need a shower and a change of clothes."

Dory dropped Billy Jo off at Rosedale Investigations, feeling frustrated at missing a chance to catch Molly with her lover. She was headed back to her home in the Flower Pot neighborhood when she changed her mind. It was still possible Dr. Manning would show. He undoubtedly knew George was out of town. She turned around and headed back to the Powell house.

IT HAD BEEN AN INSPIRED MOVE, SHE TOLD BILLY JO the next morning, because when she got there, Dr. Manning was just pulling in. Molly must have given him a garage door remote because when he drove up her driveway, the garage door opened automatically and then closed behind him. Dory settled down for a long wait, but the man backed rapidly out of the garage just half an hour later. The motion lights flipped on and she caught his license plate perfectly. When he drove past her, she snapped his face in profile, surprised to see him looking miserable. The images would prove uncontestable. George Powell would have his evidence.

"We don't usually do this, but I'm going to have Molly come in and tell her what I know before I give George the photos," Dory said.

Billy Jo had made her a flat white coffee and handed her a blueberry donut. Warmed in the microwave, the food was a belated apology for her stupid move the night before. "That way she'll be prepared at least," she said.

"Unlike your ill-prepared performance last night," Dory said, giving her a look.

"I know. I'm still cringing about trying to pee without hitting my jeans or undies when Molly was shining that flashlight at me," Billy Jo flushed.

"We won't have to go back. My photos were perfect. What are you doing on the Broadchurch case?"

"Trying to find the woman Hilary told me Grant dated in college."

"Still thinking Aimee Anderson is some relation?" Dory asked.

"Unlikely, I know," Billy Jo said. "Hilary told me Grant was sterile from having mumps when he was a kid, but it's the only explanation I can come up with. She got his college girlfriend's married name and texted it to me."

Wayne arrived with Nightshade and they walked into the kitchen. The window was open and the morning breeze twirled the sheer white curtains. The scent of purple lilacs wafted into the room.

"I thought you were getting his hair cut?" Billy Jo said, looking at the boy who had gathered his long dark hair into a man-bun.

"Lucy was not pleased," Wayne said, frowning. "My barber wouldn't cut his hair after he refused to sit in the chair. He said it was against his ethics. Who knew barbers had ethics?" He shook his head.

"Well, I like it," Dory said. "Way to stick up for yourself, kid."

"Want something to eat Nightshade? We have donuts, coffee and blueberries." Nightshade grinned and helped himself.

"What's happening with our cases?" Wayne asked.

"I caught Molly Powell with her lover last night. She's coming in this morning," Dory said. "I decided to tell her about the evidence before giving her husband the photos."

"I don't think you've ever done that before. How come?" Wayne asked.

"She's a woman of color, and a friend of a friend. Have to uphold the sisterhood you know," Dory said.

"What's happening with the Broadchurch case, Billy Jo?"

"Hilary Broadchurch-Miller left me a text with the last name of Grant's girlfriend from college. Her married name is Cindy Anderson. Luckily she lives locally, just outside Mount Blanc. Hope to get something out of her," Billy Jo said.

"Can I come?" Nightshade asked with a hopeful note in his voice.

"Need to escape the big man?" Dory asked, grinning.

Nightshade nodded and Wayne said if Billy Jo wanted the boy, she could have him all day as far as he was concerned.

BILLY JO AND NIGHTSHADE SET OUT TO MEET CINDY ANDERSON later that morning. They were headed to the Food Court in the Mount Blanc shopping mall. Reaching the mall, they parked the car and walked inside. The scent of Chinese food, pizza, Italian subs, and McDonald's flooded the air. The place was a large interior courtyard with food kiosks side-by-side surrounding the perimeter of the glass-ceilinged room. The center of the space was filled with tables and chairs. Large tropical plants made a pleasant addition.

"Here's the photo of Cindy Anderson that I printed off, Nightshade. If you spot her, just tell me. I'll talk to her while you get yourself something to eat," Billy Jo said, handing him $20. "You can get your food as soon as we spot Mrs. Anderson."

It didn't take the boy long to identify the woman from the photo. "That's her over there, by the Chinese food counter," he said, before taking off at a trot toward McDonald's.

Cindy Anderson was a petite blonde in her early forties. She wore a light summery sweater in pink and melon tones with white slacks and sandals. When Billy Jo had contacted her earlier, she said she was a reporter for their small-town paper assigned to write an article about yoga classes. Her name was Jo Hadley, she'd told her. She hadn't used her real name in case the woman called her daughter.

At first, Cindy had refused to meet with her, saying she'd have to call the paper to be sure a reporter named Jo Hadley really worked there. Clutching at straws, Billy Jo said she was freelance so they wouldn't have employment records, but she'd taken her daughter's yoga class and Aimee was a really excellent instructor.

"She's your sister, right?" Billy Jo asked, crossing her fingers. On Instagram, she'd found a picture of the two of them. They had the same last name and resembled each other strongly. "I saw a picture of the two of you dressed in identical yoga outfits. You looked like twins."

That bit of flattery must have done it, because Cindy laughed and said, "No, Aimee is my daughter." After that, it didn't take long for her to agree to the meeting.

Walking up to the woman, Billy Jo said, "Hello, Cindy? I'm Jo, the reporter. Let me buy your lunch. I'll get myself something to eat too, and we can we sit at a table and talk, okay?" With their lunches in white boxes, they left the Panda Express food kiosk and sat down at an empty table.

"Thank you so much for meeting me. I can't believe Aimee is your daughter. You definitely could be sisters."

Cindy smiled, looking pleased. "What did you need for your article?"

"If you don't mind, I'd like to record our interview." Billy Jo pulled her tiny recorder from her bag and when Cindy said it was okay, clicked it on. "Do you mind telling me how old Aimee is? You must have had her when you were very young."

"I was twenty-one and that's how old Aimee is now."

"Were you in college at that time?"

Cindy frowned. "I don't see how that's relevant. I thought this article was about my daughter, not about me." She had a suspicious frown on her face.

"Sorry. You're right of course. It's just that your daughter's so remarkable, I know she must have great parents. Can you tell me where Aimee got her yoga training?"

"She got some here and then went to Mexico to finish up her certification."

AFTER HER INITIAL BLUNDER, BILLY JO MANAGED THE REST of the interview well. Walking out to the car with Nightshade afterwards she told him, "We're looking into the reasons a middle-aged guy would be giving a young woman money every week. I'm going to refer to him as 'G' because we keep the names of our clients confidential."

"Must be a hooker," he said.

"No. That isn't it. I found out the girl's mother, who turned out to be Cindy, was a senior in college when she got pregnant. She was dating 'G' at the time. They broke up and she immediately started seeing the man she married. Aimee was born only five months after the marriage. When I asked Cindy if 'G' could have been the girl's father, she said no. He'd had a case of mumps as a kid and was sterile."

"Does that mean he was shooting blanks?"

"That's right."

"Then it must be the husband who was the father, right?" Nightshade asked.

"It's a long shot, but I still think it's 'G', the guy we're investigating. If I'm right, it would explain why he's giving Aimee money. All I have to do is prove it."

"How are you going to do that?" Nightshade asked.

"It might involve a bit of minor breaking and entering," she told him with a wink.

"I could help you. I did a stretch in juvie for boosting some food and a couple of walkie-talkies. What do you need to steal?"

"The only way to prove a biological relationship is with a DNA test. If we had some hair from each of them, that would do it. Maybe you could go to her yoga class tonight. While the class is in process, you could probably snitch some hair from the combs or hair brushes in their gym bags."

"I'm your man," Nightshade said and grinned.

# NINETEEN

It was past midnight and James Browning was taking a Lyft from the Nashville airport to the private airport in Mount Blanc. He had left his car there when he flew out of town to testify at the trial. He thought he remembered where he'd parked the vehicle, but the Lyft driver patrolled the entire long-term lot before he realized the car was missing. Someone had taken it. He could feel his fears rising and tamped them down with difficulty.

"I don't get it," he told the driver. "I left the car here. Can you take me to 6700 Park Lane in Mount Blanc?" It was the address of the condo he shared with Annabelle. He thought wistfully about Jessica, wishing he could see her, but Annabelle had always known what to do in a crisis. Right now, he needed her help. That was more important than Jessica's sweet smile. When they arrived, he got out and tipped the driver. Walking to the front door of their condo, he took out his key and slid it silently into the lock.

He was relieved to see the lights above the kitchen cupboards were on. It was critical he didn't wake Samantha. He was only going to be there a short time and hated the thought of her tears when he left. He removed his shoes and coat. Tiptoeing down the carpeted hall, he stood outside their bedroom door. Easing the door open silently, he walked in.

"Annabelle," he whispered. She didn't stir. "Annabelle, honey," he said again, louder this time.

"You're back," she said. He heard the irritation in her voice. He sat down on the bed beside her. The nightlight was on and he could see her infuriated expression.

"Please be quiet. I don't want to wake Samantha," he said.

She sat up and looked at him. "I could kill you," she whispered. "In fact, I *should* kill you," her mouth was tight.

"Don't be mad at me, Honey, I need your help. I'm in real trouble this time. Please tell me what to do." His voice sounded desperate.

"Why the hell did you get another wife? You should have waited for me."

"I know I'm not the sharpest knife in the drawer. You've always been smarter than me." He felt the muscles in his chest tighten looking at her angry face.

"We both know that," she said flatly. "What happened at the trial?"

"It ended with a hung jury and the shooter was released. The defense attorney destroyed my identification, saying it was unreliable due to the length of time, the dark parking lot, etc. I knew it was him, even though he'd grown a beard and a mustache. But, when the attorney asked me to point him out in the courtroom, for just a second I hesitated. He picked up on that and so did the jury."

"I assume you had to give your name and address to the court?"

He gave her a pathetic nod and said, "I did."

"Which address did you give them?" she asked with a dark look.

"My other one. I was afraid he would follow me here and I didn't want him to know where Samantha lived. He never got a look at her because she was in the back seat when we saw the murder, but I wasn't about to take a chance."

"That's one good decision you've made at least. The killer is most likely on your trail. You don't have long now. There's only one place you can go."

"Will you drive me? Please?" he begged.

She shook her head. "No. You are going to have to get a bus. I'll take you to the station." She pushed the covers down and got out of bed.

ONCE ANNABELLE DROVE HIM TO THE bus station and bought his ticket, she left him sitting in a row of old wooden benches. It was still very early. The room was empty, eerily quiet with only the soft vibrating sound of the fluorescent lights overhead. Wanting to be sure Annabelle didn't return, James waited a full hour before leaving for Jessica's place. He knew she'd take him in her warm fragrant arms as she always had. He experienced a sudden memory of his mother, long dead now, and how she'd always cuddled him and made a fuss whenever he skinned his knees. His father would tell her to quit babying him. To his joyous satisfaction, she never listened. He had just enough time before the bus left to see Jessica and little Trevor. To say good-bye. It was the one honorable thing he could do.

The sky was getting light when he reached the home he shared with Jessica. He'd misplaced his key sometime in the last month and edged around the house, avoiding the street lights. Taking a look at his watch, he saw that it was seven-thirty. He stood back from the shrubbery and looked in the windows. Jessica had always been an early riser. A night-light was on and he caught her silhouette leaving the bedroom. Creeping around to the back door, he knocked quietly. In just moments, the light over the door came on and he saw her frightened face.

"Jessica, it's me," he said and watched a delighted look cross her features. It was one of his favorite things about her, how she was invariably happy to see him. He heard her slide the deadbolt back and the door opened. She stood there, smiling sleepily in her soft pink robe, her blonde hair mussed, holding out her arms for him. He burst through the door and hugged her, feeling her fit perfectly against him, tidy and compact. Her hair smelled like citrus, like wood smoke, like the flowering crabapple trees he'd climbed on the farm so long ago.

"I'll get Trevor up in a little bit," she said and holding his hand she led him into the kitchen. "But, first I need you to explain." She bit her lip.

"Honey, can it wait until after you take Trevor to school?" It was a rotten thing to do, he knew. By the time she came back from dropping the boy off at school, he would be gone. He'd be walking back to the bus station, getting on the bus, and taking the long ride home.

"Of course it can. I'll get him now. He's missed you terribly." Her voice sent a bright dart of love straight to his heart. Jessica almost floated from the kitchen, her small feet in their white slippers barely touched the shining floor. He heard her open the child's bedroom door, both their voices and then the boy barreled down the hall like a cannonball, his Spiderman pajamas flapping. He shrieked with joy and jumped straight into his father's outstretched arms.

"My daddy," he said over and over again. The little guy heaved a sigh of relief and cuddled against him.

James felt the pit of his stomach clench in shame. *At least I can give him this moment,* he thought and hoped the boy would remember it—lifelong.

The two of them ate their cereal in the small bright kitchen while Jessica stood nearby, sipping her coffee with a fond look on her face. When she sent Trevor to his room to get dressed for school, he asked, "If we could live anywhere in the world, where would you like to go?" He knew he was giving her false hope. There was no chance he was coming back.

"Will you break off your relationship with the other woman and never see her again?" she asked, looking at him hard.

"I promise," he said.

He knew full-well it would be best to give them both up. To start all over again in a different place with a new identify and a new wife.

"It doesn't matter where we live, if I'm with you I'll be happy," Jessica said, and kissed him.

"You are an angel. Will you do one more thing for me?"

She nodded.

"My other woman, I didn't marry her legally you know, but we've been together for a long time. Anyway, she has a daughter named Samantha from her first husband. If you ever meet, will you promise me you'll treat her kindly? She's a good kid." He pulled his wallet from his pants and opened it, showing her a school photo of the girl.

"Of course, I will. But you have to promise me, James. I need to know you have ended it with your other . . . woman." Her voice floundered on the brink of tears.

"Of course, sweetheart. I have to leave you guys again for a little while now. When I come back, you and Trevor and I are going away somewhere." The lies came so easily.

"It won't take me long to drop him off at school. I'll be back in half an hour and we can have a real talk. I need to get dressed. I love you, James."

He watched her leave the kitchen with a wave of relief. Jessica would always find another man to protect her. A brief wince hit his gut, knowing how easily she would love again. But it set him free. And Trevor was so young, he'd bond to another father.

LATER, BACK AT THE BUS STATION, he thought he caught a glimpse of the killer who had shot the cop. Taking another look, he decided he was wrong. Even if the shooter followed him to Tennessee, he would never find the farm, he told himself. He'd be safe there. Climbing the steps onto the bus and looking down the aisle, he checked the faces of every person on the vehicle. All of them seemed like they belonged, bland white faces. One attractive woman, cuddling a baby, smiled at him. There was an empty seat beside her.

She said her name was Brittany. He said his name was James. He told her he'd always wanted a family. He said he'd had a family once, but they were estranged. She told him the baby's name was Ariel. Glancing at her left hand, he didn't see a wedding ring. He asked her if she was married and she shook her head, blushing. He told her she was beautiful. She wrote down her phone number for him. He promised he'd call. She was as sweet as Jessica. He could see them as a future couple. He reached over and touched the baby's soft hand.

Then leaning his head gently against her shoulder, as the beautiful countryside rolled away behind them on that early summer morning, James Browning, who had been awake by then for thirty-six hours, finally slept.

# TWENTY

WHEN BILLY JO AND NIGHTSHADE SHARED THEIR PLAN to get DNA from Grant and Aimee with Dory, she squashed it immediately.

"I'm not blaming you, Nightshade. Billy Jo is the *nincompoop* here. You, young lady, are absolutely not doing this. It's breaking about ten laws. Think of a better way."

The phone rang before Billy Jo could protest. She grabbed it, saying, "Rosedale Investigations." There was a short pause before she handed the phone to Dory saying, "It's Wayne."

Dory was quiet for a bit listening to him talk before she said, "Yes, of course. It's no problem. I'll get the meeting together."

"What's happening?" Billy Jo asked.

"We need to bring Annabelle Browning back in. Our new confidential informant, Lorelei, says she's moving back to Bellevue. We need to talk to her before she leaves."

"I don't know if I can get her to come in. She dismissed us from the case," Billy Jo said.

"She did, and normally we would let it go, but since it impacts Jessica, we need to follow up. Wayne thinks James Browning is on the run and came here to get Annabelle to go with him. Either that, or," Dory hesitated. "If the shooter followed him here, it's possible he's already dead. And, if that's the case, our Detective is pretty sure Annabelle knows it. I'll give her a call and see if she will come in. I'm going to ask Sheriff Bradley to join us."

NIGHTSHADE WAITED UNTIL EVERYONE, INCLUDING PD and the overweight woman they called Annabelle, went into the conference room. Knowing they would be tied up for at least an hour, he decided to take a chance and leave. Pulling open the fridge door, he saw a donut, some pieces of cheese and half a sandwich. Hurriedly, he put them in his backpack, silently opened the back door to the building and walked out into the searing afternoon sun.

He had a good sense of direction and knew he could get back to Lucy and Wayne's house easily. Huck had slipped his chain the night before and escaped from the garage. When they gave up searching for the dog during the previous night and went back to the house, Lucy told him that dogs running loose were taken to the Pound.

"What happens to them there?" Nightshade asked, his voice was tight with anxiety.

"They feed them for a week or two and if someone comes in and wants them, they pay the fine and take them home."

"And if nobody comes who wants the dog?" Nightshade asked with a clenched mouth.

"I'm sure they do their best to place them, but some of them have to be put to sleep," she said. "I'll go by there on my way to work in the morning and see if they have Huck. You need to get to bed now."

He went into his room, but once there were no sounds coming from Wayne and Lucy's bedroom, he snuck silently out of the house. It was a bright moonlit night and he spent hours calling and looking for his dog. Huck was the only one who'd loved him since his mother died. Without the dog, he felt adrift from the earth, like a balloon with its string cut heading straight up into the burning atmosphere.

"I RESENT YOU PUTTING PRESSURE ON ME TO COME IN TODAY," Annabelle told Billy Jo in a provoked voice when she arrived. "I'm packing to leave town. And I already dispensed with your services."

"We know how busy you are. This won't take long," Billy Jo said soothingly as she walked her down the hall.

When she opened the door, Wayne introduced her to Sheriff Bradley and PD.

"We wanted to talk with you about your husband. We know he's back in town. Given that, we wondered why you would leave," PD said.

"It's none of your business, but I'm going back to Bellevue. My father's very ill with lung cancer. He's only receiving palliative care now." She paused, bit her lip and then continued, "Hospice has been called in because he's only got days to live."

"My condolences," Dory said, patting the woman's shoulder. A few tears ran down Annabelle's pudgy face, she sniffled, and Dory handed her a tissue.

"Where is your husband now?" Wayne asked.

"I don't know. All he said was that he needed to disappear for a while. He thought the shooter could have followed him here. I asked him where he was headed, but he wouldn't tell me. He didn't want anyone to know," Annabelle said, taking a deep breath.

"Do you have a guess?" Wayne asked. It was obvious to him she was lying. She knew exactly where he went. She'd probably made the arrangements.

"If the shooter followed him here, I fear he hasn't long," she said, and a trace of regret spread across her face.

"Why do you say that?" Dory asked.

"Because the accused must be provided the names of his accusers at trial, and since the killer was freed as a result of the hung jury, he would come after James. My husband wouldn't be safe around here anymore. Frankly, I would be surprised if he made it out of the state."

"Was he leaving the state?" Wayne asked. "I thought you didn't know where he was going."

Annabelle took a deep breath and said, "No comment."

"Are the Mount Blanc cops looking for him?" the sheriff asked.

"No comment."

"You probably shot him yourself. I would have," Dory said.

Wayne gave her a scathing look. "Did you kill him because of the other woman?" he asked her quietly.

Annabelle said nothing.

"Have you seen his body?" the sheriff asked.

Despite the hailstorm of questions, Annabelle refused to say anything further, grabbed her purse and left the office.

The team was quiet for a bit as Billy Jo topped up their coffee cups.

"The woman's not doing herself any favors by clamming up. If she killed him, her best bet is to tell us everything," PD said.

"The man badly needed shooting," Dory said. "I, for one, consider it justifiable homicide."

Looking around, Wayne turned to Billy Jo and said, "Where's Nightshade?"

She shrugged and said she didn't know. They searched the building, the backyard and Billy Jo's apartment. The boy was nowhere in evidence.

Wayne opened the refrigerator in the kitchen. The sandwich he'd bought the previous day was gone.

"If I'm going to stay married, I've got to find him," he said desperately and dashed out the door into the hot afternoon.

# TWENTY-ONE

REACHING THE EDGE OF TOWN, NIGHTSHADE STOOD in the intense heat on the shoulder of the highway in a patch of cattails. He held his thumb out. It wasn't very long before an old guy in a rusty pick-up truck offered him a ride.

"Hi there. My name's Bobby. Where are you going, son?" The man wore a blue baseball cap and Levi overalls. He had a friendly look about him. Nightshade had gotten pretty good at telling the good guys from the dangerous types. Sergeant Roscoe had taught him what to look for.

"My dog's lost and I'm looking for him."

"Hop in. Where do you think he might be?"

"I've been staying with these people who live off County Line road. He might have gone back there."

"That's the direction I'm headed. What's the dog look like?" Bobby asked.

"He looks like a German shepherd, and he's got a white bandage on his right ear."

"I think I just passed him. He was running down this road in the other direction, heading toward the freeway. I'll turn around and see if we can catch him."

They spotted Huck several miles later. He was running frantically, his tongue hanging out. Bobby slowed his pick-up down and Nightshade was so happy to see his dog, he jumped out while the truck was still moving. When the dog stopped, he grabbed him by the collar.

"I got him. Thanks a lot, Bobby," he called.

"Where are you headed now, son?"

"Homeless City."

"Sure you will be okay there? It's about ten miles away from here and I've heard it can be kind of a rough place."

"I'll be fine. I've got friends there," Nightshade told him.

"Okay. I just remembered something. I've got a little piece of rope in the cab. You can use it as a leash. Good luck," he called as he tossed the rope out the window.

Nightshade caught the rope, tied it to Huck's collar and thanked him again. As he took a U-turn, Bobby waved good-bye.

*I'll be fine in Homeless City*, he thought, but it would be a long thirsty walk and they would both be hungry again. It didn't matter. He had his dog. And he needed to keep himself strong. Sergeant Roscoe said it was the only way to make it in this world.

WAYNE BACKED RAPIDLY OUT OF THE DRIVEWAY and turned toward home. He felt his anger building. By the time he got out of town he was in a towering rage. Damn kid had run off *again*. He forced himself to simmer down, to think like a detective, to be logical. He knew Nightshade had gone in search of his dog. Since he was only five miles away from home, he'd check there first. As he drove, his phone pinged with an incoming text.

*Come back. Jessica is here,* Dory's message read.

*PD and the sheriff will have to handle,* he texted back.

She sent back a scowling red emoji face.

A few minutes later, he drove up his driveway. Theirs was a neat three-bedroom ranch with flowering shrubs around the foundation. The dark purple-leaved bushes were in full magenta bloom. Soft gray shutters bracketed the clean windows. Whenever Wayne arrived, the house always felt as if it reached out to welcome him. His breathing slowed. He parked the truck in the garage and walked inside. If Nightshade had been in the house, there would be evidence. Something would be out of place.

He walked through the back entry into the white kitchen. It was immaculate. The cupboards and granite countertops shone; everything was put away. Nightshade hadn't been there. To be certain, he walked through the rest of house slowly, checking the living room, the recently added sunroom, the office and the guest bedroom. Nothing was disturbed.

When he reached their bedroom he smiled, remembering Lucy getting into bed the previous night and reaching for him. Her body was cold from being outside for hours searching for the boy's dog. She snuggled close saying she needed him to warm her up. He was amused, remembering how aroused he'd been.

"Not a chance, Buddy," she'd told him with a low laugh in her voice. He knew that laugh. It meant he would have to wait, and he didn't really mind. It was late, they were both tired. And it had been good working as a team. For the first time, he'd felt it was going to be okay having Nightshade around.

Lastly, he checked the backyard for the dog, but there was no sign of him. Getting back into the truck, he headed for Homeless City, knowing it was most likely where he'd gone. As he drove, he reluctantly acknowledged the parallels between his life and the boy's. Nightshade was nearly sixteen. Wayne had run away from his foster parents when he was seventeen. He was Native American and was pretty sure Nightshade was part First Nations, too. The boy's mother died of an overdose. Wayne's mother had left him when he was a toddler. Nightshade didn't know who his father was. Wayne had only recently learned that his father joined the U.S. Army in the 1970s and died in the Vietnam War. There were even similarities in their names. Wayne's middle name was Nighthawk.

Since Homeless City was ten miles away, he suspected the boy would have hitched a ride. He parked his truck on the side of the highway and waved two cars down, asking if they'd seen the kid. They hadn't. While he was talking with one woman, an old guy in a junky pick-up wearing a blue baseball cap roared past. Wayne waved his arms, trying to get the man to stop, but wasn't successful. At that moment, he received a second text message. It was from Billy Jo.

*"Have you found him yet?"* she'd asked.

Before he left the office he'd hollered at her, saying she was supposed to be watching the boy. Now he felt ashamed of his outburst and knew he would have to apologize. Nightshade wasn't Billy Jo's job. Keeping track of the boy was his responsibility. Lucy had made that clear.

*"Not yet. Watching him wasn't your job. Sorry,"* he texted back.

JESSICA BROWNING ARRIVED AT ROSEDALE INVESTIGATIONS as Wayne was leaving. When Billy Jo opened the door, she was pleased to see her looking better. She was dressed becomingly and although her smile was a bit shaky, it was clear just looking at her that James Browning had come home.

"Come on in. The whole team is waiting to meet with you," she said.

"I'm not sure that's necessary. James came home this morning."

"That's great news and I'm happy for you, but we have some final questions. Okay?" Billy Jo asked. When Jessica nodded, she walked her down the hall. When she opened the door, PD greeted them and introduced her to Sheriff Bradley.

"We know your husband is back in Rosedale. Have you seen him yet?" PD asked.

"Yes, he appeared at the house this morning. Our son was delighted to see his dad. After we had a little time together as a family, I took Trevor to school. He was gone when I got back," she said and a shadow crossed her face. "But, I'm not worried this time. I know he'll return soon."

"How did your conversation go?" Dory asked, shooting PD an oblique glance. They both knew they would have talked about Browning's other family.

"I'm sure you've figured out by now that James is married to two women." Her mouth tightened. "He didn't marry the other woman legally, but they had been together for years and it was considered a common law marriage. Before he moved here, James and the woman's daughter witnessed the murder of a narcotics officer. I knew very little about this, but it explained a lot about his behavior. He left me a note saying he had to leave for a while, that it wasn't safe for him to be in Rosedale."

"He's been safe living here for years. Why did he think he was in danger now?" PD asked.

"He said that the man who killed the police officer got off when the trial ended in a hung jury. James feared he had been followed back home. He's probably just lying low for a few days."

"Did you talk about Annabelle?" Dory asked.

"Yes. He said he had ended their relationship. The only thing he asked of me was to be kind to her daughter if we ever met. He showed me a picture of her."

"Thanks for coming in, Jessica. That's all we needed. Please notify us when James comes back," Sheriff Bradley said.

ON HIS WAY TO HOMELESS CITY, Wayne stopped at a fast-food place and loaded up on hamburgers for the residents. When he reached the settlement, he looked down on the beehive of activity. Soon enough, he saw the dog. It had a trailing piece of rope hanging from its collar. The boy walked over and petted the animal. Wayne watched him for a while, remembering living with his foster mother as a child.

A few years after Wayne came to the family, a younger boy arrived. Over time, he became the younger boy's big brother, if not through blood, then through love and commitment. He recalled a day when his little brother's puppy disappeared. He'd followed the sound of its faint high-pitched cries and crawled under the porch where the frightened pup was hiding. When he handed the puppy to his joyful brother, pride had filled his chest. Recalling that day, he acknowledged how important a dog could be to a troubled kid.

Remorse still ate at him when he recalled leaving the house of his foster family early in the morning when he was seventeen. The younger boy had begged him to stay. He returned years later, but was too late. By then, his brother was dead, at the hands of his foster father. Lucy bringing Nightshade into their lives meant the universe was giving him a second chance to do things right. He knew with that chance came an obligation to care for and guide this young man.

It was hard for him to admit, but he was starting to think Lucy was right. He loved her so profoundly and wanted to make her happy. It had been a shock when she said Nightshade was the son God sent them, but if Lucy believed finding him was the work of the Almighty, he had no choice. His own reservations about taking on an adolescent with a record would have to be set aside.

# TWENTY-TWO

As WAYNE HEADED DOWN THE HILL TO HOMELESS CITY, the sun beat down on his head and shoulders. High temperatures made his anger flare, but he knew better than to let it take over. He took deep breaths as he walked, knowing he needed to be calm in order to properly handle the situation. Nightshade looked up and spotted him. The boy stood stock still, folded his arms across his chest and tugged on his dog's rope, pulling him a bit closer. When Wayne reached the crumbly paved pad with its battered tents and smoldering burn barrel, he stopped and waited.

Sergeant Roscoe approached and said, "The boy wants to stay with us. You need to leave."

"I will, but not until I hear it from him," Wayne said calmly. Then turning to Nightshade, he pitched his voice low and asked, "Is that true? Do you want to stay here?"

The boy looked a bit uncertain but didn't respond. He plunked himself down on the broken concrete, pulling his dog close to his side.

"Looks like I need to give him some time to think. I brought food," Wayne said and held out the white paper bag. "Help yourselves, folks. Women and children first."

The old woman called Rosie gestured to the two women who lived in the camp. One was holding the hand of a child who looked to be about ten years old. It broke Wayne's heart to see the youngster living there, but at least he had one parent. He'd mention it to Lucy. Perhaps Child Protection Services could do something for them. Both women walked up and quickly snatched the sandwiches.

"Take two for the boy," he told the ten-year-old's mother. She looked at him a moment, unsure whether he meant it, but then grabbed the extra burger. Wayne then handed Sergeant Roscoe the bag with the rest of the food. He wanted to show respect to the man by having him distribute the food to the remainder of the group. The sergeant called the men over and told them to help themselves. Wayne noticed that he didn't take anything for himself and shook his head at Nightshade when he approached. Wayne's veneration for the former soldier increased.

"I won't take the boy unless I have your permission, Sergeant."

"Come over here, Nightshade," Sgt. Roscoe said. "You have a decision to make. These people, this man and his lady, are willing to take you in. They have come twice to collect you. They won't come again. That's right, isn't it?" he asked Wayne, who nodded. "You need to decide right now and whatever you choose will determine your future." A long silence ensued.

"I'll go then, I guess," Nightshade said at last.

"Is that your decision? You are coming with me?" Wayne asked and the boy nodded. He cast a quick look at the Sergeant as if to ask his permission.

"On your feet, Soldier," Sergeant Roscoe ordered. "This is no longer your place."

"Good luck to you, sir. And respect," Wayne said as he saluted the King of Homeless City.

"I'M GLAD YOU FOUND YOUR DOG," he said as they hiked the hill side-by-side to the truck. Nightshade didn't respond. He loaded Huck into the back seat. The dog settled, giving a sigh of contentment. Once in the driver's seat, Wayne put the keys in the ignition, started the air conditioning and looked directly at the boy.

"I have something to say and I'm only going to say this once. I'm not going to watch you any longer, but if you *ever* leave us again, you will break Lucy's heart and I will never forgive you." It was the voice he used with young offenders who had been given a second chance. He saw the impact the words made in the boy's eyes.

"Fine, but I'm only staying for her," Nightshade said in a combative tone, raising his chin defiantly.

"Be that as it may, Nightshade, I am staying for both of you," Wayne said quietly, and they drove slowly home. A pact had been made. They understood one another. There would be other confrontations, he knew, but he'd handled this one right. More issues lay ahead: school, girlfriends, the awkward talks about drugs, alcohol and sex. But when Lucy came home that night she would smile. He would hug her and for the first time, he would also hug the boy.

KNOWING THAT SOLVING THE BROADCHURCH CASE could be her ticket to a partnership, Billy Jo sat down at her workstation and pulled out her notes. The critical question was whether Aimee was Grant's daughter. She'd read that males infected with mumps *could* be permanently sterile. The key word was "could." More information was needed, but nobody would give her Grant's medical records and Dory had squashed the idea of Nightshade stealing some hairs to get their DNA.

Who would possibly know? A sudden idea hit Billy Jo, and a delighted grin crossed her face. Grant's mother would know. A mother would remember if her son had mumps as a child, how bad a case it was and other relevant details. She picked up her phone and dialed Hilary Broadchurch. There was no answer, so she left a voicemail message. "It's Billy Jo from Rosedale Investigations. I need your mother's name and phone number. I believe she would have some information that could be vital to solving the case."

Then she called for Dory, asking her to come out of the kitchen. When she appeared, Billy Jo stood up, twirled around and gave a happy shriek. "I've had a brainstorm. You were right to tell me to find another way to check whether Aimee Anderson might be Broadchurch's daughter. I'm getting in touch with Grant's mother."

"Good thinking," Dory said, patting her on the back. "Changing the subject, you seem like you've adjusted to PD's retirement by now. Have you?"

"Mostly, I guess. I still have some hard questions to ask him, though."

"What questions?"

"Remember when we talked about the time after my mother and Grampa died?"

Dory nodded.

"They both passed away the summer after my junior year in high school, and I got a job at the Creamy Scoop, the ice cream shop in town. The job gave me a little spending money, but I was so dumb, I didn't even know I had to pay rent. I never picked up our mail from the Post Office either, so I didn't pay the utility bills. I couldn't figure out why the air conditioning didn't work." She shook her head. "Anyway, after a few weeks, the landlord evicted me. He called me a squatter. There was nothing left for me in Rosedale, and I wanted to go to college, so I drove to Knoxville."

"Would they admit you without a high school degree?" Dory asked.

"At the Admissions office, I found out I had to take the GED first. I got a job in a little pizza place and sat for the exam. I passed it and applied to college. I went to school part-time there for almost two years."

"Hold on a minute. I want to get the timeline right. Do you mean that you were evicted only a few weeks after they died?" Dory asked.

"That's right. The landlord said the rent hadn't been paid in several months. Mom probably forgot because she was so sick."

"At that time, did you have a cell phone or a credit card?"

"No. I was only seventeen."

"What about a car?"

"I did have a car, but it wasn't in my mother's or my grandfather's name. I think it was a gift from a friend of Mom's."

"Without a cell phone or credit card it would have been pretty hard for PD to chase you down. You know the way we locate missing people is through credit card purchases, cell phone calls and pings on cell phone towers. Or, by locating their cars."

"True," Billy Jo said thoughtfully. "I hadn't thought of that."

"It seems to me that if the man has anything to apologize for, it's only that he didn't find you in the short time you were still around here."

"You're right, Dory, because it was almost immediately after I returned to town two years later that he found me," she said.

"Which leads me to think he'd been looking for you all along," Dory said, giving Billy Jo a meaningful glance. "You need to cut PD a break about this. Knowing him, I would bet he was trying to locate you that whole time."

Billy Jo sat back down at her desk, deep in thought. The only issue left was the short period after her grandfather and mother died. But, it was still confusing. The man was running Rosedale Investigations at that time. *Even if he didn't have time to find her himself, he employed two other detectives. Why didn't he assign the task of finding her to one of them?*

She took a deep breath, knowing she'd made her decision. She had to ask him why he hadn't found her earlier, or the question would never stop burning holes in the deeply folded crevices of her memories.

Just then her cell phone pinged with a text. It was from Hilary

Broadchurch Miller, who sent the name and address of her mother and a message. *"I already told Mom you would be in touch. She's home this afternoon and expecting you."*

Billy Jo sighed, setting aside her issues with PD. There would be enough time to ask him why he hadn't come for her sooner, once the case was solved. Switching the office phones to the answering machine, she headed out the door.

# TWENTY-THREE

BILLY JO HEADED SOUTHWEST OUT OF ROSEDALE, checking the directions for the Broadchurch address on her phone from time to time. Half an hour later, she'd reached open country with only occasional houses scattered across the massive granite escarpment. She sped past the address the first time, missing it in the thick vegetation. Backing up, she turned into a lane so narrow, the trees touched above the road. Tall shrubs scraped against her car. Bumping along the gravel track, she came to a crossroads. A wooden sign tacked to a tree listed the names of several homeowners. The Broadchurch residence was indicated with an arrow. She turned left, heading down a narrow ribbon of a trail that was cut like a step into the rocky hill. Then the road veered off and almost immediately terminated. Ahead of her was a cement driveway that ended at a two-car garage.

She got out of her car and looked up the hill into the ranks of ascending trees. The temperature had fallen and trees with gauzy skirts of mist marched up the hill in layers. The colors of the leaves ranged from chartreuse to a deep glass green. Looking down, she felt she could step off into the tops of lower trees and would never fall. It was like floating in a magical amphitheater made of leafy trees and the cool white shoulders of fog.

Most people probably entered the house through the garage, Billy Jo assumed, but decided it wouldn't be polite. Walking along the bluestone sidewalk in front of the one-story residence with its large windows, she came to a heavily carved wooden door and rang the bell.

Mrs. Broadchurch, a tiny birdlike woman with bright blue eyes appeared and said, "You must be Billy Jo. Hilary said you would be coming. Follow me." She was one of those women whose filmy hair had turned white while her face remained tanned and youthful.

The woman walked briskly through the living room, kitchen and down a hall. When she'd answered the door, Billy Jo noticed her long white shirt was spattered with tiny spots of colored paint. The woman was probably an artist. Music played in the distance and she smiled, recognizing the melody. It was from a French opera called Lakmè. Her confidence rose as she absorbed the gorgeous lilting tones of the "Bell Song." Listening to opera always helped her come up with ideas relevant to solving cases.

The last room in the house had windows on three sides. Paintings were hung between the panes. They were small, framed pencil sketches of birds, the perfect addition to the cluttered but charming art studio. The windows on the front side of the home looked down into a thickly wooded canyon. Through the open windows at the back, she could hear a trickle of water moving over rocks in a stream. She heard the plaintive song of the mourning doves and inhaled the pleasant fragrance of pine trees.

Mrs. Broadchurch sat down on a tall stool in front of an easel on which rested a partly completed portrait of a dog. "I'm a pet artist. Find somewhere to sit and tell me why you are here." She picked up her brush, looked carefully at a photograph of the dog she was using for reference, and started painting.

Billy Jo gazed around the room with its built-in shelving units filled with tiny cans of paint. On the back wall was a counter with a sink, a scattered pile of cardboard boxes lay on the floor. In the middle of the room was a chair in the final stages of being refinished. She decided she'd stand.

"I don't know what your daughter has told you so far, Mrs. Broadchurch, but Hilary came to Rosedale Investigations asking us to look into a relationship between her older brother, Grant, and a yoga instructor named Aimee."

"She told me," the woman said, sounding annoyed. "Unfortunately, my daughter is not terribly self-aware. She envisions herself as a social butterfly in the upper echelons of Nashville society. That's why she started hyphenating her name to Broadchurch-Miller. She wants those two dullard sons of her to go to Harvard and Yale. Ha!" she snorted. "Those boys will be lucky to make it through high school. I'm sure you're shocked, but it's the God's truth."

"Not at all," Billy Jo said who had, in fact, been deeply shocked. "Are you aware that Grant has been giving Aimee money?"

Mrs. Broadchurch continued to work, precisely capturing the texture of the fur on the dog she was painting. "I'm sure Hilary's worried that this girl will end up with all Grant's money and she won't get another dime. It would serve her right. She's always bugging him for more, usually to buy clothes or jewelry. He already paid off their house. She tells everyone her husband owns a Mercedes dealership, when in fact he sells used cars."

"Go on," Billy Jo said, making notes on her pad.

"You seem like a smart girl and by looking around this house, you can see how my children were raised. My home is filled with music, art and surrounded by some of God's most beautiful nature. I have no idea why Hilary turned out to be so shallow. So what if Grant is having an affair. Good for him. It's about time he had a woman in his life."

Billy Jo, still startled after hearing Mrs. Broadchurch's critical remarks about her daughter and grandsons, was struggling to maintain control of the interview. To gain time, she cleared her throat and said, "We originally thought they were having an affair, but apparently Grant is not sleeping with Aimee. She has a serious boyfriend, and your son has been seen at fancy restaurants squiring both of them around town. He always picks up the tab."

"What does Hilary think is going on then?" Mrs. Broadchurch asked. She set her paint brush down and turned around to look at Billy Jo. For the first time, she seemed interested in the subject. Her bright eyes narrowed in concentration.

"She thinks Aimee is blackmailing Grant, but for a forty-year-old bachelor he's led a pretty blameless life. I checked his record with the police and he only has a couple of parking tickets. Frankly, I couldn't find anything she could blackmail him with."

"So, what do you think is happening?" The woman ran her fingers through her hair, sprinkling it with touches of color.

"I may be wrong, but I think Aimee is his daughter. However, I understand that Grant had mumps as a boy, and the disease could have left him sterile. I'm hoping you can confirm the case of mumps and provide your opinion on whether your son is able to have children."

"I remember the mumps, of course. Grant was twelve and his testicles did swell up a bit. One was larger than the other, about the size of a plum. Orchitis, the doctor called it."

Billy Jo was irked to feel herself blushing. She really hadn't needed that much detail.

"Too much information, girl?" the woman laughed. "Anyway, I assumed that Grant had his semen tested when he got serious with his girlfriend, Cindy, in college. She wanted a family and he told me they broke up when he told her about his condition. Why would he have given up on the relationship if he had viable sperm? It doesn't make sense. He was deeply in love with the girl."

"Perhaps he just accepted the doctor's original diagnosis and never checked."

"That's possible, I guess, or maybe he had some reservations about marrying her. I had a long talk with our family doctor after Grant recovered from the mumps. We saw old Dr. Pierson then. He's long gone now, but at the time he told me that when only one of the testicles . . ."

*Not that word again*, Billy Jo thought, cringing in embarrassment.

"Are you okay?" Mrs. Broadchurch stopped speaking for a moment, seeing Billy Jo's obvious discomfort. "Anyway, he said Grant could be sterile, but it was also possible that his sperm count would just be low. Is that all you wanted to know?"

*Way more than I wanted to know, really*, Billy Jo thought and took a deep breath. She hated turning scarlet in front of this woman who could discuss her son's reproductive system so unblushingly. "There's one other thing I wanted to ask. Has Grant ever discussed Aimee Anderson with you, or his reasons for the sudden relationship?"

"Not yet, but I suspect if she were his daughter, he would have. I've always wanted a granddaughter, especially after seeing Hilary's little rapscallions," the woman said, rolling her eyes.

"Thank you for your time and the information, Mrs. Broadchurch. I'm going to leave you my card. If you have any more thoughts of what might be going on, I'd appreciate you calling me. On another note, the portrait you are working on is excellent, almost photographic. You really captured the soul of that little dog."

"I should probably raise my prices," Mrs. Broadchurch said with a pixie grin. Then her face turned a bit serious as she said, "If it turns out I have a granddaughter, I wish to be informed."

"I think it would be best to talk directly with your son. And if you learn anything relevant, I'd be most appreciative if you contacted me," Billy Jo said.

She walked back through the cluttered artistic dwelling feeling bemused. The lovely opera music wrapped itself around her all the way out to her car. Putting the keys into the ignition, she decided she'd call her personal physician. Perhaps he could shed some light on the likelihood of male sterility after a case of mumps. If he couldn't, she was pretty much out of ideas.

# TWENTY-FOUR

NIGHTSHADE AND HIS DOG HUCK ARRIVED at the dog obedience class offered by Everything Pets right on time. Dr. Lucy had promised that Huck could start sleeping in the house once he'd received a passing certificate from the course. He'd begged Lucy to attend the class with him. She shook her head.

"Huck is your dog, and your responsibility. You'll be fine. Don't forget to introduce yourself to the other members of the class," she'd said, patting him on the shoulder.

Head down, with Huck on his leash, he walked into the large store, spotting a sign for the obedience class that met in a room toward the back. The sign read Kim Douglas, Instructor. When he got to the room, a heavy-set, cheerful girl with thick glasses welcomed him. She immediately got down on her chubby knees to greet Huck. She was wearing tight jeans with holes in them and a red sweatshirt that said, "For the love of God, Woman! Eat a salad!" Nightshade felt his mood lightening. He got a kick out of her ability to make fun of herself.

"What a beautiful dog. What's his name?" Kim asked.

"It's Huck. I'm Nightshade."

"Nice to meet you. I'm Kim. There are only four dogs in this class. I don't like to take on too many when we are focusing on commands, obedience, and controlling aggression. There's a pit bull named Chester, a young lab named Blackie, and a Doberman named Lincoln in the class. I never bother with the names of the owners, just memorize the dog names," she chuckled. "How long have you had Huck?"

"I found him in a dumpster when he was about two months old."

"How horrible. Poor baby Huck. What made you open the dumpster?"

Kim asked.

"I heard him crying. The garbage company is called Junk Removal and I almost called him Junk, but one of the people I was with said not to name him that. Anyone who heard his name would think he was trash. He told me there was a famous book called *Huckleberry Finn*. When he told me the story, I decided to call him Huck."

"Much better. Here are our other attendees," she said, turning to greet the dogs who were being led in. Kim steered the group toward chairs that had been arranged in a semi-circle with plenty of space between them. "Take a seat and have your pets sit beside you," she said.

Nightshade sat down and told Huck to sit. The others nodded to him as they got seated. The man with the big boisterous lab was having a hard time getting his dog under control. Kim walked over and said, "Blackie. Sit," in a loud voice. It worked. The woman knew what she was doing.

"Welcome, everyone. I always start these classes by saying that if a dog is out of control, it's *never* the dog's fault. I'm going to say that again. If a dog is out of control, it's *never* the dog's fault. It's always the dog's *owner* who is mishandling the animal. Dogs fundamentally want to please you. They do need discipline, especially when they are young, but that means consistency and firmness, never harshness or abuse. I only use positive reinforcement in my classes and if I ever hear of, or see you, hitting a dog, I will report you. Hope that is clear," Kim said, making eye contact with each person in turn.

Nightshade grinned. He was used to Sergeant Roscoe. Miss Kim could have been him in female form. The class was going to be interesting.

IT WAS NEARLY FIVE O'CLOCK WHEN MR. GEORGE POWELL, a handsome, middle-aged, African American attorney, stopped into Rosedale Investigations with an unusual request. Dory had given him the evidence of his wife's infidelity several days earlier, after first showing the damning photos to a horribly embarrassed Molly. George said he wanted Dory to be with him when he confronted his wife.

"Why on earth would you want me there?" Dory asked with raised eyebrows.

"I want to save my marriage, not end it," he said.

"That's commendable of you, George, but I don't need to be present while you two thrash this out."

"If Molly wants to stay married to me, she has to apologize, agree to get another job, never see that bastard Manning again, and tell me why this happened," he said.

"You seem to have this all thought out, although Molly might have conditions of her own, you know, if she agrees the marriage is worth saving . . . which she might not," Dory said, giving him a meaningful sidelong look.

"Molly and I already had a short talk. I said I knew about her affair with Dr. Manning. She was obviously humiliated. I told her I wanted to save our marriage. We have two children in college and have been married twenty-five years."

"Sounds like you have made a good start. I'm sorry, George, but I'm a private investigator, not a marriage counselor. I can recommend a good therapist if you like," Dory said. She pulled out a small pad of paper and started writing a name and phone number.

"The woman made a fool out of me." George smacked Dory's desk hard with his fists. Clearly striving for control after the outburst, he said, "I'm sorry. I shouldn't have reacted like that. If you'll do this for us, Dory, I'm willing to pay double what you charged me to investigate my wife's extra-marital activities."

Despite her reservations, Dory acquiesced. As CFO for Rosedale Investigations, and with PD's recent needs for money to cover his retirement, she wasn't in a position to turn down his offer. After George left, having agreed to return later that evening, Dory dialed her friend Rebecca, the marriage counselor who picked up the call.

"I need some advice, my friend," Dory said. "One of my clients wants me to do a marriage intervention. I planned to give him your number, but he insists on me being there. His wife cheated on him, but he wants the marriage to survive. Any guidance?"

"It's hard to say much without knowing the couple, but make sure they are talking to each other and not to you," she said. "And I never start the conversation. Let them begin. It will give you a clue to their dynamics. The one who talks first is the dominant person in the relationship. And make sure that each of them gets about the same amount of time to present their points of view during the appointment."

MR. AND MRS. POWELL WERE SCHEDULED TO MEET WITH DORY in the Rosedale Investigations conference room at six p.m. Knowing the encounter was likely to be emotional, Dory had bought wine, Brie, fruit and crackers. She was putting wine glasses on the room table when she heard the tinkling bell on the front door. The couple had arrived. They were talking quietly as they came down the hall. It seemed a good omen.

George held the conference door open for Molly, his other arm rested around her waist. It was a nice gesture and evidence he was sincere in wanting to save the marriage. To Dory's surprise, Molly shrugged his arm away, looking irritated. Their non-verbal behavior was intriguing. The wife was the guilty party and yet it looked like George was the person making the overtures. Dory felt for the man.

After greeting the couple, she said, "I wonder if you would both like a glass of wine. I thought it might help ease the tension." As they got seated, she passed around the Brie, sliced apples and crackers. Following Rebecca's advice about not starting the conversation, she waited. It didn't take long.

George looked directly at Dory and said, "As I have told my wife, I don't want a divorce. I do have certain conditions, however, if the marriage is going to be saved. On the way over here, I told Molly she had to get a new job, never see Manning ever again, and tell me why this happened."

Speaking to her, instead of to his wife, was exactly what her friend the marriage counselor had warned her about. "You aren't married to me, George. Please address your remarks to your wife," Dory said.

"Okay." He turned to his spouse. "In order for me to forgive you, Molly, I have to know this will never happen again. After twenty-five years of marriage, I can't believe you would betray me like this," George said, clenching his jaw and shaking his head. He was barely under control. Dory didn't blame him, but he needed to tone it down a bit.

"It's just so typical," Molly said bitterly.

"What is that supposed to mean?" George asked in an offended tone. "I've been faithful for twenty-five years while you have been carrying on for God know how long."

"A month," Molly said. "I never cheated before. And the night Dory took her photos, was the night I broke off the relationship."

"So it's over?" George asked and Molly nodded. "Are you going to say you are sorry at least?"

"No, George, I'm not, and here's why. All you ever do is work. You leave at seven in the morning, even on Saturdays, and you don't come home until after seven at night. You eat the dinner I've worked hard to prepare and never once give me a compliment. I do all the grocery shopping, the cooking, the cleaning and laundry, even though I have a challenging job and work full-time. You don't even speak to me during dinner and afterwards you go immediately into the living room and bury your nose in the newspaper or turn on the news. You don't even help clear the table. And it's been years since you've asked me about my day," Molly said.

"Is this the case, George?" Dory asked, looking at him inquisitively. She was beginning to see Molly's side of things.

"It is. And there's more. My husband hasn't given me a birthday or Christmas gift in decades. I don't need to tell you, Dory, that as a black woman you are married to a family and a community. I do a lot of vol-unteer work which my husband refuses to help with. We haven't gone on vacation since the children finished middle school. And, let's face facts, George, we haven't had sex in months."

George looked deeply uncomfortable. He squirmed, shifting in the chair. "I've provided this family with a good living. Our children attend fine colleges. You don't have to work," he said, sounding defensive.

"First of all, I want to work. I'm a nurse and enjoy my profession. I care about my patients and they respect me. I agree you have been a good provider, but I haven't felt appreciated since the children were born."

"I suppose that bum Manning was big into appreciation," George said. He sounded disgruntled.

"He was, but as I said, I ended it the night Dory took her pictures. So, if you want to stay married to me, it's going to take a lot more than being a good provider," Molly said firmly. She took a sip of wine. George looked at Dory. She tilted her head at Molly, reminding him to speak to her.

An hour later, the couple had agreed to try again. George even admit-ted that he'd failed Molly and that her relationship with Dr. Manning was in part his fault for neglecting her and the marriage. Watching the couple walk out hand-in-hand into the moonlit night, Dory felt pretty good about herself.

"*Guess I could always get a job as a marriage counselor if this private eye gig doesn't work out,*" she thought, grinning.

# TWENTY-FIVE

B ILLY JO'S CALL TO HER DOCTOR THE NEXT MORNING had been a total waste.

"The only thing I can tell you is that sterility *can* occur when the male child is pre-pubescent, but it isn't inevitable. There are many times where the sperm count is just lower than optimal," he said.

She clicked off the call feeling irritated. Her idea about Grant being his yoga instructor's father seemed impossible to prove and Hilary had given them nothing but suspicions about the blackmail. Having already talked with Mrs. Broadchurch, Grant's mother, and confirming the case of mumps, her next step was to talk with Grant directly. And for that, she needed Wayne. He arrived about an hour later with Nightshade.

"Good morning, guys," Wayne said. The boy nodded and headed directly into the kitchen.

Billy Jo, knowing the boy's appetite, had started buying extra muffins and fresh fruit. She followed them, offered Wayne coffee, and got Nightshade a paper plate. "Any chance you would interview a client for me today?" she asked.

"I was planning on getting the lawnmower out and showing Nightshade how to use it. He's going to mow and trim the lawn here this morning. While he's doing that, I could talk to your client. Who's coming in?"

"Grant Broadchurch had agreed to pay us a visit," she said.

"Remind me of the specifics, will you? His sister thought he was being blackmailed, right? What have you discovered so far?"

"Grant Broadchurch has been giving his yoga instructor money every week for two months. I thought they were sleeping together, but that turned out not to be true. My next supposition was that she was his illegitimate daughter, but he had mumps as a kid and doesn't believe he can have children. I met with his mother who confirmed the mumps diagnosis, but since then I learned some boys who have the illness can still father a child. I wanted to get ahold of Grant's hair for a DNA test, but Dory absolutely forbids me from doing that."

"Dory is right," Wayne said, looking at her incredulously, and shaking his head. Then he asked, "Do you want me to find out if he thinks Aimee is his daughter?"

"Yes, please," she said.

GRANT BROADCHURCH APPEARED AT THE OFFICES of Rosedale Investigations an hour later. Billy Jo had seen him in the yoga class, but was again struck by what a handsome man he was. Having visited his mother, Billy Jo could see he had her twinkling blue eyes, the color of a bluebird's wing. Unlike many middle-aged men, he didn't have a paunch or beer belly and was a lanky six feet tall. He was wearing a nice pair of charcoal gray trousers, a periwinkle blue shirt and a sport coat. He smiled cheerfully when she greeted him at the door.

"Am I in the right place?"

"You are. I'm Billy Jo and I want to thank you for coming over."

Grant held out his hand to shake hers, saying, "I remember you from yoga class. You are much better than I am."

"I'm just a beginner. Aimee is a great instructor," she said, hoping it would elicit some reaction.

"She sure is, but I'm wondering why you wanted to talk to me. Isn't this a private detective agency?"

"It is and if you will follow me to our conference room, I want to introduce you to my colleague, Detective Nichols. He'll tell you why we wanted you to come in. Would you like something to drink? We have tea, coffee and a few sodas."

"Do you have iced tea?"

"We do. Would you like sugar or lemon?"

Having provided Grant with lemon and sugar for his tea, they walked down the hall. When she opened the door, Wayne stood up, introduced himself and thanked Grant for coming.

"I'm sure you're confused about why we asked you to stop by," Wayne said.

"Indeed I am."

"Our agency was contacted a while ago by your sister, Hilary. She was concerned about your recent relationship with Aimee Anderson."

Grant's mouth tightened and he clenched his jaw, saying, "My personal life is none of my sister's business."

"We agreed," Wayne responded, "and told her intimate relationships between single people was a private matter."

"It's not an intimate relationship, if by that you mean sexual. I'm not sleeping with Miss Anderson," Grant said firmly.

"But you are giving her money," Wayne said. "We were confused by that."

Grant took a deep breath, struggling to control the frustration that showed in his reddened face. "That's none of your business or my sister's."

Wayne's hazel eyes bored into Grant's as he said, "Your sister believes you're being blackmailed. That's against the law and if that's the case, no matter how difficult it may be, you must report it to the sheriff."

Grant shifted uncomfortably in his seat before saying, "Miss Anderson is a fine young woman. She is *not* a blackmailer and I refuse to discuss this further. My money and how I spend it is my business, not yours and definitely not my sister's." He stood up, flushed and irritated.

"I agree with you and apologize for my questions. They were inappropriate. I'd very much appreciate your staying just a bit longer. We have one or two more questions," Wayne said, and his apology must have registered because Grant, somewhat reluctantly, sat down. "We wondered if perhaps Miss Anderson was a relative, someone you wanted to help."

"She's trying to start her own business, rather than working for Power Zone. I've agreed to help fund her own studio. If that's all, I need to get going."

Afraid Grant would leave before they got to the heart of the matter, Billy Jo quickly asked, "Is Miss Anderson your daughter, sir?"

Grant gave a disbelieving cough before saying. "She is not. In fact, I can't have children, the result of a bout of mumps as a child."

"Does Miss Anderson think she's your daughter?"

There was a long pause and Billy Jo was about to ask another question when Wayne gave her a warning glance. They were silent as the obviously uncomfortable man struggled to respond.

"She does," he said after a painfully long interval. "I've told her repeatedly that I'm not her father, but she says she has evidence."

"What evidence?" Wayne asked.

"It's important that you hear me about this. I am not the girl's father. Miss Anderson is not asserting a relationship with me to obtain support or to become my heir. She is acutely uncomfortable about the money I've been giving her and the only reason she accepts is because I've agreed to be a silent partner when she opens her own studio. In fact, when Aimee told me she thought she was my daughter, she was unable to do so without crying."

"She wept," Wayne said softly as a painful silence settled in the room.

Grant swallowed and said, "Aimee had to obtain a blood test when she travelled to Mexico to complete her yoga training. She learned then that she has type 'A positive' blood. She found her birth certificate and realized she was born only five months after her parents married. She recalled her mother talking about me, saying that we broke up prior to her marriage and tracked me down. When she found out I have type 'A positive' blood, it led her to believe she's my daughter, although literally millions of people, including myself, have that blood type."

"Why would that information make her cry?" Wayne asked. His voice was low and kind.

"Because she's believed all her life she was the daughter of her mother, Cindy and her mother's husband, Nick. If that isn't true, it would tear her family apart."

"Does she know their blood types?" Billy Jo asked.

"Yes, they are both type O. I checked with my doctor and learned it is technically possible for two O-type parents to have a child with A or B blood. Extremely rare, but possible."

"Perhaps there's another reason Aimee believes you are her father," Billy Jo said. "When I talked with her mother, she said the two of you were in a committed relationship in college."

"That's true. Cindy wanted a family and when I told her I was sterile, she broke things off with me and started dating my good friend, Nick. Obviously, she was sleeping with him before we broke up," Grant said. "Are we done here?" He reached for his cell phone and keys.

"Almost. I want to thank you for talking with us. I can see how hard it's been for you. One last question, if I may. Are you dating anyone at present?" Wayne asked.

"I'm not, although I'm always willing to do so if the right woman comes along. Now, I'd appreciate you informing Hilary that you have talked with me and that she has no cause for concern," Grant said.

When he opened the door to the hall and walked out, Wayne followed. The two men talked for a few minutes before Billy Jo heard him leave.

"Well, that was a bust," she said when Wayne reappeared. "Aimee thinks she's Grant's daughter, but he maintains it's not possible. Why did you ask him if he was seeing someone?"

"Because it gave me an opening to raise something else."

"What?"

"I told him if Miss Anderson was correct, and he was in fact her father, he could also get anyone he dated pregnant. I said he really needed to get tested. He was taken aback, but said he would consider it."

Billy Jo stood up and hugged Wayne enthusiastically. "That was brilliant! I never would have thought to do that," she said.

"Don't you even *think* about trying to get the man's medical records," Wayne said looking at her through narrowed eyes.

Billy Jo lowered her gaze, but her mind was dancing. She probably couldn't get the result of a sperm viability test, but by checking his credit card charges, she might find out when and where the test was done. And then she would go back to see Grant's mother—the woman who had no reservations about discussing her son's reproductive capabilities and who had always wanted a granddaughter.

# TWENTY-SIX

BILLY JO FINISHED HER REPORT FOR HILARY BROADCHURCH and ran a quick spellcheck before printing the document off on Rosedale Investigations stationery. It was standard practice to include the client's bill with their reports. Dory always prepared the bills, but she wasn't there. In fact, Billy Jo realized, she hadn't been in the office for more than an hour or two for a week.

"Dory has all but disappeared recently," Billy Jo told PD when he called.

"She's probably working on a cheating spouse case," PD said.

"I don't think so. I could find no pending cases when I went through the files. Mark and I were having dinner at the Brookshire Inn last night when I spotted a woman peering into the windows of a building at the end of Main Street. I was virtually certain it was Dory, so I ran outside and called her name, but she scooted around the end of the building and disappeared."

"Did you check her house in the Flower Pot neighborhood?" PD asked.

"Yes, I went over there this morning. I peered in the windows and saw a cereal bowl on the kitchen table and an empty coffee cup. Her little dog was asleep on the couch, so she's in town."

"Sounds to me like she's on some private mission. Keep checking. And, since we recently put Lorelei Vail on the payroll as a confidential informant, you could call her as well."

"I will. When will you be back at the cabin?" she asked.

"Liam and I are leaving today to go back to Knoxville for the spring semester. As a matter of fact, I was going to ask you if you would like to house-sit for a few days. It's fine with me if Mark wants to join you."

"Is there some reason you are uncomfortable leaving the cabin uninhabited?"

"No, just thought you might enjoy some time there. The wildflowers are budded and a bluebird had made a nest in the little dogwood tree outside the kitchen window."

"Thank you. I'd love to. Don't know if Mark is busy, but I'll check," she said, ending the call.

A FEW MINUTES LATER, THE BELL ON THE FRONT DOOR TINKLED and Wayne came in with Nightshade, who accompanied him everywhere of late.

"Greetings, Billy Jo. Nightshade and I are going to Rosedale High School this afternoon. He's getting tested to see what grade he should be placed in when school starts in the fall."

Billy Jo glanced at the boy, who'd already headed for the kitchen. "Have you seen Dory lately?" she asked.

"Not in the last few days. How are you coming on your application for partnership?"

"I've made a start. PD asked me to housesit for a few days while he's in Knoxville. I'm headed out there tonight."

"Want some company?" Nightshade asked as he approached her workstation holding a plate piled high with cheese slices, crackers, two stale donuts and a peach.

"You have an appointment with the guidance counselor at the high school today," Wayne reminded him.

"You are welcome to come out to the cabin any time though," Billy Jo said. The boy gave her a grateful look.

WHEN WAYNE AND NIGHTSHADE LEFT, BILLY JO OPENED the partnership application document on her computer and flipped back through her handwritten notes pertaining to the last three major cases the agency investigated: the Blind Switch, the Blind Split, and In the Frame. During the investigation of the Blind Switch case, she remembered saying Daniel Parrish's death could have had something to do with the racehorse he was training. Her comment had sparked merriment in the team.

Dory had said, "So what is the horse then, a prime suspect?"

And PD had added, "What we have is a far-out theory from the peanut gallery."

Even though she'd been right about the horse being a critical factor in the case, nobody was going to support her application for partnership unless she'd made a major contribution to either identifying the *means*, finding the *motive* or isolating the *opportunity* for the killing. Those were the three major components necessary to solving a murder.

Unable to think of anything she'd contributed to those factors, and still feeling troubled by Dory's absence, Billy Jo put the office phone on voicemail and headed back to the Flower Pot district, determined to track her down.

Dory wasn't at home when Billy Jo arrived, but her little dog was outside in the fenced backyard. When she stopped by earlier, the dog had been sleeping on the couch, so she was definitely in town. Opening the side gate to the fenced yard, she petted the pup and re-filled her water dish from the garden hose. Then tearing a little piece of paper from her notebook, she wrote a message asking Dory to call her and shoved the note in the screen door.

*Where the heck was the woman? And what was she up to?* The image of Dory peeking into the windows of an empty storefront in town and then darting guiltily around the corner of the building continued to trouble her.

WAYNE AND NIGHTSHADE ARRIVED AT ROSEDALE HIGH SCHOOL, parked the truck and walked inside. Wayne spoke to the receptionist in the main office saying they had an appointment with the guidance counselor. They were asked to sign in and directed to a space in the library that was reserved for individual testing. The library was a large room with the pleasant scent of books and a hushed atmosphere. Bookcases covered the outer walls between the floor-to-ceiling windows. Off the main library was a computer lab with multiple desks and computers. Students were browsing or talking quietly. Some looked their way curiously.

"Isn't Lucy coming?" Nightshade whispered. He didn't want to do this stupid testing thing anyway and having Wayne take him made it doubly embarrassing.

"She'll be here soon," Wayne said.

As they waited by the check-out desk at the student library, the counselor came out of her office.

"Hello. I'm Eleanor Robson. You must be Mr. Nichols, and this is

Henry, right?" she was a woman in her fifties with glasses, salt and pepper hair and a pleasant face.

Wayne nodded and said, "His given name is Henry, but his nickname is Nightshade."

"Do you prefer Henry or Nightshade?" she asked.

"Nightshade," Wayne said, answering for him. The boy still had a hard time talking with strangers and confined himself to nods or headshakes. Nightshade gave him an appreciative glance.

A wind-blown Lucy arrived at that moment and introduced herself.

"Glad you could join us, Dr. Nichols. I was just going to ask Nightshade when he last attended school regularly?"

"He was twelve, but I believe his schooling was somewhat sketchy throughout his life," she said.

"Given that, I'm going to give him two tests. The Basehor-Linwood Virtual School offers three-minute reading assessments. This test requires the student to read a passage while mistakes and self-corrections are recorded."

"How does his performance on these tests help you determine grade level?" Lucy asked.

"For example, if the student misses just two words from the fourth grade word list, and three from the fifth grade word list, the student would be considered to be at a fourth grade level for reading."

Nightshade cast Lucy a horrified open-eyed look and whispered, "Fourth grade?"

"Don't worry. I'll be giving you the high school level tests," Mrs. Robson said.

"What about math?" Wayne asked.

"For that I'm going to use Goldstrum assessment which allows us to ascertain his mathematics competence."

"This all sounds good. How long will this take?"

"It will take about an hour and a half to do the testing," Mrs. Robson said. "There's a nice little coffee shop down the road."

"Thank you. We will see you later. Bye, Nightshade," Lucy said and gave him a hug.

# TWENTY-SEVEN

B ILLY JO WAS LISTENING TO THE WEATHER REPORT on the radio while driving out to PD's place. It had been a dramatically colored sunset, as it often was before the onset of summer storms. The rain was supposed to start soon and was predicted to last all night. The gravel trail that led back to the cabin often washed out in heavy rains. She had practically ripped the undercarriage off her car once during a storm. Just then her phone rang and Dory's face appeared on the screen.

"Where in heaven's name have you been the last few days?" she asked, exasperated.

"I am at the office now and see that you typed up the report for Hilary Broadchurch-Miller. I've made out her bill and I'll put both in the mail. I know I've been out of touch lately. Sorry about that, but there was nothing happening in the office and I was working on a personal project," Dory said. She sounded extremely pleased with herself, which made Billy Jo feel even more annoyed.

"What project is this?" she asked.

"I'm not quite ready to tell you yet, but it's something to do with my future and maybe yours, too."

"Please tell me you're not thinking of retiring. Are you?" Billy Jo's voice practically squeaked.

"Not a chance, but if this project works out, it will be a very fun venture."

"I certainly hope this project isn't going to take long to finish up. It's bad enough with PD staying in Knoxville with Liam, and Wayne being taken up with Nightshade. I never thought I'd be working solo and I don't like it."

"I know you don't. Don't worry, Lorelei and I are just about done."

Billy Jo bit back the bitter remark she almost made about Lorelei. She was jealous; there was no getting around it. The woman was taking Dory away from her, like Liam was taking PD away. She'd struggled to contain her feelings of abandonment that had dogged her steps ever since her mother and grandfather died. It seemed to her, since PD decided to retire, she had been trying to walk through a deserted raspberry patch where the thorns on the long purple canes ensnared her and kept her trapped, unable to break free.

"Are you going to be in the office tomorrow?"

"Yes, except for a two-hour stretch after lunch."

"Okay, I'll be in around nine. Sorry, have to go. I'm just about to turn into PD's drive and the rain has started," Billy Jo said and clicked off the call.

Turning her thoughts to more pleasant matters, she envisioned the upcoming evening with Mark. They would light the candles on the table and watch the summer rain turn the ravine into multiple shades of indigo. It would be perfect sleeping, wrapped in his arms and listening to the rain on the cabin's metal roof.

THE NICHOLS FAMILY HAD ARRIVED HOME after receiving Mrs. Robson's report on Nightshade's academic level. He stormed into the house after them, ran down the hall to his room and slammed the door. They had stopped by the bank and grocery store and hadn't gotten back until nearly dinnertime.

"What's his problem?" Wayne asked.

"You heard Mrs. Robson say he can go into high school at the freshman level," she said.

"Given that he was out of school for years, I thought it was good news. I don't get this door-slamming behavior."

"At his age, he really should be a sophomore or even a junior, not a freshman. It's going to be hard enough attending school six or seven hours a day, without the teasing he's going to have to deal with. Even with all the emphasis on getting rid of bullying in the schools, he's bound to encounter mean kids."

"Having dropped out of school at seventeen, I was harassed when I started at the police academy," Wayne said.

"How did you handle that?" Lucy asked.

"I settled it pretty quickly. Only took a couple of beat-downs," Wayne said.

"Oh my god, I certainly hope you aren't going to suggest that Nightshade beat up kids from his school!" She flashed furious eyes at him.

"Given your reaction, I'm guessing that would be a pretty bad idea," Wayne said, looking chagrined.

"It certainly would," Lucy said. She gave him a long look before adding, "Actually, I've got an idea. We have all summer before school starts. Mrs. Robson gave me a print-out of the areas he needs to improve. I'm going to call the school and get him a tutor."

"Now that, my brilliant wife, is a wonderful thought. Come here and give me a hug," Wayne said. But as he took her in his arms and bent his head to kiss her, Nightshade came skulking into the kitchen.

"I suppose this is how it's going to be now," he said in an irritated voice. "I'm going to be living with disgusting adults who are always kissing and hugging. Or worse!"

"This is the least of your problems. Lucy has made you doctor and dental appointments and she's going to hire you a tutor," Wayne said and grinned.

"There's a bit of light at the end of the tunnel, though. I've enrolled you in driver's training. It starts tomorrow. And, I've got a girl in mind to tutor you," Lucy said.

"Is she cute?" Nightshade asked and Wayne hooted in laughter as he slapped him on the back.

"Out of here, both of you. There's way too much testosterone in this kitchen."

THE FOLLOWING MORNING, AFTER DROPPING NIGHTSHADE off at driver's education, Wayne drove to Jessica Browning's house. He'd been thinking about where James was hiding out and she was the last person he saw before he disappeared. When he knocked, Jessica answered the door, saying she was desperate to talk to someone and was so pleased he had shown up. He felt a qualm, knowing he had never been good at handling women in despair.

"Come in, Detective. I've just made a pot of coffee," she said.

"Thank you, I would appreciate the coffee," he said and followed her into a bright kitchen with sage green cabinets, a yellow linoleum floor and white Formica countertops. He took a seat at one of their chairs. A cream-colored pottery bowl filled with orange Clementines was centered on the table.

"Help yourself to the fruit," she told him, setting down a cup of black steaming coffee for him and taking a seat herself. She ran her fingers through her curly hair and took a couple of ragged breaths.

"Did you have some questions I could answer?" he asked, hoping to avert the likely storm of emotions she wanted to unload.

"I can't believe I'm married to a man who had to identify a murderer," Jessica said. She sounded overcome.

"James was just unlucky enough to witness the death of a narcotics officer. He didn't do anything wrong." *Except for marrying two women,* he thought. "Did you ever learn why Samantha was with him that night?"

"Yes, he was going to pick up some groceries. Her mother was still at work, so he took the child with him. He tried desperately to keep her from seeing the man fall and the pool of dark blood spreading beneath his head." She winced and swallowed. She was breathing so hard, her chest almost vibrated.

"Are you okay?" Wayne asked. An instinctive part of him wanted to put his arms around her, to hold her tight until her breathing slowed. A still deeper drive made him feel frantic to escape. He knew it was ridiculous to feel his masculinity was threatened by female anguish, but he couldn't help squirming in desperation when women poured out their hearts to him.

"He told me he didn't love her anymore, but I *hate* that he has this other woman. I was so happy to see him again when he arrived, but I've had more time to think since then, and I can't believe he kept this from me for so long. We weren't supposed to have secrets."

*Everyone has secrets, although not usually of this magnitude,* Wayne thought. "I think theirs was a pretty contentious relationship for many years. And if it makes a difference, he never legalized his marriage to Annabelle. It was what we call a common law marriage."

"Annabelle, is that her name?" Jessica asked in a high voice. "I don't want her to have such a nice name. Is she pretty? Prettier than me?"

*If the idiot hadn't married two women, this whole mess could have been avoided,* he thought, experiencing a fierce jaw-clenching indignation. *How long did the jerk think this situation could hold without a shattering into a million pieces?*

"Do you think that Annabelle still loves him? Or that he still loves her?" Jessica's voice was filled with despair. She was openly weeping now, tears running down her face.

Wayne took a deep breath. He felt he'd handled things clumsily. Rarely certain about exactly how a woman felt, or what would possibly help, he said, "She is angry, I know that."

"I'm angry, too, damn it! He split his time between two women and two children for years! I'm worried that he'll go back to her," she bit her lower lip. "There are many days I know I would be better off without him. I would divorce him, but I still love him and so does Trevor." She sniffled and started to cry again.

Afraid he would make things worse for Jessica no matter what he said, and wanting to identify a friend she could be with, he asked, "Do you have any family around here? Any women friends you could talk to?"

"I don't have any close girlfriends and I'm an only child. My parents died in a car crash shortly before I married James." She brushed her eyes with her hands, wiping away tears.

"I'm sorry," he said. "You said James was your first husband's cousin, right? Where is that branch of the family located?"

It was always to family that people ran when times were the toughest. There was an invisible cord that stretched between individuals and their loved ones. He knew that cord. For him, it stretched north to encircle the Native American reservation where he spent his childhood. More recently, that cord also encircled the people he'd learned to care for in Rosedale, enfolded his beautiful wife and now he could feel it pulling Nightshade inside its circle.

He forced himself to attend to what Jessica was saying.

"Yes, the family is from southern Illinois. They have a farm there."

"Do you have their address by chance?" *This was why he had come.*

"I'll get it for you. But can't you stay and talk to me a little longer, Detective Nichols? Please?" She raised imploring eyes to him.

"I'm sorry, Jessica, but I have to go."

Her face crumpled and he could hear her sobs as she walked down the hall. As soon as she returned with the address, he thanked her and left.

Walking out to his truck, carrying the small piece of paper with the address for the Browning farm in his hands, he exhaled in relief. Despite the risks he was heading into, this was old, familiar territory. Finding a person who was in fear for their lives and keeping them safe—that was what he was good at, not comforting broken-hearted women. He sent a quick text to Lucy saying he was going to be away for a few days. Knowing how much she worried about him, he didn't say he was going after James Browning, or that he was determined to bring him back dead or alive.

It had taken the bearded man in the black van several days to drive to Tennessee from Washington and he feared Browning could have escaped in that time. His only lead was the address of his home that he'd obtained from the clerk after the trial. Once he got to Rosedale and found the house, he'd parked nearby, watching the attractive woman and her little boy out in the yard and following them as they did errands, but he hadn't seen hide nor hair of Browning.

Then he caught a break. A big man who carried himself like a cop appeared, knocked and went inside the house. Slipping his car into gear and cruising by the driveway he saw a bumper sticker on the man's truck that read 'To Protect, Serve, and Defend—The Rosedale Sheriff.' He'd been right. The guy was a cop and the only reason he would be visiting Mrs. Browning was to locate her husband. Watching the man leave the house a little later, he noticed he had a slip of white paper in his hand. He'd looked at it several times before climbing into his truck.

In his entire career, the bearded man had never left a witness alive. James Browning wouldn't be the exception. Waiting until the cop drove around the corner, he shifted his van into gear.

# TWENTY-EIGHT

MARK PULLED INTO THE CIRCLE DRIVEWAY in front of PD's cabin as the sun slipped down beyond the horizon. He parked his car and reached into the backseat for the bottle of wine and the paper sack containing the corn-on-the-cob he'd bought at a local farm stand. Stepping out of the car, he inhaled the scents of the beautiful forest, smiling to himself, knowing he was a lucky man. The screen door squeaked as he walked into the kitchen. Billy Jo raised her face from the dish she was cooking and smiled at him. She must have just showered as her hair was damp and she wore a silky kimono-type robe in peacock blues and greens. The robe was tied with a sash.

He set the grocery sack down on the counter and moved toward her. When she turned away from the stove to greet him, he slowly and deliberately untied the sash at her waist. Her silky robe fell open revealing her beautiful slim body. He clicked the burner on the stove off and drew her closer. She kissed him and slid her hands up under his T-shirt. He buried his hands in her hair that smelled like lemons. He found himself whispering her name, stroking the little beads of her vertebrae, running his hands along the curve of her hips.

Taking her by the hand, he led her to the bedroom. Opening the door, he felt a brief moment of uncertainty, wondering if she would stop him, but she laid down and raised her arms to him smiling. He joined her in the white embrace of the bed.

AN HOUR LATER, THEY WERE STANDING in the kitchen together. She was stirring gnocchi and cherry tomatoes in olive oil in a frying pan. Little bottles of red pepper flakes and cloves of garlic were on the cutting board. He poured them each a glass of wine and pulled the fresh corn on-the-cob from the paper bag. He stripped off the papery husks as Billy Jo cooked. She was listening to her favorite opera, Mozart's *Magic Flute*. He'd struggled to appreciate the music, knowing how much it meant to her.

"Dinner is just about ready," she told him. "Set the table and light the candles, will you?"

He nodded. In his mind, he still touched the softness of her skin. The scent from her hair was on his hands. *It could all end tonight and I would leave this earth knowing I found the person I am supposed to be with*, he thought. He took the pillar candles she handed him, placed them on the table and lit them. They shone, making the dining table an island of light in the dark forest.

"Shall I open the sliding glass doors?" he asked, and she nodded. He slid the doors open to the evocative sounds and smells of the spring evening, just as the rain began to fall.

"I HAVE A SURPRISE FOR YOU," MARK SAID, when they woke the next morning.

"What's that?" she asked, still drowsy. She lay on her side turned away from him and he looked at her naked back folded in the white sheets and wished he could paint her like that.

"I have gotten permission to work remotely this week. Why don't you try to do the same?"

She rolled over and looked at him thoughtfully. "I can check with Dory. It might not be possible. But, if she will commit to spending time in the office, I might be able to escape the tyranny of the phone."

"I could transfer the office calls to your cell. I am a computer geek, you know," he grinned.

"Maybe tomorrow. I've promised to be in the office by nine this morning, so I have to get going."

"Try to get off early this afternoon. It's going to be a beautiful day and we could spend some time together."

"I'll see what I can do. On a work matter, do you remember me telling you about a phone call James Browning made to the Nashville police post the day he disappeared? Did you ever get a chance to check on that?"

"I did. The call was to the main desk and Browning asked to speak to a detective. He was transferred to Detective Strong. When I talked to

Det. Strong, he remembered James coming into the post. He'd witnessed a murder a long time ago and asked if he could go through some mug shots."

"That makes sense. It was the day Browning left town. He came back after the trial ended in a hung jury, and now he's disappeared again. I've got a bad feeling Wayne has gone off in pursuit of him," she said, sitting up and pulling the sheet across her breasts. A tense look crossed her face as she added, "I worry when he takes off like this. I wish he hadn't gone alone."

"He's a tough guy, try not to worry. I'll make us some coffee," Mark said, as he stood up and reached for his robe. Grinding the coffee beans, he realized that every day they spent together he fell deeper in love with her. When she came out from the shower wearing a white terrycloth robe with her wet hair curling, he handed her a cup of coffee.

"I think we need to take a little trip sometime soon," he said. "It's past time."

"Time for what?" she asked.

"Time you met my mother."

She didn't speak, just opened her eyes very wide, her mouth in a startled "O".

BILLY JO LEFT THE CABIN AN HOUR LATER. The woods seemed to glow with the warmer temperatures as spring moved into summer. The white trillium lit the shadows under the ivory-trunked poplars. Driving past the cottonwood tree where the pileated woodpecker was busy finding insects for its breakfast, she smiled to herself, remembering Mark saying it was time for him to meet his mother.

He'd been a late baby, born when his parents were in their early forties. Mark's father had passed away long ago and there were no siblings. His mother was currently residing in an independent living facility in Ohio. They had spoken on the phone several times and Mark sent her pictures of the two of them, but meeting her in person meant their relationship had moved to another level. He wouldn't have mentioned it unless he was serious about her. Remembering him untying her sash in the kitchen the previous night, and the thrill that ran through her body, she felt a pulse of happiness beat in her throat.

WHEN BILLY JO ARRIVED AT ROSEDALE INVESTIGATIONS, she saw Dory's car parked in the driveway. There was a second vehicle too, one she didn't recognize. Walking inside, she asked, "Whose car is that in the driveway?"

"Mrs. Broadchurch's," Dory said.

"Do you mean Hilary?"

"Nope. It's her mother."

"Did you tell her we had concluded there was no blackmail?"

"I did, and that we'd sent Hilary our final report. She said to consider her a new client. I put her in the conference room."

"Okay. Let me hang up my jacket and I'll go find out what's up."

Opening the door, Billy Jo greeted the woman. The room felt stuffy and she opened one of the windows. A warm breeze ruffled the napkins on the sideboard beside the coffee urn, bringing the scents and sounds of spring into the room.

"What can I do for you this morning, Mrs. Broadchurch?"

"As you suggested, I talked to my son and asked him to bring Miss Anderson to meet me. He did so. She's a lovely girl and I got her talking. She blushed when she told me, but maintains my son is her father because of her blood type. He seems abashed by her insistence and extremely tickled, but maintains she can't be his because of the mumps. Apparently, your Detective urged him to have a test to determine if he was fertile, but he says it's not necessary. Over the years, he's dated quite a few women and none of them ever got pregnant. He's perfectly content to have a relationship with Aimee without taking it further. She is comfortable with that as well, because if she finds out Grant is her biological father, it will create havoc in her family."

"I don't see how we can help you then, other than urging your son to be tested, because we've completed our work on this case. As I believe my colleague mentioned, we've sent Hilary a report and a final bill. There is nothing more to be done," Billy Jo said.

"I'm surprised at you, Miss Bradley. I thought you were a bit smarter than that," she said, slanting her blue eyes at her obliquely. "As you are well aware, even if it turns out my son *can* have children, it doesn't prove that Aimee is his daughter."

"True," Billy Jo said. "What do you have in mind?"

"DNA, is what I have in mind," she said and her eyes sparkled. "I've brought you my son's comb in this plastic bag. Wrote his initials on the outside. I wore clean plastic gloves to pick it up."

"And you're asking me to have his DNA profile created. You know that's only one side of the equation."

"I do, and I've brought you something else as well." She reached into her large purse and scuffled around a bit before coming up with a teacup. It was also inside a clear plastic bag with the initials AA written on the outside. There was a perfectly visible lipstick print on its edge.

"I take it you served Miss Anderson tea," Billy Jo said, squashing her amusement. "This will definitely work, but as you mentioned, both Grant and Aimee are content to let sleeping dogs lie. Why do you want them to know?"

"It's not for them to know, it's for me. I'm getting older and am not in the best of health. Grant promised to leave the royalties from his software to Hilary's sons, but if Aimee Anderson is my granddaughter, I intend for her to inherit my estate," she said with an impish grin.

"Such a will could be challenged by Hilary or Grant, you know. As your children, they have the legal right to take it to court."

"Grant wouldn't do that. He adores that girl. Hilary might, but I've talked to my attorney and he's promised to make my Last Will and Testament watertight. Frankly, I think it would do my daughter a world of good to have to get a job."

"Did you get their permission for the DNA test?"

Mrs. Broadchurch shook her head.

"Hmmm. That's too bad. I may have problems getting it analyzed, but I'll give it a try," Billy Jo said, pursing her lips to hide her amusement at the woman's audacity.

"How long before you'll know?"

"If I can get permission for the analysis, they can do it in less than a week. On another matter, I have a commission for you. My colleague, Dory, whom you met, has a little white dog named True. She named her that because the job of a private investigator is to get to the truth. She was a lot of help to me with a recent problem I had, and I want to give her a thank-you gift."

She realized as she said the words that her regret about PD retiring had seemingly melted away. Whether it was Mark saying it was time for her to meet his mother, the possibility of becoming a partner in the firm, or just putting the needs of others before her own, she'd gotten over her reaction to his decision. It had been a blessing to have the love of three wonderful adults who had held her hands through the last few years. She smiled to herself.

"It will be my pleasure to paint True's portrait," Mrs. Broadchurch said. "All you need to do is send me a good photo. You can attach it to an email, or a text."

Walking past her station as she escorted Mrs. Broadchurch out of the building, Billy Jo set the two plastic baggies down on her desk. When she closed the door behind their client and turned around, Dory, clad in royal purple with strings of gold necklaces, was waiting.

"She wants you to do DNA tests on her son and Miss Anderson, I take it," Dory said.

"Brilliant deduction, Investigator Clarkson," Billy Jo said.

"I'm not merely a sex goddess, you know." They both chuckled.

# TWENTY-NINE

**B**ILLY JO KNEW IT WAS UNLIKELY THE PRIVATE LAB that did DNA tests would analyze the specimens Mrs. Broadchurch brought her without the client's permission. During the 'Blind Split' case, when she got the results that showed Lexie Lovell and Teddy were siblings, she'd provided the lab with professionally obtained swabs collected at the hospital. Now, all she had was a lipstick print on a cup and hair from a comb. She decided to call the lab and come at the question from a different direction by asking if they did paternity testing.

"Good morning, I'm Billy Jo Bradley and I have used your services previously. I need a paternity test done."

"We do paternity testing here," the woman said.

"I don't know if you can do the test from what I have, which is a comb with hair on it and a lip print on the edge of a cup. Can you get DNA from that?"

"We probably can, but every lab has rules. In our facility, either the mother or the father is needed to start the process. If this is for a legal situation, however, it's best to have both come in so that their buccal swabs can be professionally obtained. That's what we require. Often the couple's legal representative is met with before the parents come into the lab."

Billy Jo felt her stomach fall as the woman talked. Mrs. Broadchurch had taken her son's comb and Aimee's teacup without their permission. Doing the DNA test from such materials was quasi-legal at best. While the woman said she had no intention of sharing the results with her son or potential granddaughter, Billy Jo knew that there could be a legal dispute in the future. She'd taken a shine to the amusing woman and didn't want her wishes to be set aside. She left the building and drove to the sheriff's office hoping Detective Rob could help.

MRS. COFFIN WAS SITTING AT HER DESK IN THE FRONT OFFICE of the sheriff's office. The purple heliotrope Billy Jo had given her on her previous visit was still blooming on the counter.

"Good morning, Billy Jo. What can we do for you this morning?"

"I need to see Detective Rob. Is he around?"

She reached to buzz him, just as he walked into the lobby.

Billy Jo greeted him and said she had some DNA samples she needed analyzed but the situation was a bit problematic.

"Let's go to my office," he said, and they walked in together. "Have a seat. Tell me what's going on."

"Remember when I asked you to run a check on Grant Broadchurch to see if he had a record?"

"Sure do. Guy was clean as a whistle."

"That's the man. Anyway, his mother wants his DNA compared to a woman's for a paternity check. She brought me her son's comb and a lipstick print from the woman."

"And I gather you think the results could be a problem."

"Yes, and it gets worse. Mrs. Broadchurch didn't have permission to take either her son's comb or the lip print from the woman's teacup."

Rob frowned. "Can't you use the local DNA lab?"

"They require professionally obtained buccal swabs, so no, I can't use them. As I said, it's the man's mother who wants to prove the relationship. Neither the man, nor the young woman are requesting the information."

"I'll have to check with Sheriff Bradley about this."

"If he says it's okay, Rosedale Investigations will cover the cost. Can you let me know what he decides?"

"Yup. As it happens, our lab folks have had it easy since they finished processing Browning's car. Hasn't been much crime in Rosedale of late. Even the small-time crooks seem to be on vacation. One would almost think we lived in a civilized society," he said, giving her an ironic grin. "I'll call you after I speak with the sheriff."

"No hurry. If he agrees, could you get results in a week?"

"Our people are definitely not overworked at the moment. When I stopped down there yesterday, they were doing the *New York Times* crossword puzzle."

"Thank you so much, Rob. One other thing. I'm afraid Detective Nichols is on the hunt for James Browning. PD is in Knoxville and he's gone on this trek alone. Macho jerk," Billy Jo said, turning a worried face to Rob.

"I'll mention it to the sheriff," Rob said. His mouth tightened as he added, "You need to tell Dory and PD."

WAYNE HAD BEEN DRIVING EAST FOR SEVERAL HOURS, heading to the Illinois address Jessica gave him for the Browning farm. His plan was to find Browning and convince him to come back to Tennessee to face the music. He'd knock on the door of the farmhouse, talk to the owners and ask if they'd seen Browning. They would lie and say they hadn't. Then he would park his car somewhere out of sight, probably take a nap and then return. Once night fell, Browning would start to feel restive. He'd feel safe emerging from the farmhouse after dark and would come outside.

Wanye's GPS showed that the Browning farm was located out in the country between Jonesboro and Carbondale, Illinois. He got off the freeway at Jonesboro for help with directions. The town was a prosperous and attractive village with a connected set of two-story historic brick buildings at its heart. He parked his truck, waved down a man driving a U.S. Post Office vehicle and showed him the map on his phone. "I'm trying to get to this address."

"You have to get back on IL-146 and keep driving for another twenty minutes. Before you get to Carbondale, you come to the small town of Makanda. Take the exit off the freeway and get directions there. It's a region with a lot of small lakes. You'll need somebody local," the postman said.

Merging into traffic on the freeway, he drove deeper into the rolling Illinois farm country. Farms were spread out here, with red barns, black and white Holstein cattle, and tractors disking up the fields for planting. The plowed land behind the tractors shone black and fertile in the sun. It was the breadbasket of America. Wayne felt himself relaxing. He found the landscape pleasing, evocative of his years as a child in Michigan's Upper Peninsula.

He was almost to the Makanda exit when he noticed the black van behind him. He remembered seeing a similar van earlier and wondered if he'd been followed, but told himself not to be paranoid. Nobody knew where he was headed. The population of Makanda was only five hundred and fifty, too small a place for random people to visit. Deciding to stay on the highway and take the next exit, he was relieved when the black van swung off the freeway at Makanda. The driver was local.

At that moment, he got a text. He knew Lucy would have figured out what he was doing and would be furious and frightened. *"Don't you leave me a widow, God damn you, Wayne. I'm not cut out to be a single mom,"* she'd written.

THE BEARDED MAN HAD NOTICED THE COP checking his rear-view mirror. It was obvious that he was looking to see if he was being followed. Not wanting the cop to see his license plate number, he decided to get off the freeway. Checking his GPS, he found an old two-lane road that paralleled the freeway at Makanda. If he got off there and put on some speed, he could get to the next overpass and watch for the truck. He got there just in time to see the cop drive beneath the crossing and pull into a rest area. He smiled, noticing that the only vehicle in the lot was the man's truck.

When he glanced over at the passenger seat at the tracking device, he congratulated himself on how smart he was. The dumb cop wouldn't notice a thing. Waiting until the cop went into the building, he rapidly drove to the rest area parking lot, got out of his van, knelt down to attach the tracking device to the underside of the truck and drove off. Looking in his rear-view mirror, he didn't see the cop; he was still inside the building.

Knowing how the police worked, he assumed the man would want to check out the address on the white piece of paper during daylight hours. He'd probably wait until nightfall before taking Browning into custody. That would be the perfect moment for him to strike. The bearded man thought of the high-powered deer rifle in the back of the van with a sense of satisfaction. It was the perfect weapon. It would be a perfect crime.

IT WAS LATE AFTERNOON WHEN WAYNE DROVE UP the driveway of the Browning's farm. There were two houses on the property. One was older, probably the residence of the original couple. The second house, often called a tenant house, would have been let to seasonal help but might also be the home of a married son or daughter of the family. He parked his truck and got out. A shirtless young guy in overalls was sitting on the porch of the tenant house drinking a beer.

He walked up to the somewhat ramshackle place and said, "Hello, I wonder if I've come to the right place. I'm looking for James Browning."

"Haven't seen him."

"Seems like you know who I'm talking about though," Wayne said calmly. He pulled out his private investigator identification and showed it to the guy. "I'm a private detective who's been hired to track him down."

The young farmer had a shock of yellow-colored hair. He stood up with a resolute expression on his narrow face and took a step toward Wayne. At that moment, an attractive woman came out on the porch carrying a baby. The baby had his father's light hair, the color of wheat chaff.

"Hello, who are you?" she asked in a pleasant voice. Wayne felt relieved. The man had been about to boot him off the property. Turning to her husband, she asked, "Sam, have you offered this man a beer? Or would you rather have lemonade, sir? Just made some."

"Thank you. Lemonade sounds perfect for this hot afternoon." He wanted to prolong the visit and if she went back into the house for the beverage, it would give him a bit more time. "Could I have a seat?" he asked.

"Offer the man a seat, Sam," his wife said briskly before going back inside.

Not having been offered a seat, Wayne nonetheless sat down on a kitchen table chair that had been brought out on the porch. "That must be your little one with your wife. Cute kid. Looks just like you," he said. He knew young fathers were proud and such comments often made them more receptive. It didn't work with Sam Browning.

"Told you already, I don't know a James Browning," Sam said. He was still standing.

"Actually, what you said was that you hadn't seen him," Wayne said and looked hard at the man. He'd been caught out and flushed. At that moment, his wife came outside with the baby on her hip. She was carrying a glass of lemonade and held it out to Wayne. Handing the baby to her husband, she said her name was Jenny.

"Thank you, Jenny, this looks delicious. I'm looking for a guy named James Browning. I believe he's your husband's cousin. Have you seen him around here?"

A sudden shadow crossed the woman's face. She glanced at her husband who turned a fierce narrow-eyed glare on her. "Sorry. We don't know that person. When you've finished your lemonade, you best be on your way."

It was exactly the lie he'd expected. He gulped down the beverage, thanked them both and walked toward his pick-up. He looked back once, seeing them standing side-by-side on the porch. Sam was holding the baby, who was kicking his chubby legs. He checked the windows on the second floor, to see if anyone touched a curtain, but nothing moved. So far, everything was going to plan. All he had to do now was wait.

# THIRTY

Mrs. Coffin called Billy Jo that afternoon to tell her the sheriff had denied her request to analyze Mrs. Broadchurch's DNA samples. It was what Billy Jo had expected, but still frustrating. She decided to leave the office for a bit.

"I'm going to do some errands. Back in an hour," she told Dory.

As soon as Billy Jo pulled out of the driveway, Dory dialed their new CI, Lorelei Vail.

"Good morning, are you ready to go?"

"You bet," Lorelai said.

"We have to leave right now because Billy Jo's only going to be gone an hour. We're meeting our realtor, Maureen, at the new coffee shop in Rosedale. Java Zone, it's called. I'll get started with her if you can grab us a couple of coffees."

"No problem," Lorelei told her. She was already up, showered and dressed, wearing white Capri pants and a pink T-shirt sprinkled with images of strawberries and earrings that looked like strawberry slices. Picking up her keys, she walked outside, locked her townhouse door and headed to the carport. It was exciting that their realtor, Maureen, would be there to meet them. The woman was totally thrilled to be handling the sale of the property on Rosedale's main street. The building had been empty for three years and its sale would represent a nice commission for her.

She was lucky to snatch an angled parking spot in front of Java Zone from a patron who was just leaving. Getting out of the car, she spotted Maureen, who was sitting at a table under an umbrella to ward off the sun. Greeting the woman as she passed, she told her she was getting coffee for herself and Dory. "What can I get you?" she asked.

"I'm all set," Maureen said. "Java Zone certainly is boosting business in downtown. It's going to help you once you get started. I've brought the contract."

"Lots to do before opening day," Lorelei said with a smile. Working with Dory on their special project was a dream come true.

THE LINE MOVED QUICKLY AS THE BARISTAS FILLED CUPS. The scent from the coffee, the hissing from the machines and the cheerful chatting customers were a good sign for their future. Lorelai was next in line to be served when she glanced out the front window of the coffee shop and caught sight of Dory, who had joined Maureen at table. The realtor was flipping through the pages of the sales contract. Then her heart almost stopped. Billy Jo was getting out of her car across the street. Gesturing madly, Lorelai tried to get Dory's attention. The other customers looked at her oddly. She felt like she was watching an oncoming train heading right toward them.

Billy Jo got out of her car, saw Dory and walked toward her and Maureen. Lorelei grabbed their coffees, exited the line (while bumping into some irritated customers) and dashed out the door. She had to distract the girl from spotting the real estate contract.

"Morning, Billy Jo. Nice morning, isn't it," Lorelei said, quickly positioning herself to block the girl's view of the table. "Dory and I are interviewing Mrs. Walters this morning. She's a potential new client for Rosedale Investigations." Knowing that conducting first interviews with clients was Billy Jo's responsibility, she thought saying they were talking with a new client would distract the young woman. It worked.

"Since when did you two interview new clients?" Billy Jo asked, putting her hands on her hips and looking piqued.

"Since Lorelei has been using her contacts to build our business," Dory said. She smiled somewhat guiltily, sliding her purse over the contract.

"It's nice to meet you, Billy Jo. I'm Maureen," the realtor said, standing up and holding out her hand.

Billy Jo shook hands with the woman and said, "I'm just going to get some coffee. I'll come back and join you."

Once she was inside the coffee shop, Dory said, "Whew! That was close. Nice work, Lorelei. Quick thinking, Maureen. We are keeping our plans quiet for the moment. It's going to be a surprise for the whole team on the Fourth of July weekend."

LEAVING THE FARM WITH THE LATE AFTERNOON SUN beating down on
his truck, Wayne headed to the interstate and drove back to the roadside
rest stop he'd stopped at earlier. It would be a good place to park until
it got dark. He turned off the ignition and got out. There was a fountain on the paved cement court and he bent to drink the cool bubbling
water. Then he checked all the cars parked in the lot. No black vans. He'd
been right that the guy who got off the freeway at Makanda was a local.
Settling himself back in the truck, he felt the reassuring pressure of his
gun in his shoulder holster.

Then he envisioned the faces of the people who would be worried
about him. He needed to answer Lucy's text. Getting back in his truck,
he picked up his phone. *"I'm fine,"* he wrote. *"Please tell everyone I'm
checking on something for the Browning case. Should be home tomorrow."*
Sometimes little white lies were the way to go.

Wayne hadn't gotten much sleep in the last few nights and the slanting
afternoon light made him feel warm and relaxed. When he woke several
hours later, startled by a vehicle pulling in beside him, it was completely
dark. He felt a quick pulse of anxiety, before noticing it was a pick-up, not
a van. He started his truck and pulled out of the rest stop. Driving back
toward the Browning farm, he kept checking behind him, but the dark
road was completely empty. He parked his truck off the roadside before
reaching the couple's driveway.

ON FOOT NOW, WITH THE SOUNDS OF THE WARM COUNTRY NIGHT all
around him and the moon rising, Wayne walked toward the farmhouse.
A white barn owl rose from his tree into the dark. He flew off so silently
he might have been made of wood ash. He wondered whether Browning
might be staying in the larger house, but no lights were on and it looked
deserted. He took a position standing between some trees on the edge
of their property. He heard the baby cry for a little bit, the sounds of the
young mother singing to him and then nothing.

Half an hour later, Sam Browning came out to the porch. He pulled a
beer from the cooler and sat down. There was something in his lap. When
the moon came out from under the clouds, Wayne could see the long
circular tube pointing upward. Sam Browning was holding a rifle. That
rifle could be a problem. A lot of farmers who used rifles to kill pheasants
and rabbits for food, and to rid the property of woodchucks and raccoons,
were excellent shots. Wayne pulled his own gun from its holster.

When clouds covered the moon, Wayne darted to his new hide-out. Stepping into the cluster of shrubs to the left of the driveway, he inhaled the delicate scent of wild honeysuckle. A car went past on the road. He turned to take a look, but it was too dark to see anything . . . except that it was a van. He felt the hair prickle on the back of his neck. He'd been a cop for too long to ignore such promptings.

He knew he hadn't been followed from the roadside park to the farm, but then he got a sick feeling. While he was in the restroom, the person who was hunting James Browning could have attached a tracking device to his vehicle. A frantic need to get back to the truck and destroy it raced through his mind, but it was already too late. In that moment of indecision, wondering whether he could safely leave his position, James Browning came out onto the porch and spoke to his cousin, Sam. He caught the words, "stretch my legs." It was the moment he'd been waiting for.

His luck held. James Browning started walking down the driveway. Unless his quarry veered off into the field, he would walk right past the shrub where Wayne was hiding. He waited, forcing himself not to jump the gun. The man had to be almost parallel to his position before Wayne spoke. James was closer, nearly there now.

In a harsh whisper, Wayne said, "Browning, stop right there. I'm here to take you back to Tennessee. I've gotten the sheriff in Rosedale to offer you protection. It's not safe for you here."

Browning hesitated, uncertainty in his every tensed muscle. "Who the hell are you?" he cried out loudly, and all hell broke loose.

A sudden ricochet of bullets shattered the night all around them. In the house, the woman screamed and the baby wailed. Sam stood up and got off two shots in the direction of the shooter. Then the world went silent, and he waited, hearing running footsteps in the distance. Pinned down with his heart pounding, Wayne knew he couldn't get to James, whose body lay twisting in the driveway, or go after the shooter without risking his own life. In the past he would have taken the chance, but he was a married man now and had made a promise to Lucy.

He heard the sound of a vehicle starting up, a wheel yanked too hard, and knew the shooter was getting away. Adrenaline flooded his bloodstream, forcing him into action. He yelled, "Hold your fire, Sam. I'm going after the shooter."

"Okay," he heard Sam say in a choked tone of voice.

Running as fast as he could, Wayne reached the road. But all he could see were the taillights of the van, looking like evil little red eyes in the distance. With a heavy heart, he headed back to the unmoving body lying in the dusty driveway. Sam was kneeling beside his cousin. Patches of inky black blood oozed slowly from Browning's chest, soaking into the dusty earth.

"I'm calling an ambulance," Wayne said, keeping one finger on James's jugular pulse and reaching for his phone, but even as he dialed 911, he knew he was too late. The pulse throbbed once, twice and then stopped dead. Both men knelt beside the body in silence, counting the minutes as they waited in darkness for the sound of the ambulance siren.

# THIRTY-ONE

IT WAS FIVE O'CLOCK THE NEXT MORNING before Wayne finished dealing with the forces of law and order and walked out of Carbondale's State Police Department. The round bowl of the sun was just above the horizon and the clouds were glorious, soft white billows. Knowing it was far too early and that she'd be furious, he dialed Dory's cell phone.

"What the hell, Wayne," she said in a sleep-fogged voice.

"Sorry to call so early. Browning was shot and killed last night. The shooter was probably the guy who killed the cop ten years ago. Anyway, once I reported the murder, I spent hours with officers from these little one-cop towns trying to convince them to call in the state boys. They finally came, took my statement, and one from Sam Browning, who owns the farm where James was hiding. He got off a shot or two at the killer. We hope he wounded the guy, but I heard running footsteps, so he wasn't hurt badly, if at all. They found the 30-06 shell casings from the semi-automatic, but they came from a high-powered deer rifle, so I doubt they will be much help."

"Stop, stop, stop. Where the hell are you? And are you okay?" Dory asked.

"Illinois. I'm okay. Now, if I might continue," he paused before saying, "everyone has agreed that Browning's body requires a formal identification. He's going to be transported to the morgue at Rosedale General today. One more thing. The shooter put a tracking device on my truck. That's how he found Browning." Wayne paused, took a breath and added, "You need to get a sweep done for our offices at Rosedale Investigations. Probably unnecessary, but I don't want to leave anything to chance."

"Okay, I will. Other than this update, which I appreciate, even though you did *disrupt* my beauty sleep, why are you calling? You wouldn't have called me unless you wanted something," she said in a deeply suspicious tone of voice.

"You're right. I need you and Billy Jo to tell Jessica and Annabelle that James is dead."

"You know I hate the death knock."

"I know, but since Browning changed his identity when he moved to Tennessee, there has to be a formal identification. In Billy Jo's original background work, she found out that Browning assumed the name of a dead child. I still haven't learned his original name, or how he was related to the Browning family."

"Fine," she said grudgingly, "I'll do it. But you will owe me."

"One other thing. Please call Lucy for me. I need you to defuse the thermo-nuclear blast that is coming my way. You can tell her I'll be back this afternoon, if you think that will help."

"Stop being such a freaking coward. Call your wife yourself. And I recommend flowers, candy, jewelry and a groveling apology," Dory said and broke the connection.

Climbing into his pick-up, Wayne decided he'd hold off on calling Lucy. Before he left the state of Illinois, he still had two mysteries to solve. He needed to know James Browning's original name and how he was connected to the long-dead child.

It was only 5:30 a.m. but by the time he arrived at the Browning's farm, he knew Sam and Jenny would be up. Most parents of small children were woken early with imperious demands for food from their offspring.

DORY ARRIVED AT THE OFFICE OF ROSEDALE INVESTIGATIONS that morning by eight o'clock. Noting that Billy Jo was not in evidence, she walked upstairs and knocked on her apartment door.

"Get up, Kiddo. We have a job to do for Wayne this morning."

"Hang on, just getting dressed. Down in a minute," Billy Jo called. Dory went back downstairs. She'd stopped by the grocery store on her way in and bought Starbucks coffee, strawberries and pastries. Her young associate would need caffeine to take on their new task. Washing the berries and pulling off their little green tops, Dory wondered if Annabelle had already left Rosedale to return to her hometown. She sent her a text saying she needed to see her ASAP. There was no answer. She knew Annabelle would be resigned to the news of James' death, but that Jessica would be devastated. Bracing herself, she dialed Jessica's phone number.

"Hello?" Her voice sounded rushed.

"Good morning. It's Dory from Rosedale Investigations. We have some information for you about James. You're probably about to take your son to school. Could we stop by in a bit?" She could hear the woman talking to her son, telling him to grab his school folder and lunch.

"Can we make it 9:00?"

"Of course. We will see you then," Dory said. She clicked off the call as Billy Jo appeared in the kitchen wearing a T-shirt in a watermelon-slice print, cut-off jeans and flip flops. Hardly the appropriate outfit for a delivering such dire news.

"What's up?" she asked.

"Browning was shot and killed last night."

"Oh dear," Billy Jo's expression turned sad.

"Wayne thinks the shooter was probably the guy who shot the cop ten years ago. He's on his way back here, but we have to tell both Browning's wives this morning."

"I hate this part of the job."

"Me too. They need to know because later today there will be a formal identification of the body at the Rosedale General Morgue and they need to be prepared. You aren't dressed appropriately to deliver this kind of news."

"Couldn't this wait until Wayne gets here?" Billy Jo asked in a strained tone of voice.

"He won't be here until it's time for the body identification. It's on us. Go find something navy or black and real shoes. I'm going to call Sheriff Bradley to see if he will go with us."

Billy Jo nodded, grabbed a pastry and headed back upstairs.

When Dory reached the sheriff, he said he was swamped with the paperwork related to the murder of James Browning and couldn't get away. He'd be at the Rosedale Morgue for the formal identification of the body.

BY THE TIME WAYNE PULLED INTO THE BROWNINGS' dusty driveway, he knew both members of the couple were awake. He could hear the baby crying and Jenny's voice soothing him. Sam was standing outside on the porch. He was holding his rifle across folded arms and his tense body radiated an uncompromising ferocity. Recognizing the truck, he set the 12-gauge rifle down, but didn't look at all welcoming.

"Hello," Wayne said as he walked up to the porch. "I'm sure you're none too happy to see me, but I have some questions."

"When the cops wanted me to come into the station last night, I refused. I wasn't about to leave Jenny and Sam, Jr. here alone. I only went in after an officer agreed to stay here to protect them." Witnessing the shooting had left Sam wrung out and exhausted. Wayne felt for him.

"I can assure you and your wife that the shooter is long gone by now, he's likely left the state or even the country. Do you mind me asking you a couple of questions?"

"I have questions of my own," Sam said, his jaw was clenched.

"Go ahead."

"When James showed up here, he said he needed a place to hide out. He told me about the murder he'd witnessed and that the perpetrator was released after his trial ended in a hung jury. If anyone came for him, he told me to say he wasn't here. I told Jenny he was visiting for a few days. Do you think it was the murderer from ten years ago that killed him?" His eyes bored into Wayne's.

"I'm assuming so."

"You say the shooter is gone, but what if he thinks James told me something that could identify him?"

"In the language of the law, anything James told you is considered hearsay. It isn't admissible in court because it can't be proved. Your family is safe."

Sam made a frustrated sound.

"May I ask, was James your cousin?"

"He was."

"His last name wasn't originally Browning though, was it?"

"No. He's a cousin on my mother's side. Her maiden name was Browning but she married Ray Sutton. They were the original owners of the farm and only had one son. The man you call James Browning was originally named James Sutton."

*That made sense. When James decided to change his name to make it harder for the killer to find him, he'd picked Browning. It was a family name.*

"The computer person at our office discovered that name when she was looking into James' background. Was there an infant in the family named James Browning who died a half century ago?"

"Yes, my great grandparents' first son died in infancy. That was his name. He's buried on the farm."

Wayne nodded. "I assume the original folks are all gone now, and you inherited the property."

"We all lived on the farm together once," Sam said, and Wayne heard the raw nostalgic ache in his voice. "My Aunt Sue Ellen and Uncle Richard lived in the big house. It's vacant now. My parents, my brother Chris and I, always lived in the tenant house."

Wayne recalled hearing the name Chris. It took a moment, but then it clicked.

Sam's brother, Chris, had been Jessica Browning's first husband.

Sam continued saying, "All three of us boys grew up together. Chris later married Jessica. He was killed in a traffic accident when they had been married just a year. I'm the only one of the three of us alive now," he said. His face darkened with pain.

Wayne's mind connected the dots, seeing the three little boys in dungarees living and playing on the farm. James must have moved out West, got together with Annabelle and witnessed the crime that dogged his steps up to the final moment. Like a faultlessly guided laser missile racing down a long trajectory to its final target, the murderer had returned. Browning must have been afraid every day of those ten years thinking that his time had come. Perhaps, knowing he could die at any time, partly explained how he justified marrying two women.

"I'm very sorry you and your family had to go through what happened last night and for the loss of your brother and your cousin. My plan was to talk to James, get him off your property and to a safe place before anything like this happened," Wayne said.

Remorse clogged his voice. A shard of cold ice seemed lodged in his chest—like a jagged piece of bone it cut into his heart with every breath he took.

"How the hell did the bastard find us?" Sam asked. His eyes pierced Wayne's.

Wayne took a deep breath. This was the worst part of what he had to say. "The shooter must have put a tracking device on my truck when I pulled over at a rest stop. I didn't catch on quickly enough and," he paused, "I led him straight here." Shame made him grit his teeth. It dominated his voice.

It was always fear of botching a dangerous situation that drove him. And now the worst had happened. He'd endangered a family, a woman and a child. His conscience pierced his soul and the icy pain in his chest grew heavier.

"Jenny is talking about leaving me," Sam said. He cast Wayne a hungry desperate look.

"You can tell your wife she's safe now, I give you my word. And I will do everything in my power to get protection for you and your family until the perpetrator is caught," Wayne said. But in his mind he wondered whether it was even possible to ensure the family's protection in this quiet rural area of single-officer towns.

"Jenny's going back to her parents' house and taking little Sam with her. I don't think my wife will ever feel safe here again." His voice trailed off as he looked across their yard toward his fields. He hadn't ploughed yet and the remnants of bent and broken corn stalks, pale and desolate, spoke of the previous year's harvest. "I want you off my property."

"I'm going," Wayne said. He walked down the porch steps and headed toward his truck. When he opened the driver's door, he turned around, wanting to offer the man some vestige of hope. "Maybe you and Jenny could take a break, a short vacation, just until the killer is in custody."

"Ha!" Sam snorted. "I can tell you're not a farmer. It's time to plant corn. There are no breaks in my life," he said, as he picked up his rifle. He walked inside and the screen door slammed shut behind him. Wayne could hear Jenny's frightened voice as they argued. Looking through the windows, he saw Sam reach for her. She turned away. The baby was crying.

WHILE THE FORCES OF LAW AND ORDER IN ILLINOIS were processing evidence and fighting over jurisdiction the night before, he'd secured an evidence envelope and plastic gloves from the station. Then he'd gone out to his truck, and accompanied by the lead detective for the case, ducked down underneath the chassis and spotted the tracking device. Putting on gloves, he detached the device and dropped it into the envelope. It was a long shot, but if the killer was bare-handed when he stuck the device to his truck, there would be fingerprints. The murderer who devastated the Browning family had to be nailed or the ice-cold talons of shame that bent around his heart would never let him go. Identifying the shooter and bringing him to justice was his only hope for forgiving himself.

Heading back to Rosedale, Wayne passed the rest stop where he assumed the shooter had attached the tracking device to his pick-up. A mile further down the highway, an idea struck him. Taking the next exit off the freeway, he turned around and headed back. Pulling into a parking spot, he looked up at the eaves of the building and felt a rush of self-satisfaction. Due to the number of crimes being committed at rest areas, the state of Illinois had recently installed closed circuit cameras at their stations. Because he knew the exact time and date he'd parked there, the Illinois police could request and receive that portion of the tape. They would be able to see the full license plate number of the van and likely the shooter's face as well. Together with any partial fingerprints from the tracking device, they would have him. He pulled his phone from his pocket and dialed the Carbondale police post.

# THIRTY-TWO

D ORY DECIDED SHE AND BILLY JO SHOULD SPLIT UP to tell Browning's wives about his death. Dory would inform Annabelle—if she could find her. She assigned Billy Jo to tell Jessica.

"That's not fair, Dory. You are pulling rank on me. All you have to do is break the *news* to Annabelle. I have to break Jessica's *heart*," Billy Jo said.

"Sorry, Kiddo," Dory said. "I did call Jessica and said you would be coming by."

They set out in their separate cars, dreading what lay ahead of them.

On her way to Mount Blanc, Dory called Lorelei, who picked up immediately. "Could you help me with something this morning?"

"No problem. What's up?" Lorelai was in an upbeat mood, enjoying the assignments from Rosedale Investigations and looking forward to working with Dory on their new venture.

"I'm assuming I don't have to remind you that you can't share anything about our cases."

"Absolutely."

"James Browning was murdered last night. His body is being transported to the morgue at Rosedale General and I have the unenviable task of telling his common-law wife, Annabelle, that he's dead. She told us a few days ago that she'd decided to leave the area. I hope she hasn't left already. Have you seen her?"

"Sorry, my friend. Annabelle Browning left last night around ten o'clock, pulling a U-Haul trailer."

"Dammit. We need her to identify his body. She's going to have to turn around and come back. I left her a message earlier. I'll be at your house in about fifteen minutes. See you then," Dory said.

Clicking off the call, Lorelei walked upstairs and knocked on her guest room door. "Samantha, get up, Honey. Come down and have something to eat. Dory from Rosedale Investigations is coming over."

Walking across the landing to her bedroom, Lorelai opened her closet doors. If it turned out that Annabelle couldn't return in time, and Samantha had to be the one to identify her father's body, she wanted to be properly dressed to go with her. *Poor kid,* she thought as she replaced her lemon-yellow blouse with a black one.

BILLY JO WAS FUMING. DORY HAD PUT HER IN A TERRIBLE POSITION by assigning her to inform Jessica. Jessica was the one who had actually loved the man. Annabelle never acted like she gave a damn. Delaying as much as reasonably possible, she stopped to get an espresso. The bitter taste of the dark liquid would be in accord with what she had to do. A fine misty rain had begun, sprinkling the pink geraniums planted outside the grocery story that housed a coffee dispensary.

When she reached the Brownings' neighborhood, she spotted Jessica and her little boy walking down the sidewalk away from their house. Jessica was carrying a navy umbrella. Trevor was pulling a red wagon filled with white boxes. Several school children carrying those same white boxes (filled with candy bars) had stopped by Rosedale Investigations asking for donations. It was a fundraiser for the local school.

Billy Jo parked her car, swallowed the last dregs of her espresso and grabbed her umbrella. She felt like an assassin sent to destroy the woman's world. Mentally rehearsing what she would say, she jogged to catch up with them. "Mrs. Browning," she called and the woman turned back to see who had called her name.

"Hello, Billy Jo. Are you here to help us with the candy sale this morning?"

"I'm so sorry, Jessica, but your husband...I'm terribly sorry to have to tell you last night James met his death . . ."

She hadn't needed to say another word. All the color leached from the woman's face and she turned away. She thrust her fist into her mouth to silence her sobs, her thin shoulders heaving.

Quickly turning to the child, Billy Jo said, "Trevor, honey, I'm going to go with you to this next house. Your mom needs a little time to herself."

"Okay," he said, smiling up at her. He hadn't noticed his mother's anguish.

The two of them walked down the sidewalk in the misty rain, pulling the wagon behind them. Bending down to ruffle the little guy's short hair, she felt its softness, like the fluff of dandelions. Trevor was only six, she remembered, the same age Samantha was on the day she witnessed a murder that destroyed her innocence. Looked back at Jessica, she saw her bent over beneath her navy umbrella, trying to muffle her cries.

The killing that had destroyed Samantha's childhood had refused to leave either of the families of James Browning in peace. Like an evil apparition, it had roared across a thousand miles and a decade of years, to shatter the life of a second child. She experienced a brief moment of fierce satisfaction that Browning was dead and could no longer hurt either family.

WHEN LORELEI USHERED DORY INTO HER CONDO, Samantha was sitting at the bar munching on buttered toast and wearing pink shorty pajamas.

"What the heck?" Dory asked, turning toward Lorelei with a perplexed expression.

"Samantha is staying with me for the time being," she said, giving Dory a quick penetrating glance telling her not to ask questions. "Samantha, say hello to Miss Dory."

"Morning, Dory," the teenager said sleepily.

"Well, isn't this nice," Dory said, gathering her thoughts. "Is that coffee brewing?"

"Certainly is. Shall I pour you a cup?" Lorelei asked.

"Thank you. I'll sit here at the counter with Sleepyhead."

The women chatted for a while about the weather. They speculated on how long the rain would last, spoke of the fundraiser for the school and the meeting they had with the owner of the building they were purchasing. Samantha wasn't listening. Teens normally considered anyone over thirty to be adult white noise, not worthy of their attention.

"I need to tell her now," Dory said softly, catching Lorelei's eyes.

Taking a deep breath, Lorelei said, "Samantha dear, Dory has some sad news for you this morning."

"What?" Samantha asked. She was pouring milk into her cereal.

"Set that bottle of milk down, will you? Don't want you to drop it. I'm so sorry, honey. I do have awful news. Your father died yesterday."

"No, no. That's not right. He's just had to leave us for a little while to . . ." Her voice trailed off, but looking at them both, tears began running silently down her face.

At five o'clock that afternoon, Sheriff Bradley and Detective Wayne Nichols stood in the hall outside the door to the Rosedale General Morgue. The hospital's pathologist, Dr. Katherine Lange, wearing a long white lab coat with her glasses on a cord around her neck, had been told about the situation and was expecting two family members to provide an identification of the body. She emerged from the morgue where she had been preparing the body and joined the group.

"The bullets only hit his torso, so his face looks okay. Is the wife coming in first?" she asked.

"That's right," Sheriff Bradley said. "Her name is Jessica."

"Dory told me there's a second wife who has left the state. I understand her sixteen-year-old daughter, Samantha, is coming later to confirm the identification," Dr. Lange said.

"Correct," Bradley said.

They waited, glancing at their watches from time to time. Fifteen minutes later, Billy Jo came down the hall, leading a tear-stained woman by the hand.

"Jessica Browning?" Dr. Lange asked. When she nodded, the pathologist said, "I need to see some identification."

With a shaky hand, Jessica pulled out her wallet and gave it to Billy Jo, who handed the woman's driver's license to Dr. Lange. She looked at it briefly and gave it back.

"Please come in now. These gentlemen need to accompany us for legal purposes."

As they walked into the facility, Billy Jo shot Wayne a look that begged him to save her from having to enter the morgue, but Jessica never let go of her hand and she was pulled inside.

The body, totally covered with a white sheet, lay face-up on the dissecting table. The unique scent of death and embalming chemicals permeated the air. Billy Jo experienced an instinctive visceral recoil and had to force herself not to bolt from the room. The domain of the dead was not a place anyone, except perhaps those accustomed to the work of the facility, could remain for long.

"I'm going to pull the sheet back now, Mrs. Browning," Dr. Lange said, and with a gentle practiced motion, drew it carefully down to reveal the man's face.

Jessica swallowed and moved closer to Billy Jo.

"Can you identify this person as James Browning, your husband?"

Jessica touched her lips and nodded.

"I'm sorry, Mrs. Browning. You need to identify the body aloud. These gentlemen need the information."

"It's my husband, James Browning," Jessica said. She was clutching Billy Jo's fingers so tightly, they had turned white.

"Thank you, Mrs. Browning. I'm sorry you had to go through that," Sheriff Bradley said. "If you want to spend a bit more time with him, we can leave you alone for a while."

Jessica nodded and everyone started to depart. "Please stay," she said pitifully to Billy Jo.

IT WAS FIFTEEN MINUTES AFTER FIVE when Jessica at last agreed to leave. Billy Jo had been surreptitiously checking the time on her cell phone, hoping desperately to get the woman out of the hospital before Samantha arrived. It was going to be tight.

"I assume you'll be having a funeral and will want to know when the body will be released," Sheriff Bradley said when they emerged.

Jessica nodded. She was so pale, Billy Jo was afraid she was going to pass out.

"There's some paperwork to complete, but your husband's body can be moved to the Rosedale Funeral Home in a day or two. You can contact them about a funeral."

"Thank you," Jessica whispered.

She and Billy Jo were walking down the hall toward the elevators, when they saw Dory, Lorelei and Samantha coming toward them. To Billy Jo's surprise, Jessica stopped dead in her tracks.

Taking a deep breath, she said, "You must be Samantha." Her voice quavered, but she straightened her shoulders and added, "I'm Jessica Browning. Your father told me about you and showed me your picture. There will be a funeral for him and I hope you will come." It was obvious it had taken every bit of her inner resources to greet the girl.

The shocked Samantha shot a quick glance at Lorelei, but then rallied. Turning to Jessica, she raised her chin and said, "My mother has left the area, but I am staying here for the school year. I will attend my father's funeral."

"I have a little boy named Trevor," Jessica's said and her voice broke.

Samantha managed not to cry as she said, "I look forward to meeting him."

# THIRTY-THREE

AFTER LEAVING THE MORGUE, WAYNE STOPPED at the grocery store, picked up three Sirloin steaks, some potato salad and a nice bottle of wine. He also added a package of Lucy's favorite candies, cashew nuts dipped in dark chocolate. Then he visited the floral department, taking his time picking out magenta tulips, pale yellow daffodils and blue hyacinths. The girl behind the flower counter added a froth of white baby's breath and ferns, wrapped them in lime green tissue paper and tied a little white ribbon around the bouquet. Dory had told him to bring jewelry too, but there wasn't time.

Driving into their driveway, he saw Nightshade playing fetch with Huck in the back yard. *Good*, he thought. It would give him a few minutes alone with his wife. He brought the groceries in from the car and set them on the kitchen counter. Lucy appeared as he was putting away the provisions. He looked carefully at her expression, which gave nothing away.

"How was your day?" he asked, taking two wine glasses from the cupboard and filling them with red wine.

"I'm little more interested in what you have been up to, Wayne. Dory called this morning and said your man of two families was shot and killed. I thought," she said, looking at him with disappointment in her voice, "you were staying out of dangerous situations. You promised me."

"I try. Really I do," he shook his head. "I went after Browning hoping to get him to come back here where we could protect him. I failed." He swallowed and a surge of guilt spread across his features. "He was staying with his cousin, a young family with a baby, and was murdered on their property."

"Then it wasn't your fault," Lucy said. Her voice had softened.

Wayne took a deep breath. "No, you're wrong. It was. When I stopped to use the bathroom at this roadside rest stop, the killer put a tracking device on my truck. I led the murderer right to his quarry. Sam Browning's wife is leaving him and taking the baby with her. He doesn't think she will ever feel safe on their property again. I feel . . ." He swallowed and took a deep breath. "Ashamed."

"Oh, Honey. I'm so, so sorry," Lucy said and put her arms around him.

He pulled back and said, "I saw a black van behind me earlier that day, but didn't think it was anything to worry about because he left the freeway at this tiny town of Makanda. Now I know I was wrong."

"Is there any hope the cops will get the shooter?"

"I pulled the tracker off my truck and gave it to the Illinois state cops. If the man wasn't wearing gloves when he installed it, it's possible they can get fingerprints or some trace DNA. Hopefully he'll be in the system. Plus, there were CCTV cameras on the rest area building where I stopped, and I gave the cops the date and time that I was there. They should be able to pull the tape and see his full license plate number. If the shooter looked at the building, they can run him through facial recognition. Bringing him to justice is the only way I will ever be able to deal with my guilt." He gritted his teeth. He thought of Sam, Jenny and their baby, standing on the rickety porch on the farmhouse, and bit the inside of his cheek to keep back his tears. "I'm wondering if I've lost my edge. Do you think I'm too old for this job, Lucy?"

"Not for a moment," she said and hugged him.

Her kind words brought forth the tears he'd been desperately trying to hold back. Lucy saying he still had it, had helped him. The icy shard of shame didn't hurt quite so much. At that moment, Nightshade and his dog came into the kitchen. Wayne turned away quickly, before the boy could see his face.

"We need to leave pretty soon for Huck's class," Nightshade said.

"Get the leash and treats and load him in the car. I'll be right out," Lucy said.

ONCE IN THE CAR, LUCY DECIDED TO SHARE SOME of what had happened to Wayne with Nightshade.

"Detective Nichols lost a man he was trying to get to a safe house. The shooter put a tracking device on his car and followed him to the farm of a young couple, where the man was killed. Wayne blames himself because he didn't realize he was being tracked."

Nightshade's eyes widened. "So, he was trying to save the guy and couldn't? That's awful. We had a shooting in Homeless City once. Nobody got shot, but it was pretty scary."

"I'm sure it was. I've had gunshot victims come into the ER from time to time. It's a big job patching them up," Lucy said. "I'm so glad you weren't shot, Nightshade. I never would have gotten to know you if you had."

"Me too," he said. "You wouldn't have found me then and I probably would have lost my arm."

"Be kind to Wayne now, please, son. He's having a rough time and needs us both."

"I will," the boy said, impressed with the gravity of Lucy asking him to be sensitive and surprised she felt he could be of any help at all.

ENTERING THE PET STORE WHERE THE DOG OBEDIENCE CLASS was held, Lucy asked Nightshade to introduce her to the trainer.

"She's back this way," he said, leading her through the racks of pet supplies, food and cages to the far corner of the room. They walked into an interior room, hearing a cacophony of barking.

"That's Kim over there talking to the guy with the retriever," he said over the noise.

Lucy walked over and introduced herself. "Hi, Kim. I'm Lucy Nichols and I wanted to ask you something. Nightshade's dog is a rescue, and I'm wondering when he will be ready to be inside during the day. We've been working on his potty training and he's getting better, but so far I'm not letting him loose in the house. He wants the dog to sleep in his room at night. What do you think?"

"I think when Huck finishes the class, two weeks from now, he can be in the house for short periods during the day with supervision. He's still pretty young, probably only about a year old. As far as sleeping with the boy is concerned, that's okay, provided he's taken out for a final pee before bedtime and that the door to the room is kept closed until he can be let out again in the morning."

"Thank you for what you are doing for Huck," Lucy said.

"Thank you for what you are doing for Nightshade," Kim said. "I understand he's something of a rescue himself."

"Indeed he is," Lucy said with a winsome smile.

As soon as they got back to Lorelei's house after the morgue visitation, Samantha dashed upstairs to call her mother in private.

"Hi, Honey," Annabelle's voice was soft when she answered the call.

"Mom, why didn't you come back? I needed you. Did you know that Dad was murdered!"

"I know, Dory called me."

"I had to go to the morgue and identify dad's body all by myself," she wailed. "Lorelei drove me to the hospital, but she didn't go inside where they keep the bodies."

"I'm sorry, I was too far away to have made it. I'm still driving and I'm almost out of power on my phone, so I can't talk very long. Was it pretty awful?"

"It was terrible. I had a hard time looking at him at first, but Detective Nichols said I had to be sure it was him."

"Were you?" Annabelle asked.

"Yes, it was him. He was lying under a white sheet on a table but they made me look at his face." She swallowed.

"Poor guy was headed for this ever since you two saw the murder of that cop ten years ago. It was like that night never left him."

"It never left me either," Samantha said, anger rising in her voice.

"I'm really sorry you had to do that, Sweetheart," Annabelle said. "I'm in the mountains and your voice is cutting out. I'll call back when I have more power."

"Bye, Mom," Samantha said and set her phone down on her bed. Trying to make herself feel a bit better, she went into the bathroom and washed her face. After a few minutes, she walked back downstairs.

Lorelei was at the island sipping a mug of hot chocolate. "Want some cocoa?" she asked. Samantha nodded. Pouring hot chocolate from the pan simmering on the stove into the girl's mug, she said, "How are you doing now?"

"I think it's going to take me a long time to get over this."

"I'm sure it will. Give yourself some time. I was very impressed how you handled meeting Jessica. That was a tough thing to do."

"I could tell she loved my father. She'd been crying," Samantha said.

After a long silence, Lorelai asked, "Did you know Detective Nichols and his wife are fostering a teenage boy?" Samantha shook her head. "He's almost sixteen and will be starting at Rosedale High in the fall. He needs tutoring in math and English because he's been out of school for a while. Your mom told me you're an excellent student. Maybe you could help him."

"Maybe," Samantha said and added, "so much has happened to me lately—with Mom going back to Bellevue and now losing Dad." She started to cry.

Setting the mug of cocoa down on the counter, Lorelei reached over and hugged her while the girl sobbed and sobbed. When she finally stopped crying, Lorelei handed her a tissue. She wiped her eyes and blew her nose.

"What's the boy's name? The one Detective Nichols and his wife are fostering?"

"It's Henry Knight, but he goes by Nightshade."

"Pretty cool name," Samantha said.

# THIRTY-FOUR

"**I** WAS IMPRESSED WITH JESSICA AT THE morgue yesterday. She handled meeting Samantha very graciously," Dory said. She and Billy Jo were standing in the kitchen of Rosedale Investigations the day after the identification of James Browning.

"Jessica told me that James had showed her a picture of Samantha. He asked her to be kind to the girl, if they ever met. Even knowing he was with Annabelle, she's honoring his requests. It was due to her first husband's wishes that she even agreed to marry James. She's a bigger person than I could be." Billy Jo shook her head.

"I'd have shot the jerk myself," Dory said. "Lorelei took Samantha back to her house after the visit to the morgue. The girl was trying to hold it together, but identifying her father, her mom not being there, and then meeting his other wife was a lot for anyone to handle. Changing the subject, what are you doing today?"

"I need to get out to Mrs. Broadchurch's house and tell her we weren't able to do the DNA analysis she wanted." The phone rang and Billy Jo picked up the call. She was quiet for a bit before saying, "You don't need to come in. Dory and I have it under control. Bye, Wayne." She clicked off the call.

"Poor guy, he's really struggling. What did he say?"

"He said Lucy has hired Samantha Leigh to tutor Nightshade. They are meeting her here tomorrow."

"Funny how life turns out, isn't it," Dory said in a sentimental tone. "Samantha was originally headed back with her mother to Bellevue and Nightshade was planning on returning to Homeless City. Now they will be doing their homework with their young heads close together. It's a blessing."

MRS. BROADCHURCH WAS SITTING AT HER EASEL painting outdoors on the cement driveway when Billy Jo arrived.

"Hello," she greeted the tiny bird-like woman with her floating white hair. "What are you working on today?"

"I'm painting a chickadee. He and his mate have a nest in the apple tree. I love painting *plein air*. It's a term coined by the French Impressionists who attempted to capture light by painting outside. He's hard to get right because chickadees are always on the move. The pairs stay together all summer while they are raising their chicks. I think it was his little black cap that attracted her originally," she said with an amused smile.

"He's a lovely symbol for courtship," Billy Jo said. "I'm sorry, but I couldn't get the sheriff to run the DNA test you wanted. He said it was unethical to do the test without permission of the people being tested." She handed the woman the two plastic bags containing the teacup with Aimee's lip print and Grant's comb.

"Well, that's too bad."

"I wondered if any of those commercial sites that do DNA analysis would work."

"That's a really good thought."

"I wanted to be sure you were okay with the idea. Since you are, I'll check and see if any of them could help. Do you mind if I walk over to the stream by the end of your house? It's so beautiful, I'd like to see it again."

"Enjoy," Mrs. Broadchurch said.

Leaving the woman seated by her easel, Billy Jo skirted the front of the single-story house. Beyond the end of the dwelling, a tiny stream trickled through boulders on its way to the base of the ravine. Kicking off her flip-flops, Billy Jo dipped her toes into the water. It was icy cold and translucent. A tiny frog, the color of polished jade, jumped into the stream.

Looking down, she saw layer after layer of leafy trees descending the escarpment until the forest joined the dark blue crevasse at the base of the canyon bisected by the Little Harpeth River that shone like a slice of hammered silver in the afternoon sun. Then she gazed upwards, taking in the ascending ranks of trees with their cumulous of green leaves until the forest reached the top of the ridge and touched the incandescent sky. If she lived in this place, she would never want to leave.

She put on her flip-flops while looking up a site on her phone and was tickled to see that the 23 & Me site had something that could work.

Walking back to the artist she said, "It turns out that the 23 & Me test has a component for finding relatives. All you need to do is purchase the kit and then use the buccal swabs on the inside of your mouth, swipe the second Q-tip on Aimee's lip print and send it in."

"What about Grant? Don't I need to get him tested?"

"All you are trying to do is find out if Aimee is your granddaughter. If there's enough of her DNA on the swab, the test will tell you that."

"So what is Grant in this process then?"

"Immaterial, since you don't plan to tell him the results," Billy Jo said.

"Good plan," Mrs. Broadchurch said, and her elfin face broke into a smile. "Send me a photo of True when you're ready to have me paint her picture. Grant is going to cover my bill and Hilary's from Rosedale Investigations. He'll stop by the office in the next few days to give you a check."

"It's been a pleasure," Billy Jo said. Then taking a final look at the exquisite natural beauty in which the woman lived, she walked to her car. Opening the driver's door she looked back, seeing the artist already seated at her easel, a picture of concentration in her speckled white paint shirt and black tights. She'd picked up her paintbrush again, trying to capture the busy little chickadee who had been successful in his courtship.

MARK STOOD BACK AND LOOKED AT HIS EFFORTS. He'd set the table with the cabin's sage green dishes on blue placemats and added a white vase he'd found on the shelf above the washer/dryer. On his way out to PD's place, he'd picked up a bunch of tulips from the Floral Café in Rosedale. Their bright pink petals shone in the dim dining room. He'd also purchased a frozen lasagna casserole and put it in the oven to cook. Setting out two glasses for wine, he slid a key under the one by Billy Jo's place. Then he looked around the cabin to see if he missed anything when he cleaned. It looked pretty good to him.

Opening the sliding glass door to the deck, he felt a cool breeze brush against his cheeks, and reveled for a moment in the exquisite pleasure of being a young man deeply in love. Ever since the last night he and Billy Jo spent together, he felt ready to take the next step in their relationship. Hearing a car coming up the hill, he walked out to the porch to greet his girlfriend.

"Hi, Mark," Billy Jo called. "I have groceries."

He walked over to help her unload. She was dutifully impressed when she walked in. "Lovely job on the table. Thanks for putting the casserole in the oven. I'll just put on jeans and then we can take a walk," she said and headed for the bedroom to change.

Walking down one of the trails, they saw a male pheasant with his iridescent green neck and red head. He strolled across the path in front of them, in no hurry at all. As they crested the hill returning to the cabin, three deer crossed their trail—all young males with budded antlers. Once back inside, Mark and Billy Jo took their seats in the red and purple Adirondack chairs on PD's deck.

"What happened with Mrs. Broadchurch's DNA analysis?" Mark asked.

"I wasn't able to get it done. Sheriff Bradley said he wouldn't do it without permission of Grant and Aimee. But, I think she can get what she wants from the 23 & Me DNA testing kit."

"That's great news. And now, I have a surprise for you."

"What is it, you know I love surprises," Billy Jo said.

"It's on the table," he said.

They walked inside and he poured the wine. When Billy Jo lifted her wine glass, she looked confused. "What's this key for, Mark?"

"It's a key to my condo. I want us to move in together." He bent his head to kiss her, running his fingers through her curly hair. She smelled delicious, like the wildflower meadow they had walked in, like blue wood smoke rising from a campfire in the cool spring air.

"Are you sure about this?' she asked him. "It's a big step."

"Ever since the last night we were together, I can't stop thinking about you. Please say yes, sweetheart."

"I want to," she hesitated, "but, I need to be in my apartment during the week so I can be at my desk by eight o'clock."

"How about this? I will stay at your apartment at Rosedale Investigations during the week and you can move into my condo on weekends."

"An excellent compromise," she said and kissed him thoroughly.

After dinner, replete with the food and wine as the softly darkening evening pressed against the windows, Billy Jo looked closely at her boyfriend. "Have you thought any more about me meeting your mom?"

"I talked with her on the phone today. I told her how busy we've both been and she's decided to come here. She's going to join us on the Fourth of July. I checked with PD and she's invited to the celebration."

"Perfect," she said. "That will be just perfect."

# THIRTY-FIVE

A FTER FINALIZING THE ARRANGEMENTS FOR SAMANTHA to tutor Nightshade, Lorelei suggested she might speak with the counselor at Rosedale High. "Since you've never done this before, I think talking to Mrs. Robson would be helpful. She was the person who did Nightshade's testing."

"I'm still not certain I can do this," Samantha said. She'd never taught anyone anything, not even how to swim or ride a bike.

"Just give it a try. If after a week or two it isn't working, you can always pick up a part-time job somewhere else. I've talked to both Detective Nichols and his wife and they are willing to pay you the going hourly rate for tutoring, which is quite a bit higher than what you would get working at a restaurant. You'll need some money if you want new clothes before school starts in the fall."

"Hmm. Good point," Samantha said as she reached for the phone, dialed the high school and asked for the Library.

"Rosedale High School Library, Mrs. Robson speaking"

"Hi Mrs. Robson, it's Samantha Leigh calling."

"Nice to hear from you, Samantha. How can I help?"

"I'm going to begin tutoring a boy who is starting high school in the fall. He has been out of school a while. I think you were the person who tested him," she said.

"It is the Nichols' foster child? The one they call Nightshade?"

"That's the one. I thought I'd start with math. Can you tell me what he needs to know to start in the tenth grade?"

"You're going to have a job ahead of you to get him ready. Testing showed him barely ready for ninth. I would have said he should start in the eighth grade, but he was so tall I knew he would feel terribly out of place. He will probably struggle the most with math. I'd start with algebra. I have a text book you can use. This is a fine thing you are doing, Samantha. You're an excellent student and will be good at this. He's a smart kid, but you'll have to make him focus."

"Thank you so much, Mrs. Robson. I'll come by the school today to pick up the book and any other materials you think would be helpful. I'm going to be meeting Nightshade at Rosedale Investigations tomorrow morning."

"Let me know how it goes," she said "And good luck."

James Browning's funeral was to be held in the small chapel adjacent to the Rosedale Funeral Home.

"Our chapel is non-denominational," the kindly staff person at the funeral home told Jessica when they met. "It's a nice alternative for those people who don't have a relationship with a pastor. We held a Buddhist ceremony here once. It was lovely."

"Thank you. Will Friday mid-morning work for your schedule?" Jessica asked. She'd had to force herself to make the funeral arrangements. Her purse was stuffed with wet tissues from her tears.

"Ten o'clock will be fine. And we'll supply the officiant. Do you want an open or closed casket?

"Closed," she said firmly and shuddered. She couldn't stop thinking of James' fine strong body and the damage the bullets would have done to the man she loved.

Walking out of the Funeral Home, she raised her eyes to the dome of a cloudless blue sky. The day seemed too lovely for her sad errand. *It's the second time I've had to bury a husband and I'm not even forty,* she thought and brushed away her tears. She was driving to the offices of the local newspaper to put James' obituary in the paper, when her phone rang. "Hello," she said.

"Hello, Jessica, it's Detective Nichols. I wanted you to know that the Illinois state police are confident with the information I gave them that they will soon be able to identify your husband's killer," Wayne said. He was suddenly unable to continue as the sharp rending sound of bullets from the semi-automatic rifle returned to his mind. It had been all but impossible to erase the sounds and images of that night: the twisted body of the man on the driveway, the sound of the killer starting his car, the screech of his tires as he peeled away, the look on Sam Browning's face when he said Jenny was leaving him.

"That's good to know. I just finished arranging my husband's funeral. It's going to be held on Friday this week. Can you attend?"

Wayne hesitated, every molecule in his body wanted nothing to do with this funeral. Each day since he'd left Sam and Jenny Browning's farm, his guilt was a razor blade cutting into his chest.

"Did you hear me, Detective? The funeral is going to be on Friday at ten o'clock in the morning in the Rosedale Funeral Home."

"Yes, sorry. I will try to make it," he said, struggling to keep his voice level.

"I will see you then," she said and rang off.

WAYNE HAD CALLED JESSICA FROM THEIR KITCHEN. Checking his phone, he saw a text from Lucy reminding him to get Nightshade up in time for his tutoring appointment. She had recently given the boy her old cell phone. *Might as well take advantage of the technology to wake the kid up*, he thought and dialed the number. He heard sound of the phone hitting the floor before the boy's foggy voice said, "What?"

"We are meeting your tutor this morning in an hour. Get up." He deliberately didn't remind him to shower, get dressed, and make his bed. He would check later about the bed. He'd once read developing the habit of making your bed every morning helped instill responsibility. The most successful people in the world, the article said, made their beds every morning of their lives.

Walking out to the garage, he ousted Huck from his bed for a morning pee. It was a perfect morning with a peerless blue sky. He waited while the dog sniffed around the shrubbery, barked at a robin and finally lifted his leg against a shrub. He was so pokey, it was like having a second teenager. He called the dog over, petted him and took him inside to be fed. Huck practically inhaled his kibble. The day-to-day activities of being a parent to the boy and his dog were helping. The shard of ice in his chest was a little smaller now. He was starting to feel less ashamed, until the face of Sam Browning appeared in his dreams.

THE TWO OF THEM PULLED INTO THE DRIVEWAY at Rosedale Investigations a few minutes before the tutoring appointment. Turning off the ignition, Wayne spotted Samantha coming down the sidewalk on her bike. Riding up to the porch, she parked and stood waiting in the yard. Her backpack looked heavy, he noticed. Probably full of educational materials. The girl was taking the job seriously.

He got out of the truck saying, "Hello, Samantha. I don't know if you remember me. I'm Detective Nichols."

The girl nodded and he saw sorrow sweep across her pretty features. The last time she'd seen him was the day she identified her father's body. He knew it had been terribly difficult for her. Despite his familiarity with the facility, it was never easy for him either.

Nightshade got out of the car and slouched over. Wayne was tempted to tell the kid to stand up straight, but he stifled the impulse. There were days he longed to assume the persona of Sgt. Roscoe.

"Morning," the boy said in a laconic voice. He hadn't seen the girl yet. Then he raised his head, saw how pretty she was, opened his eyes wide and gave her a brilliant smile.

In a touching gesture, the girl held out her small hand to shake with the boy, said her name was Samantha and that she was happy to meet him. There was no need to worry now that Nightshade wouldn't pay attention. He could hardly take his eyes off her.

"Let's go inside," Wayne said, stifling his amusement.

Billy Jo and Dory were waiting and greeted the teenagers with muffins, strawberries and coffee. The women took over and, once the kids had their food and beverages, ushered them into the conference room.

Wayne waited in the kitchen. "Thanks for giving Nightshade the coffee. He needs caffeine to be fully awake," he said when they returned.

"Well, he looked wide awake to me. Was fumbling all over himself to help Samantha get seated," Dory said, chuckling.

"Let's hope what she teaches him burns through the barrage of his hormones," Wayne said. "I talked to Jessica Browning this morning. James' funeral is set for this week, Friday at ten o'clock at the Rosedale Funeral Home chapel." He hesitated. "It seems we are obliged to go. Do you think Annabelle will attend?"

"Lorelei says she's coming. Samantha called her mom and said she needed her," Billy Jo said.

"It's going to be an interesting funeral with both wives there," Dory said. "Is there anyone else we should call?"

*Would he be able to make himself call Sam Browning?* Wayne wondered. The day he first met the couple when Sam's wife brought him a glass of cold lemonade returned with a fierce punch in his core. He took a deep breath as grief filled his heart for bringing such a tragedy into their lives.

# THIRTY-SIX

Lucy and Nightshade had an appointment with the orthopedist to check on the boy's arm. The boy was agitating to have the cast removed. "It's highly unlikely the doctor will remove it yet," Lucy said, "but, if the bone is healing properly, he might consider it. I'll ask." Turning to Wayne she added, "We'll meet you at the funeral home chapel after the appointment."

Once they drove off, Wayne sat alone in the kitchen, holding a mug of cooling coffee in his hand. Huck was asleep at his feet. Reaching down, he scratched the dog behind his ears, realizing how attached he'd grown to the animal.

After struggling with his conscience the previous evening, he finally mustered up the courage to call Sam Browning. When the phone rang, the answering machine picked up. It was a relief not to hear the man's voice, although he knew what it meant. Jenny hadn't returned. She would have caught the call otherwise. Mothers with young babies who lived out in the country were home most of the time. He'd left the time and place of the funeral and said he had some information about Browning's killer. Hanging up the phone, he recalled that both Sam's brother, Chris, and now James, his only playmates from childhood were dead. Guilt weighed heavily on Wayne's spirit. Trying to cut the cycle of memories, he stood up abruptly and emptied his coffee down the drain.

Lucy and Nightshade met Wayne in the parking lot of the Rosedale Funeral Home just before the service. The boy still had his cast on.

"Do I have to go to this thing?" Nightshade asked. He looked antsy and was pacing.

"No, you can walk around town until it's over," Wayne said, handing him a $20 bill.

"Remember to keep your phone on. Is it charged?" Lucy asked.

Nightshade nodded and was about to leave when Wayne noticed a far-away look on his face. It was the look he got when he was thinking about Homeless City. "Remember why you stay," he said sternly.

"I remember," he said after a startled moment.

"Be back here in an hour," Wayne said.

"What was that about?" Lucy asked, as they walked toward the building.

"Nothing. Just trust me," he said.

"I gather that's man-code for don't ask," Lucy said as they entered the funeral home and turned down the hall toward the chapel.

Soft organ music was playing. The title of the hymn was, "Abide with Me." Wayne had heard it often and although he wasn't conventionally religious, the music usually left him feeling calm and peaceful. It didn't happen this time. Before they took their seats, he checked the people attending the service. Jessica and her son, Trevor, were sitting in the front row on the right. She wore a black hat with a veil that covered her face. Billy Jo was seated with them. Samantha and her mother, Annabelle, were sitting in the front row on the left side of the aisle. Dory and Lorelei were seated in the next row.

Looking toward the rear of the chapel, he inhaled sharply. He'd spotted Sam Browning. Sitting at the very back of the church, he had chosen a pew that light never reached. Among the disheartened group, he looked the loneliest of all. He swallowed, touching the cold place in his chest, knowing encountering the man again was part of his penance.

James Browning's casket had been placed on a low wooden platform in front of the altar. It was closed and covered with a large rectangular ornamentation made from leaves and roses. Wayne whispered to Lucy, pointing to the floral decoration and asked, "What's that called?"

"It's a grave blanket," she whispered as the officiant, wearing a dark shirt with a white band at his throat, walked into the chapel from the side door and took his place in front of the altar. He motioned to the organist, who played the final bar of the hymn, and the music ceased.

"We are assembled here today to pay respects to our honored dead—to remember the life and mark the death of James Charles Browning, who was taken from us early. He had an impact on us all, so we take this time from our busy lives to recognize his passing. It has only been a week since the Lord took him from our midst."

*It wasn't the Lord who took a high-powered deer rifle to James Browning*, Wayne thought, feeling resentment for the facile way the officiant described the man's terrible death.

As the service continued the cleric said, "In this passage from John 14: 1-6, the Lord said, 'Let not your hearts be troubled, neither let them be afraid. Believe in God; believe also in me. In my Father's house there are many mansions. If it were not so, would I have told you this? I go to prepare a place for you. I will come again and will take you to myself, so that where I am you may be also.'"

After the reading, the pastor asked, "Let us have a moment of silence in which to remember James Browning, the husband and father who lies here before us today." With the moment of silence concluded, he asked for anyone who wished to say a few words about Browning to come forward. To Wayne's surprise, Sam rose from his pew and walked slowly all the way from the back of the chapel to the podium.

"My name's Sam Browning," he said, looking out at the small group of mourners. "James was my cousin and we grew up together on a farm in Illinois. He was a cheerful boy, a smart-ass kidder with an off-beat sense of humor that often got him in trouble. It was always at James' instigation when we boys would skip school and take our cane-poles to the fishing pond. There were three of us, my brother Chris, our cousin James and myself." He hesitated, obviously struggling to maintain control, and cleared his throat. "It was a happy time and I hope to give my son as pleasant a childhood. We did a lot of work, as farm kids do, helping bring the cows in from the pasture for milking, washing the milking machines, and weeding the family garden. We never minded the work; there was plenty of time to play."

Then raising his eyes to the large stained glass window that dominated the rear façade of the church, he said, "I wish you well in the next world, Cousin, and pray that you and Chris are having a laugh together." He nodded respectfully to Jessica and her son before returning to his seat.

The service came to an end with the Lord's Prayer and most of the group straggled out of the sanctuary speaking in low tones. Annabelle and Samantha remained in their pew talking quietly. When Sam Browning walked out of the chapel, Wayne motioned him over to the side of the entry.

"It was good of you to come today, Sam, and I have some information for you. The state of Illinois has CCTV on the buildings at rest areas. I figured out the rest stop was where the shooter put the tracking device on my truck. I gave the state cops the time and date when I stopped there. It's only a matter of time now before the guy is nailed."

"I just want to know when he's in custody," Sam said through clenched teeth.

"I will let you know as soon as I do." Looking at Sam's iron expression, the icy stone in Wayne's chest grew colder.

"I saw Jessica in the church. When she married my brother, Chris, Jenny and I attended their wedding. After Chris died, James wrote to say he was engaged to marry Jessica. We were pleased about that. Now, that other woman who was in the chapel with the teenaged girl, is an ex-wife?"

*Close enough*, he thought and nodded.

When Jessica came out of the sanctuary and entered the foyer, she invited everyone to come to her house after the graveside service for the memorial reception. Turning to Sam, she said he was most welcome and invited him to stay the night. He nodded and Wayne thought a bit of the man's barely repressed sorrow had been tempered by her kindness. She extended an invitation to Lucy and Wayne as well.

"I'm sorry Jessica, I appreciate the gesture, but we need to go. We're picking up our son," Lucy said.

"Wait just a moment," Wayne said. He took a few steps toward Sam and called his name, holding out his hand. As the two men looked at each other and shook hands, something silent and powerful passed between them. Rejoining Lucy, Wayne felt lighter, cleaner, partially absolved.

"What was that?" Lucy asked.

"Nothing really. We just made a connection."

The last people to come out of the chapel were Annabelle and Samantha. Walking past Jessica, Annabelle turned and gave her a scalding look. She started to speak to her, but Samantha quickly put her arm around her mother's shoulders, whispered something and the crisis was averted. After a brief discussion with her mother in the parking lot, Samantha got into the car with Jessica and Trevor. Over her mother's objections, she had chosen to go to the cemetery and to the memorial.

Wayne's phone rang on the way home. It was Sheriff Ben Bradley's private number.

"Hi, Ben."

"I've got some good news for you, Buddy. I had an FBI agent in my office this morning. Turns out with the information you gave the Illinois state police, they identified the shooter. His name is Janislav Olgierd. Since he'd killed people in at least two states, the Illinois cops contacted the FBI. It seems that the FBI had had him on their Most Wanted List for years. They tracked him down at a rural gas station in Mississippi."

"Is he in custody?" Wayne asked. His breathing quickened.

"No. He refused to surrender and shot at the agents, wounding one of them. There was a firefight and an FBI sharpshooter nailed him. He's dead. The FBI agent said without your information, he could have gone on killing for years. The guy was a professional assassin who was known for never leaving a witness behind. Anyway, the agent told me they owed you. He said if you ever wanted to work for them, to give him a call. He left me his card."

Managing a strangled "thank you," Wayne clicked off the call. Lucy looked at him questioningly. "It's over," he said and took her hand. "The shooter is dead and I just got a pat on the back from the FBI."

Driving toward the house on that sunny afternoon, he felt his spirits rise. It had been his insight about the CCTV that identified and led the FBI right to the shooter. He'd call Sam and let him know that the shooter was dead and that Jenny and baby Sam would be safe on the farm. All he needed now was for them to be back together as a family.

"You can let it go now, Wayne," Lucy said and smiled. He nodded, feeling his guilt leave his body in a warm wave of satisfaction. He'd done his job. Now he could devote some time to his own family.

"How about we stop for ice cream?" he asked and from the rear seat, Nightshade clapped him on the shoulder.

# THIRTY-SEVEN

WAYNE, LUCY AND NIGHTSHADE WALKED INTO FAMILY COURT at ten o'clock in the morning on the last day of June. They took a seat on a wooden bench in the anteroom and waited for their case to be called. Lucy had bought the boy a suit and tie. He was wearing it, but under duress.

They'd filed the adoption petition with the help of their family lawyer, Evangeline Bon Temps. She'd worked with the sheriff's office for years and helped Wayne with a private legal matter some time ago. A small woman with a shining cap of dark hair and an ivory complexion, she came originally from New Orleans and a trace of her accent could still be heard in her voice. Sheriff Bradley and Lucy's favorite ER nurse, Soldan Channing, were joining them as character witnesses.

A harassed-looking paralegal walked up, asked them their names, checked the document in her hand and said they could go into the court. All six of them walked into the courtroom just as the Bailiff announced the entrance of Judge Carl Watson.

"All rise," the Bailiff said, and they stood until the judge was seated. Wayne had never been in family court before, although he had been in criminal court many times. It looked pretty much the same. He glanced at Nightshade who was drumming his fingers on the chair rail in front of them. Lucy put her hand gently on his, stopping the nervous behavior.

"You may begin," the Judge said, nodding at attorney Bon Temps. Judge Watson was an impressively large African American man with salt and pepper hair and piercing black eyes. He looked the very symbol of authority that morning, seated on his raised bench wearing the robe and regalia of his profession.

Counselor Bon Temps provided the Judge the background of how Wayne and Lucy met the boy and concluded her presentation on the adoption petition by saying, "In summary, Judge, our respected detective, Wayne Nichols and his physician wife, Dr. Lucy Ingram-Nichols, wish to adopt Henry Knight, known by the nickname of Nightshade, a fifteen-year-old formerly homeless boy."

"Where are the birth parents?" the judge asked.

"His mother passed away a few years ago and the father was listed as unknown on the birth certificate," she said.

"Are there any other relatives?"

"No, sir. My investigator did a comprehensive search."

"All right. Now, am I correct that the boy was discovered having an untreated broken arm?" the Judge asked, raising his face from the papers to look at her.

"That is correct, sir. Dr. Lucy Ingram was supervising her students and residents who were delivering care to the homeless the morning he was found."

"Has the boy been treated for the fracture since?"

"He has, Judge."

Turning to Wayne, the judge said, "Detective Nichols, you have had this boy living with you for just three months, I understand."

"Yes, Judge," Wayne said. Asking about the length of time Nightshade had been with them was the very thing he'd feared about moving forward with the adoption so rapidly.

"Are you fully willing to adopt this young man as your son, with all the rights and responsibilities of fatherhood after such a brief time?"

"Yes, sir, I am," Wayne said.

"May I ask why?" The judge asked drily.

Wayne hesitated and took in a breath. "Because, I love my wife, sir." A brief touch of amusement crossed the Judge's face.

"Is that the only reason?" he asked.

"No, Your Honor, I have something else to add if I may."

"Go ahead."

"When I was a young man, I left the foster home where I was staying, disregarding the pleas of my little brother who begged me not to leave. When I returned, I found he had been killed. I've always felt guilty that I failed to protect him. By coming into our lives, Nightshade is giving me a second chance, a chance to do things right. If our petition for adoption is approved, I give you my word that I won't fail him." *Nightshade is my chance at redemption*, he thought.

"Very well. I now ask you, Dr. Lucy Ingram-Nichols, are you willing to adopt this young man as your son, with all the rights and responsibilities of motherhood?"

"I am, and very proudly, sir," she said. She had worn her white coat with its embroidered insignia of Rosedale General Hospital over a navy blue turtleneck and slacks. When they discussed what they were going to wear to court the night before, Lucy said she didn't usually wear her white coat outside the hospital. It made people feel awkward and she didn't wear it in social situations for that reason, but this was a special occasion. She wanted the judge to see her as the professional she was.

"Am I to assume you were the person who spotted this boy's broken arm while providing care to the homeless?"

"Actually, it was my husband who saw him first, Your Honor. He noticed the way Nightshade was holding his arm and brought it to my attention. If not for his keen observation, I would have left Homeless City without seeing how desperately the boy needed medical attention."

Judge Watson then turned to Sheriff Ben Bradley and said, "I assume you are serving as a character witness this morning. Is that correct?"

"Yes, sir. I am willing to attest to the excellent character of both prospective parents. Detective Nichols and I worked together for seven years prior to his joining Rosedale Investigations. He was unfailing in his duties, a judgement I don't make lightly. I've known Dr. Lucy Ingram for nearly the same length of time. She's a lovely woman and will make a fine mother for Nightshade."

"Very good," the judge said. Then turning to Nurse Channing, he asked, "Are you serving as a character witness as well?"

"Yes, Your Honor. I am here as a character witness for Dr. Lucy. I'm her primary ER nurse and we have worked together for a decade. Her specialty area within ER is adolescent medicine. The other partners consult with her about their teenage patients. She has wanted to be a mother for a long time and I know she loves Nightshade." She smiled at the boy.

"Thank you. Now, as I am sure you are all aware, it is the duty of an adoption Judge to speak with any young person over the age of twelve as to their wishes in the matter of adoption." He turned his formidable gaze on Nightshade who was fitfully loosening his necktie. Lucy touched his arm and whispered for him to stand up. "Follow Attorney Bon Temps to my chambers," the judge said and left the courtroom, his black robe billowing out behind him.

IN THE FEW MOMENTS THEY STOOD TOGETHER outside the Judge's office, Attorney Bon Temps reiterated what Lucy had said. "All the Judge wants to know is whether you want to be adopted by Lucy and Wayne. Nothing to be worried about."

"Aren't you coming with me?" he asked nervously.

"No, the Judge needs to speak with you privately. It's his job to find out if you consent to this adoption."

"If I want to keep living with Wayne and Lucy, you mean?" he asked. He ran his hand through his recently cut hair that came to just above his shoulders. He was still getting used to it being shorter.

"Adoption is more than that. It means that Lucy will be your mother for the rest of your life and Wayne will be your father. You will have two parents to love you," she smiled kindly at him.

Nightshade nodded. He knew Lucy loved him, she'd proved it with everything she'd done, but he still felt on trial with Wayne. He wondered if the adoption would make things go easier between the two of them. He remembered Wayne saying he had agreed to the adoption because he loved Lucy, but then added that he'd had a little brother who was killed and he wanted to do things right this time.

At that point, the judge's clerk appeared and said, "Henry Knight? Are you Henry?"

Nightshade nodded and after a quick backward glance at Attorney Bon Temps, followed the clerk into the judge's office. Judge Watson's chambers had high ceilings, wooden paneling, and tall windows flanked by floor-to-ceiling drapes. It had been purposely designed to portray the majesty of the law. He sat down in a chair in front of the desk.

"It is my duty as a Judge in Family Court to ask you about your wishes," the Judge said, waving his clerk from the room. "I understand you were living in a place the police call Homeless City when they found you. Is that right?"

Nightshade nodded, seeing in his mind the small blue tarp that hung over a broomstick balanced between two burn barrels. He wondered if his tattered sleeping bag was still there or if his space had been taken by someone else. He remembered the day the snow fell heavily last winter and how bitterly cold he was that night. It had been a hard life. The face of his mother came to his mind, and he wished she could see him in his new clothes. A brief pang of loss hit him, for her, for Rosie, the old lady who looked after him after his mother died, and for Sgt. Roscoe. Being adopted might mean never seeing them again. He missed them, but knew he no longer missed that life.

"You are a lucky young man to have these people want to adopt you," the Judge said. "Being adopted will mean you will have all the advantages necessary to succeed in life. You will be able to get a good education and eventually become a solid citizen and contributing member of society. I ask you now, are you fully willing to become the Nichols' son?"

"I guess so," he said, but his voice trembled.

"Do they treat you well?" the judge asked. His attention was focused like a laser beam. "Do you have enough to eat? Have your own room in the house?"

"Plenty of food there and I have my own room. Dr. Lucy got my arm fixed and let me keep my dog. He stays in my room with me at night now," he said.

"What about Detective Nichols. Is he good to you?"

Nightshade hesitated for a bit before nodding.

The Judge noticed. "You need to be sure about this, young man. Do you want to become their legal son?" He brought all the power of his deep voice to bear on the question.

"I do," he said, and this time his voice was stronger.

"Do you need more time to make a final decision? It's not a problem if you want to wait a while. You haven't known them very long."

All the things that had happened to him since the day Dr. Lucy made him go with her to the hospital flashed through his mind: the doctor operating on his arm, the dog obedience classes, the steady meals, the educational testing and now his tutor, Samantha who was becoming his friend. It was like Sgt. Roscoe said when Wayne came to get him after he ran away, if he went with them, that decision would influence the rest of his life. It already had. He looked directly at the judge. "I don't need more time. I'm ready, sir," he said.

"Then we are all done here. Congratulations, son. You have a bright future ahead of you."

# THIRTY-EIGHT

THAT EVENING THERE WAS TO BE a party at the Nichols' home to celebrate Nightshade's adoption. Wayne and the boy worked together all afternoon hanging strings of tiny white lights above the back patio and in the foliage of the trees. At one point, Nightshade climbed a twelve-foot ladder to attach lights to an oak tree. The ladder wobbled a little and Wayne dashed over to steady it.

"Hold on there," he said. "I really don't want to have to take you to the ER today."

"Me neither," Nightshade said, climbing down the ladder. "Look," he said, turning his wrist back and forth. "Thanks to Lucy, it's completely healed."

"It is and you're definitely putting on some weight with her cooking," he said.

"Do you mind telling more about your little brother? How did he die?" Nightshade asked.

Wayne felt the old remorse rise in his chest and forced it down. Taking a deep breath, he said, "I was in foster care and there was a second child who came to that house after I did. He was ten years younger than me and I considered him my little brother." He paused and swallowed. "I ran away from that house when I was seventeen and left him behind. He didn't want me to go. Several years later, he was murdered by my foster father. I would have done anything to have the monster brought to justice, but by the time I found out what had happened, he was dead. All I could do was to have my brother's remains buried and a gravestone made. I had the words, *His was the Valor of a Lion,* carved on the stone. I've felt guilty about it all my life."

Nightshade looked moved by what he had heard. He nodded and said, "I've been in foster care a couple of times. It's not easy knowing nobody loves you enough to adopt you."

"No, it's not. But living in Homeless City must have been harder. I was homeless for a while as a teenager, so I know something of what you went through."

"It's something we have in common," Nightshade said in a thoughtful tone.

"As I told the Judge, you coming into our lives gives me a chance to do things right."

"I know that Lucy worries when you get yourself into dangerous situations, like you did when Mr. Browning was killed."

"She does, but I always manage to survive," Wayne said with a rueful head shake.

"I've gotten through some pretty tough times, too. Maybe if Lucy hears how I survived on the streets, she will realize how tough we both are."

Wayne smiled at the boy and said, "Okay, tough guy, let's go inside and get something to eat."

BY EIGHT O'CLOCK THAT NIGHT THE HOUSE WAS PACKED with people, all eating and drinking champagne. Nightshade was still uneasy around folks he didn't know and there were a lot of them. He tried to sneak off to his room, but Lucy kept him busy passing out food and filling people's glasses. At one point, Wayne was standing with Lucy in front of the fireplace. He tapped his champagne glass and asked for silence.

"Could I have your attention, please? As all of you know, today was a momentous day in the life of the Nichols' family. We received the decision by the Family Court and Nightshade is now officially ours. Please raise your glasses in a toast to his future. Come over here, son," he said. It was the first time he'd called him son, and it felt good.

Nightshade looked around for Huck. He whispered something to Lucy who turned to the group and said, "Hold on a minute folks, we forgot the fourth Nichols' family member. Go get him," she said.

He left the living room and went to his room to liberate Huck. The dog followed him back to the living room and sat down in front of the family.

"Now we are ready for pictures," Wayne said, as he reached down to pat the dog. "I'd like to propose a toast. Please raise your glasses *to the son God sent us.*" He looked directly at Lucy then, and all their guests cheered.

IT WAS PAST MIDNIGHT WHEN THE LAST GUEST DEPARTED, leaving the house silent. Lucy had picked up most of the party detritus before she and the boy went off to bed. Wayne walked through the house one more time, adding dishes and glasses he found to the dishwasher, when he noticed a pile of mail on the kitchen desk. He picked up the letters and circulars. Flipping through the stack, he came to one that made his heart pound. The return address read Sam Browning, 1000 Maple Rd, Makanda, Illinois. For a moment, he felt the ice in his core grow heavier. He took a deep painful breath, opened the envelope and pulled out the letter. There was only a single line.

"Jenny and Sam Jr. are back," it read.

Wayne rested his hand on his chest and exhaled in immense relief as the last splinter of ice in his soul dissolved.

The dog woke up from his nap behind the couch, wandered over, sat down and looked up at him. He wanted to go outside. Opening the sliding glass doors, Wayne released Huck into the back yard. Walking out after the dog, still holding the letter in his hand, he felt a profound gratitude for all the things life had given him. He'd come a long way from that abandoned little Indian kid in Michigan's Upper Peninsula.

All the stages of his life flashed through his mind: running away from his foster home at seventeen, his first girlfriend who broke his heart, attending the Police Academy, joining the Detroit PD, making the rank of detective early, and then his first tragic failure, little Ruthie whose abductor was never caught. He'd left Michigan in despair after that case and wandered south, landing at the Rosedale Sheriff's Office. It was where he met Lucy.

The day of their wedding he thought he had nothing more on his wish list. Thinking of her now, her body warm with sleep, and the son she'd found for them to raise, he lifted his face to whatever gods there were who had watched over his life.

"I thank you for everything you have given me," he said and rubbed his glistening eyes.

GETTING READY FOR BED THAT NIGHT, the question Billy Jo wanted to ask PD played over and over, like a broken record, in her brain. *Why hadn't PD come for her sooner?* Not knowing was driving her crazy. She had to know the reason, she decided, whatever it might be, and dialed his phone.

When he answered, she said, "Remember when we talked about my Grampa Aaron's settlement?"

"I do."

"There was one thing we didn't get to that night," she said.

"Does this need to be talked about now?" he asked, sounding distracted.

"I'm sorry, PD, but it does."

"Okay. Can you come out tomorrow morning?"

"What about this evening? I could come for dinner and stay over."

"No. That won't work. And please don't come too early tomorrow morning. Say nine o'clock? I want to sleep in."

"Okay," she said, but frowned as she hung up. To her knowledge, PD had never slept late in his life. He was always up and about by six a.m. It didn't make any sense.

SHE HAD COMPLETELY FORGOTTEN PD asking her not to arrive too early and only remembered as she approached his mile-long driveway at eight-thirty the next morning. *Oh well,* she thought. *I'm sure he'll be up by now.* It was a glorious morning, and the weather was predicted to be sunny throughout the weekend, perfect for the big July Fourth event. She'd flicked on her turn signal when she noticed a car pulling out of PD's gravel drive.

*Who could have been visiting him this early?* She wondered. His was the only cabin on the property. As the vehicle went past her, the driver turned the other way, but Billy Jo knew that car. It belonged to Lorelei Vail. *What the heck?* She wondered if there could be a business matter they were discussing, but then she started to giggle. *Lorelei Vail and PD were having an affair!* She was the reason he'd lied about wanting to sleep late. It was just too cute for words. The woman was sixty-something and PD was about to turn seventy-five, but one just never knew when Cupid would draw back his bow and send down a shower of arrows.

Her adopted grandfather was still wearing his striped pajamas when she opened the screen door to the cabin. "Did you get a good night's sleep last night?" she asked him, covering a wicked grin with her hand.

"Told you not to arrive too early," he said with an embarrassed laugh. "Guess our secret's out. Don't suppose you could keep this to yourself?"

"Not a chance, Romeo," she said.

"Dory is going to have a field day," he said, shaking his head and handing Billy Jo a cup of coffee.

They chatted about the party, how many people were expected, the food and the fireworks. He told her he planned to set off the fireworks with the help of Wayne and Liam.

"I wish you'd get a professional to do it, PD. Fireworks can be dangerous, you know."

"You worry too much, girl," he said. "Now, what did you have to talk to me about?"

Billy Jo took a deep breath. A swirl of emotions took her breath and for a moment, she couldn't begin. Then she straightened her shoulders and said, "I want you to know that whatever happened at that time, I have forgiven you. I'm grateful for all you have done for me. You saved my life."

PD nodded, but he wasn't smiling any longer. His old face, wrinkled as walnut shell, looked apprehensive.

"I know Grampa Aaron asked you to look after me and my mom before he died. But his death followed hers so closely, you had no time to help us. Is this right so far?"

"It is," PD said. "And I will spare you the pain of asking me the next question. You want to know why it took me two years to find you."

"I have to know, PD. You're supposed to be this legendary detective. Yet with all your skills, it took so long. Were you really looking? Didn't you care that I was all alone?" Her voice trembled.

"I failed you. I know," he said and turned his face away.

Seeing the pain he was experiencing, she was almost willing to let him off the hook, but then felt her conscience prod her. If he had an explanation, she wanted to hear it.

After wiping his face with a kitchen towel, PD turned back to face her. "I was in the room with your Grampa Aaron when he died. He clutched his chest, laid back on the bed and was gone. Trying to get my bearings, I went down to the hospital chapel and spent a long time remembering the days we spent together as soldiers in the jungles of Vietnam. Afterwards, still feeling shaky, I wondered if I should be driving, but decided I was okay. It was the wrong decision. Pulling onto the freeway, I was hit head-on by a speeding truck. The driver lost control and crossed the median."

"Oh no," she whispered.

"I was unconscious when they pulled me from the wreck. It was lucky the accident happened so close to the hospital but even with all their skills, I was in a coma for a long time. The surgeons fixed my broken leg, mended a smashed hip and clamped a head injury as I slept. Even now, I don't remember all of this. I was in such horrendous pain they gave me a lot of meds. They told me afterwards that I got the full cocktail, fentanyl, propofol and morphine. When I finally woke up, I had a severe headache and no memory of what had happened. I found out later I had what's called retrograde amnesia. It's a condition that takes away a person's memories of what had occurred prior to the head injury."

"I don't need to know any more," Billy Jo said, rubbing her stinging eyes. "I love you, PD. I had no idea you were dealing with such an appalling medical tragedy. I moved to Knoxville shortly after Grampa and Mom died. I didn't have a phone, credit cards or a car in my name. There was no way you could have found me."

"Hang on, I need to tell you all of it," PD said and took a shaky inhale. "Bits and pieces of what happened kept returning to my memory. When I finally recalled Aaron asking me to look after you, I felt horrible. I went to your apartment, but you were gone by then. That's when I learned your mother had died of ovarian cancer shortly before your grandfather passed. I talked to everyone who knew you—your mom's doctors, your neighbors, your teachers, your landlord, even your Grampa's priest. I left my card with all of them. Finally, one of your neighbors contacted me. She remembered you working at the Creamy Scoop. I went there and a girl behind the counter told me you'd left town. She didn't know where you went, but said you'd talked about working at a pizza restaurant. You thought you'd make more money waitressing. I followed that clue to the earth. I went to every pizza restaurant in every city, town and village in Tennessee within two hundred miles—only to find you here, back in Rosedale two years later."

"When, like Sir Lancelot from Camelot, you came riding to my rescue," she said, smiling through her tears. It was an enormous relief to know that he had tried so hard, that he had never given up searching for her.

"Does this help you, Sweetie?" he asked.

"It sure does," she told him.

"I'm so sorry you had to go through that without any family. I'm your family now, you know. I'm always going to be here for you."

"I know and I will always be grateful," Billy Jo said with a sweet smile.

"Grateful enough to keep you from telling Dory about my little romance?" he asked with a chuckle.

"No way," she said, wiping away her tears and grinning.

# THIRTY-NINE

DORY KNOCKED ON BILLY JO'S APARTMENT DOOR ridiculously early on the morning of July fourth. She could hear the girl's feet as she stomped angrily toward the door.

"Seriously?" Billy Jo said, partially opening the door. Mark sat up in the tumbled bed and waved.

"I'm here to address the most important decision you are making today."

"Which is?"

"What you are going to wear to the party. I've purchased you a dress."

"Oh my God," Billy Jo said. "Go away! I'm wearing blue jean cut-offs and a T-shirt." Her dark hair was tousled from sleeping but her dark eyes were wide awake and snapping.

Turning toward the boy in bed, Dory said, "Mark, you need to leave. I have spoken to your mother. She requires your presence."

"Fine. Come in then," Billy Jo said. She flung the door open and trudged off toward the bathroom. Dory walked into the studio apartment with its minimal kitchen tucked under the slanted roof, a skylight covered in vines, a table that also served as a desk and a queen-sized bed. The bathroom door was ostentatiously slammed.

Mark pulled the sheet off the bed. He held it in front of him as he struggled to get up without revealing himself. "Is my mother really here?"

"No, but I have spoken to her. She will be arriving at your place within the hour and I suspect, being a mere male, that it isn't clean enough for motherly inspection."

"Probably not," Mark said. Still holding the sheet in front of him, and trying not to trip over it, he followed Billy Jo toward the tiny bathroom.

"I'm going downstairs to make coffee," Dory called. "Come down as soon as you are decent."

Billy Jo, Mark and the sheet were wedged so tightly in the bathroom that the door hardly closed. Part of the sheet had caught in the door jam. The young couple looked at each other and could only laugh.

DRESSED IN BLUE JEAN CUT-OFFS, a red bandana-print shirt tied at her slender waist and white sneakers, Billy Jo tromped downstairs to see the dress Dory had purchased. She was determined to go to the party dressed as she was, to assert her own style for once. But when she pulled the gown from the shopping bag (with its black and white piano keyboard logo), there was no contest. It was a midnight blue summer evening gown with wide straps. The straps were adorned with silver stars and it had a sheer organza skirt over a nylon underskirt. A narrow belt, bejeweled with smaller stars, was the finishing touch. Raising her eyebrows at the likely cost of the fancy outfit, Billy Jo asked Dory if she could pay her back over time.

"Not necessary. I am your fairy godmother today," Dory said and with a magician's flourish produced a pair of sparkly shoes from the second shopping bag. Digging deeper, she pulled out a tiny box containing long star-spangled earrings.

"Dory, you are amazing. Thank you so very much. I don't recognize this shopping bag. Is it from a new store in town?"

"Right on Main Street," Dory said, with a pursed-lip smile.

"Is something special happening that I need to be dressed up for?" she asked, thinking it was lucky Mrs. Broadchurch had finished the portrait of Dory's little dog. She would have something to give Dory in return.

"Just wanted Mark's mother to see you looking your best," she said. She touched her right eyebrow briefly with a single fingernail and her brown face was transfigured with delight.

That eyebrow touch was her "tell." It was the gesture she made when she was withholding information. Something was definitely happening and Billy Jo wondered if they were going to announce her promotion to partner at the July 4th event. She'd finished her report of the contributions she'd made to Rosedale Investigations' cases and turned it in a few days earlier.

LATER THAT MORNING, BACK IN THE KITCHEN at Rosedale Investigations, Billy Jo was making a charcuterie platter to take to the party. It was the first time she'd made one and she was using a photo from a recipe book as a guide when she heard the front doorbell tinkle.

"I'll get it," she called to Dory, who was in her office working on billing. Opening the front door, she was a bit surprised to see Jessica Browning and her son. "Welcome and come in," she said. The recent widow looked rested and more relaxed since the funeral. She was dressed attractively in a blue shirtwaist dress and had put her hair up in a twist. "How can I help this morning?" Billy Jo asked.

"It's my bill. It came in the mail and I'm so sorry but I need to pay it off monthly. James had a life insurance policy, but I haven't received my settlement yet. It probably has to be split between the two of us," Jessica said, sighing. "Frankly, I'm struggling to make ends meet. I'll get a job as soon as Trevor goes back to school in September and can start making payments then. Would that be okay?" she asked, looking a bit embarrassed.

"That's fine, Jessica. Lots of clients make monthly payments. It's not a problem. I'll tell Dory." She reached into her desk drawer and pulled out a cookie, asking if Trevor could have it. Jessica said "okay," and they both turned toward the child who had gone to the front door and opened it. Grant Broadchurch walked inside.

"I'll be with you in a moment," Billy Jo said.

"Come here, Trevor. Don't bother the gentleman," Jessica said. He scampered over and grabbed the cookie.

"He's no problem," Grant said. "Cute little guy you have there, ma'am," he said.

"It's Jessica," she told him. He nodded and Billy Jo caught the evanescent spark of attraction between them.

Grant remained standing in the waiting room surveying the framed photographs of shining racehorses, stacked stone slave walls, and the swirling Little Harpeth River.

In a quiet voice Billy Jo asked, "Do you think you'll be able to pay us $100 a month starting in the fall?"

Jessica nodded and thanked her for all the support she'd given her at the funeral. Billy Jo hugged her good-bye. The mother and son walked out the door.

GRANT CAME UP TO HER WORKSTATION after they left saying he was there to pay Hilary and his mother's bills.

"Just a moment, I'll get Dory to print them off for you," Billy Jo said.

Dory emerged from her office moments later and handed Grant the two bills. He reached for his checkbook.

"You look ready for the July 4th holiday," he said, smiling. She was wearing a navy and red flowered floor-length dress, red platform shoes and rhinestone clips in the pattern of the American flag in her hair.

"That's a heck of a lot more than you owe," Dory told him, picking up the check he'd written out and reading the amount. She showed it to Billy Jo, whose eyes widened. The check was for ten thousand dollars more than the bill.

"But, far less than your agency is worth. My mother said to tell you, Billy Jo, that she was particularly pleased," he smiled.

"So she has the granddaughter she always wanted then?" Billy Jo asked with a smile.

"She has," Grant said. "And to my delight, I have a daughter. We're keeping it to ourselves, though, as we don't want to raise problems in Aimee's family."

"Is there anything more we can do for your handsome self this morning?" Dory asked.

"I'm pretty sure that very attractive woman who just left is married, otherwise I'd ask for her phone number," he laughed.

"In fact that woman, whose name is Jessica Browning, could hardly be more available," Dory said. "Her husband passed away recently and left her pretty hard up."

"A real rat then," Grant said.

"A better description than you could possibly imagine," her voice was heavy with sarcasm. "Billy Jo, could you run outside and catch Jessica? They walked over here this morning so I'm sure she's still nearby. Ask her if she would be willing to give her phone number to our fine-looking Mr. Broadchurch here, will you? And be sure to tell her he is single and found her shall we say, incredibly attractive? Correct?" He nodded, smiling in amusement.

"Will do," she said and dashed outside. When she came back in, she had a little piece of paper with a phone number on it. "All part of the service," Billy Jo told him, laughing.

# FORTY

MUCH LATER THEY ALL AGREED THAT the term "get-together" had literally been true in the case of almost everyone who attended PD's famous Fourth of July party (even long-single Dory made a startling announcement, telling the group that she . . .) But, no. I shan't spoil the ending, Dear Reader. You deserve a last chapter.

PD's CEDAR-CLAD CABIN HAD BEEN BUILT amid a grove of gray-trunked beech trees, each topped with a cumulus of silver green leaves. On the west side of the cabin, a large deck floated over a deep ravine. The east side bordered a cleared field that Liam had cut with the mower, creating a meadow where the dining table would be placed. Beyond the meadow, the land dropped down to a graveled area, perfect for setting off the fireworks. When dark descended, guests would be entertained by a beautiful blazing display.

Billy Jo had driven out with her charcuterie platter, the fruit for dessert fondue and some wine. She grabbed her contributions out of the car and walked into the kitchen.

"You're just in time," PD said. "We need a hand taking the table out to the meadow. It's solid walnut and pretty heavy. Liam and I can carry the table, but if you could bring the extension leaves, that would be a help."

After lugging the table to the meadow, they inserted the leaves making it sixteen feet long. They men went back to the cabin for chairs.

Lorelei drove in and after giving PD a quick surreptitious kiss, produced a white cotton tablecloth printed with exploding fireworks. She'd also brought red pottery plates, hand-painted stemless wine glasses, silverware and Chinese paper lanterns that were intended to be lighted just before fireworks. After adding a candelabra to the table, she and Billy Jo stood back to survey the result. Standing in the sunny meadow, with pink clover and purple knapweed growing around its carved walnut legs, the table was right out of a movie set.

"Once the moon rises, it's going to be perfect," Lorelei said.

*Clearly, this relationship with Lorelei was going to elevate PD's parties from informal pizza get togethers to sophisticated happenings,* Billy Jo thought.

"Why so many chairs?"

"PD and me, you and Mark, Wayne, Lucy and Nightshade, Samantha, Mark's mother, Dory and Liam."

"Which makes eleven."

"Dory and Liam are bringing guests," Lorelei said.

"Interesting," Billy Jo said, wondering if Liam had a girlfriend now and if Dory had invited her on-again, off-again boyfriend, Al. If so, it would be a surprise as she had complained a lot recently about him visiting his condo in the Caribbean more frequently than usual. She'd even announced it was high time she did something about the situation.

"Sorry, I have to run back to the office. Dory and I are driving out together later."

"I've got to go home and get Samantha. We'll be here in time," Lorelei said with a smile.

DORY AND BILLY JO SET OFF TOGETHER FOR PD'S CABIN AT DUSK. Guests were expected to arrive at seven p.m. Dinner would be served at eight. Fireworks would be kindled once it was completely dark. Billy Jo was still wearing her original outfit of blue jean shorts and a red bandana-print shirt but was planning to change into the dress Dory bought for her before fireworks. They were in PD's kitchen putting food away when Wayne, Lucy and Nightshade pulled in. Lorelei and Samantha arrived at virtually the same time as the Nichols' family. PD greeted his guests and he and Wayne walked out to the meadow carrying the grill. Nightshade and Samantha were walking behind them, although they soon veered off, chatting as they headed down the mown trails through the forest.

In the kitchen, Lorelei said, "We are doing Bratwurst and veggie hot dogs on the grill and I've made my famous potato salad. Samantha baked a pan of brownies."

"I'm going to take my melting pot and forks out to the dessert table," Billy Jo said.

As she opened the front door, Liam pulled up on his red motorcycle. He had a rider on the back. They parked the bike and pulled off their helmets. The girl who got off was skinny with straight mahogany-colored hair.

"Hi Liam. Who is this you have brought to our party? I'm Billy Jo," she said, walking over to greet the couple.

"This is my friend, Maeve," Liam said. At the word, *friend*, Maeve cast Liam an ominous look. "Whoops, sorry. I meant to say I've brought my *girlfriend* to the party," he said.

"Nice to meet you, Maeve," Billy Jo said. "We are just about to carry food out to the tables. Liam, you know where the beverages go."

She left the couple unloading beer from the motorcycle panniers. Depositing her fondue pot and forks on the dessert table, Billy Jo continued walking down the dusty lane in gathering twilight. When she reached the terminus of the mile-long driveway, she saw Mark's car approaching. To her dismay, it looked like he was alone. She'd been so looking forward to meeting his mother, and now it seemed she hadn't come after all.

"Where's your mom?" she asked, disappointment in her tone when he pulled up level with her and lowered his window.

"She'll be out later. I drew her a map. This place is a bit hard to find unless you know where you're going."

"You should have brought her with you," Billy Jo said, frowning. "It's not very gentlemanly of you, Mark, to make her find her way out here alone at night. You need to go back for her."

"Shhh. I'm under orders. Another one of the guests is bringing her. It's all part of Dory's plan," he said and grinned. "Hop in the car, Sweetheart."

"Dinner is served," Dory announced at eight and the group picked up their plates and circled the serving tables. The sizzling bratwurst smelled delicious on the evening air. The sun had vanished below the horizon and dusk settled on the meadow. The first fireflies appeared, blinking on and off above the breeze-blown grasses.

"I'd like to propose a toast," PD said after everyone got seated. He was standing with Lorelei at the head of the table.

"I was going to say we should raise a glass to another successful year at Rosedale Investigations," Wayne said, "But, I defer to our host."

"Thank you Wayne, but looking around at the assembled on this perfect summer evening, I'd like to propose a toast to all the couples here. To our young lovers, Mark and Billy Jo. To the newly-weds, Wayne and Lucy. To Liam and his girlfriend, Maeve, and to our teen-age . . ." his voice trailed off as he looked at Nightshade and Samantha. At his words, they looked at each other in acute embarrassment. "Lastly, I ask you to raise your glasses to Lorelei, who I am thrilled to say has given me a last chance at love. So, let's all toast Cupid. To whenever he may arrive and whomever his arrows may strike."

They all clinked glasses together and cheered.

"Before we move on," Wayne said, "I want us to raise our glasses to our leader, PD. With his retirement, he leaves behind a legacy of commitment and trust in our team, in our clients and the community. I know he will continue to mentor all of us from afar and that this will not be the last 4th of July celebration in this beautiful place. To Detective Patrick Devlin Pascoe." He clinked his glass against PD's and everyone applauded.

"And I have something to say to our Investigator, Dory Clarkson," PD said. "She is taking on an expanded role with me retiring. In the years we've worked together, I've grown to profoundly respect her strong work ethic, intuition and excellent insight into the criminal mind. She'll now be her own boss who can hire and mentor any new employees of Rosedale Investigations, as well as keeping an eye on Billy Jo, who has come a long way but still needs her guidance." Everyone chuckled. Billy Jo rolled her eyes and grinned.

"I appreciate that, PD," Dory said. "I've put up with a lot from some of my prior bosses and appreciate the freedom and respect you have given me. The one thing you failed to mention, though, is that I'll be Wayne's boss now, too."

"Hold on just a minute here," Wayne said but was drowned out by Lucy's laughter and cheers from everyone else.

"Now that we have officially established the new pecking order at the office, I have a surprise announcement," Dory said. "Lorelei and I have just opened a new dress shop on Main Street in Rosedale. It's called the Nightspot because we're selling evening gowns. We're going into partnership and after dinner Billy Jo is going to model one of our outfits."

"Our grand opening is tomorrow at noon. The store is at 312 Main Street and all of you are invited to attend. I'm the Manager and Dory will

join me as Assistant Manager on weekends," Lorelei said. She was holding PD's hand and looked blissfully happy.

"One last thing before we dig into all this wonderful food," Dory
added. "As we all know, Billy Jo has wanted to become a partner in
Rosedale Investigations for several years and recently submitted a formal application for partnership. Both Wayne and I think that Billy Jo
will ultimately make a very fine criminal investigator. We support her
sitting for her Certified Legal Investigator's exam when she graduates
from college and although we don't think she's ready to be a partner yet,
we want to recognize her potential, salute her persistence, and acknowledge her savvy and intelligence. I hope you're not disappointed, Billy
Jo. Would you like to say a few words?"

"Yes, I would," she said, standing up. "Hearing this wonderful trib-
ute, I'm surprised to realize I'm *not* disappointed in your decision. The
last few years of my life have been graced by the presence of Dory,
Wayne and PD. These three amazing people have helped me cross the
bridge from adolescence to adulthood. I know I still have some learning to do about life and relationships, but thanks to them, I know what
family is and what it means, which is . . . everything. I also want to
congratulate both Dory and Lorelei on their new venture," Billy Jo said,
and hugged Dory.

"Take your seats people and enjoy," PD said.

Turning to Dory, Billy Jo said, "It all makes sense to me now, seeing
you peeking into empty store windows on Main Street and having coffee with the woman I found out later was your realtor. I love the logo
of the black and white piano keys on your shopping bags and that the
store is called the Nightspot." She reached down and pulled a flat package from under her chair. "This is for you."

Dory unwrapped the painting of True and her face lit up. "This is just
perfect. I assume this is the work of Mrs. Broadchurch. She's amazing.
True's fur is so lifelike it's positively pettable. Now don't forget, as soon as
you're done eating, Billy Jo, go change into the dress. I left it hanging in
the bathroom of the cabin."

"What happened to your guest?"

"Oh, he'll be along," she said with a quick mysterious grin.

THE GROUP WAS FINISHING DINNER WHEN THEY SAW A CAR coming
down the lane. It was almost completely dark by then and while the car's

headlights prevented most of the party from identifying the vehicle, Mark and Dory immediately rose from their seats and walked toward the car, directing it to the area where the driver could park.

Assuming Mark's mom had finally made her appearance, Billy Jo dashed back to the cabin. There was just time to change into her dress. Once in the bathroom, she removed her shorts and top before reaching for the midnight blue gown. Enjoying the silky feel of the fabric as it slid over her shoulders, she added the sparkly belt and slipped on the shoes. Looking into the mirror above the bathroom sink, she ran a comb through her hair, touched up her lipstick and put on the earrings. "Looking good there, girl," she said, smiling at her reflection.

Hearing someone open the squeaky screen door to the cabin, she walked out into the living room. Mark was standing before the split-stone fireplace in the living room. His mom, a sweet little dumpling of a woman with twinkling eyes, was right beside him.

"You must be the girl my son is hopelessly in love with," she said and gave Billy Jo a hug. "That's a beautiful dress you are wearing. You can call me Milly."

"I'm so happy you could join us, Milly. It's wonderful to meet you at last. There's plenty of food left and I'll take you out to the table. Did you have a hard time finding us?"

"No, I caught a ride with a gentleman that Dory sent to pick me up."

*Probably Al*, Billy Jo thought.

The three of them walked through dew-drenched grass toward the meadow. Reaching the food table, they saw Dory standing beside an African American gentleman Billy Jo had never met before. It definitely wasn't Al.

"Hello," Mark said. "Thanks for bringing my mother out tonight."

"It was my pleasure," the man said, pulling a saxophone case from the back seat.

"I'd like to introduce you to Elmer Clarkson," Dory said and at their confused expressions added, "Elmer is my husband. He's a fine musician and plans to play for us later. We never finalized our divorce and we're happily getting back together," she chuckled.

"I really have to hand it to you, Dory," Bill Jo said, shaking her head in amazement. "A new store and a reconciliation with your husband. And you kept them both a secret until tonight when you could spring both surprises on us. I'm guessing you arranged for Elmer to bring Mark's mother out so I'd be wearing the dress when she got here, right?" Billy Jo asked.

"I did indeed," Dory grinned mischievously.

Maneuvering their chairs into a line along the edge of the meadow later, they all remarked at never having seen so many blinking fireflies.

"Did you know that the purpose of their blinking is for male fireflies to find potential mates?" Mark whispered as he took Billy Jo's hand.

She shook her head with a smile.

Lorelei passed out the Chinese lanterns. Once lit, they rose into the still air, golden paper orbs that stood out against the velvety night like a myriad of suns. The moon came out from behind the clouds, turning the meadow grasses silver.

BELOW THE EDGE OF THE KNOLL, THE MEN WERE GETTING READY to set off the fireworks. Wayne had carried a large bucket of water down to the sandy area at the bottom of the knoll earlier. Lucy had insisted on it, in case sparks spread and caused a fire. PD, flashlight in hand, was locating the fuses on the fireworks. He had purchased several of the fountain types that, once lit, rose from a central point into a colorful, sparkling, V-shaped spray. Five of them were set in a row.

"We're about to start," he called to the group and Billy Jo could see Wayne, Nightshade and Liam standing with PD. They struck their lighters at virtually the same time and backed rapidly away. All she could see of Mark was his dark silhouette on the edge of the meadow. It looked like he was kneeling down. There was a fizzy sound, the scent of smoke and the bright fountains exploded.

Billy Jo was about to walk over to Mark when she noticed Elmer Clarkson, Dory's husband. His black outline was visible against the brilliant wall of fireworks as he bent his head to his saxophone and the hauntingly beautiful notes of Kenny G's "Forever in Love," swelled in the moonlight. At that moment, Liam trotted up the hill with his camera in his hand as more and more fireworks exploded.

All of this, Billy Jo realized, the fireworks, the beautiful gown, the arrival of Mark's mother, the luscious saxophone music, and Liam's camera poised to record the event, had been for Mark to propose. Her breath caught. Tears rose in her eyes as she walked forward slowly and deliberately, treasuring every single step as she absorbed the love of everyone who had created this wondrous surprise.

Mark was down on one knee at the edge of the meadow in front of the backdrop of still-fizzing fireworks. He looked up at her and his eyes were filled with joy.

"Miss Billy Jo Bradley, I would rather have had one kiss from your lips, and one single moment of your love than to live an eternity without you. Will you marry me, Sweetheart?"

Just as she bent to kiss him, she whispered, "Of course, I will."

He slipped the ring with its square ruby stone on her ring finger. It was a perfect fit. Billy Jo's filmy dress floated in the evening breeze as Mark rose to stand beside her and Liam took a dozen pictures.

"I have an early wedding present for you," PD said, walking up and handing her an envelope. She opened it to see a cashier's check. "It's the remainder of Aaron's estate. I hope you will use it to pay for your wedding," he said as Billy Jo's eyes filled with tears.

"Somehow, I doubt you will ever feel abandoned again," Mark whispered.

"Somehow, I believe you're right," she said as the rest of her family came up to congratulate them.

L YN FARQUHAR—PENNAME LYN FARRELL—holds a PH.D. from Michigan State University and is an experienced author, having published the seven-book series (the Mae December mysteries) with Epicenter and three books to date in the Rosedale Investigations series: *The Blind Switch*, *The Blind Split*, and *In the Frame*. This book, *The Family Man*, concludes the series. She also published one women's fiction book, *The Cottonwoods*. Seven of her books have been picked up by secondary publisher, Harlequin. Sales to date from primary and secondary publishers total 30,000. Lyn worked for Michigan State University's College of Human Medicine for 30+ years before retiring to become an author. She is a mother of 2, has 6 step children, and 12 grandchildren. She loves gardening and playing with her Cavalier King Charles Spaniel and is always on the lookout for any of her family artist grandfather's work.

# Rosedale Investigations

Thank you for reading *The Family Man*. If you enjoyed this book and missed the first three in the series they are available at local independent bookstores, Amazon, Barnes & Noble and Bookshop.org. Good books and authors from independent presses are often overlooked. Your comments and reviews can make an enormous difference. Please consider:

- Posting a short review on Amazon and GoodReads.
- Checking out my website & joining my newsletter mailing list at lynfarrell.com
- Spreading the word on social media, especially Facebook, facebook.com/farquha1
- Asking your local library to carry this series or add them to their online portal.

The first book in the Rosedale Investigations series finds Detective Wayne Nichols and Investigator Dory Clarkson joining a private investigations firm run by Detective PD Pascoe. Their first client, Cara Summerfield, comes with a missing person's case. Cara became pregnant in high school and her son, Danny, was adopted at birth. Her husband, up-and-coming politician, was never told about the pregnancy. Cara wants Danny found. When he's located near death in the hospital, Wayne suspects attempted murder. Can the team solve this one before it's too late?

Rosedale Investigations has a new client, Lexie Lovell, whose father died and left his estate to be split between Lexie and her brother. But Lexie never knew she had a brother and nobody has a clue where the boy or his mother are. When Det. Wayne finally finds little Teddy, he's in an abandoned farmhouse and his mother isn't there. Where is his mother? Lovell's attorney was the only person in the father's hospital room when he died. Did he commit murder to get his hands on Lovell's money?

When wealthy widow Abigail Forester is reported missing by her nephew, Rosedale Investigations finds she's trying to avoid him because he's pressuring her to change her will. Then Abigail sets off to meet with her attorney to change her will, is in an accident and dies. Was Abigail deliberately targeted? A second client requests a history of ownership for a century-old painting. Billy Jo puts the painting in the safe at Rosedale Investigations. The next morning Billy Jo is missing, blood drops lead to the street and the painting is gone.